A GOOD LIFE

LEANNE LOVEGROVE

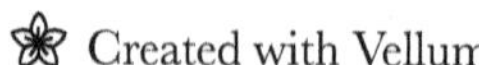 Created with Vellum

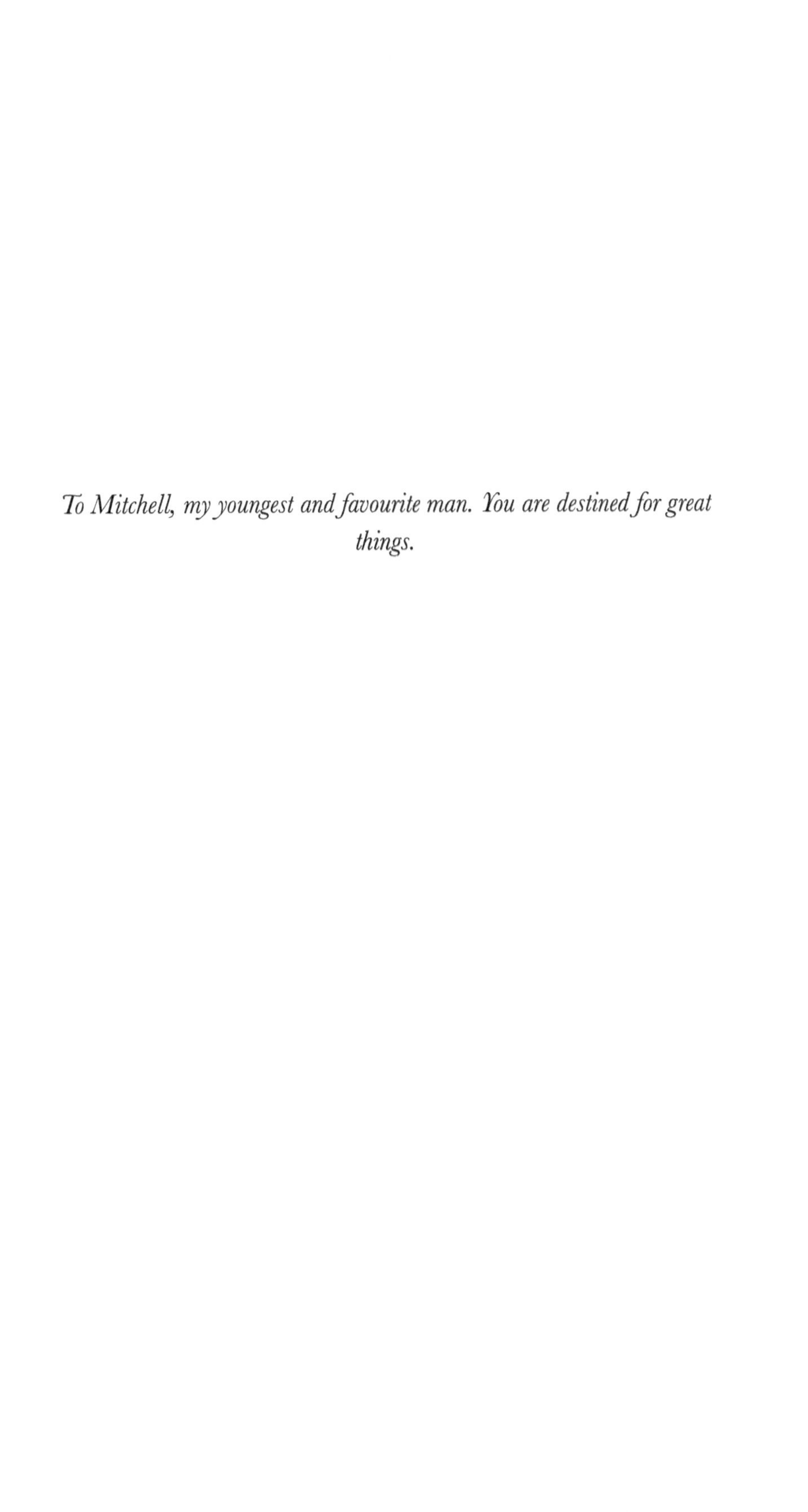

To Mitchell, my youngest and favourite man. You are destined for great things.

PROLOGUE

Shadows dance on the window and I blink. Time zeros back in. When I sat down it was daylight, the birds chirping, the grass wet with dew, the sun not yet radiating any warmth. I hear the clock ticking; it sounds loud to me.

Too loud.

My last cigarette has burned out in the tray, ashes only left. The odour lingers, on my fingers, in the air. A smoky pallor fills the room.

The pervading darkness of the twilight creeps into the room. Where have the hours gone? I look at the easel standing in front of me, the brush in my hand, paint still clumped in the bristles. The cheeks of the cherub staring back at me are full and flushed pink.

Were they ever warm? A whisper of blonde hair across the head, short, fluffy. I long to brush my hand over the wisps and feel its softness. That longing causes an ache to shoot through my chest. My arms are empty.

The eyes are shut but I imagine they are blue. Like the ocean. The lashes fair like the sand on the beach. I move my foot to brush the dog; the fur is bristly. She knows; offers me comfort. But it's too late. I'm exhausted. The pain of each stroke has kept me going, like an exorcism, releasing the agony and transporting it to the painting. It's hard to capture likeness, my memory tricks me, time so short, images fading.

It's done.

CHAPTER 1

'Well, you've made a right royal mess of things, haven't you?' Millicent Osborne swung the cottage door open.

The words hit Greta square in the chest and clean stole her breath away. Standing on the top step, she swayed and reached for the handrail. Trust her aunt to dig down deep, and to the point, immediately.

Her body buzzed; the sensation rocketed up through her shoulders, climbed her neck and thrummed at her temples. She gripped the railing tighter, and her knuckles turned white.

Not now, damn it.

Blackness threatened at the edges of her vision. She gulped in three quick breaths, kept still, allowing lightness to return and her head to clear. The dull throb remained.

Surely, now that she'd arrived, things would improve, wouldn't they?

Greta took in the familiar surrounds and a pang of something else hit her.

In the middle of bloody nowhere and surrounded by wild rainforest and unkempt gardens, the cottage was as she remembered. Neighbours wouldn't hear a cooee if you called one and the trip into civilisation was a day out. The rotten timber stairs had peeling paint curled against its boards. The narrow deck had dead potted-plants and a faded green door. A sign welcomed you to *Banyan Creek* even though the creek, or rivulet of water depending on the time of year and drought conditions, was at the far rear of the property.

But there was comfort in this place. The house had been the same for as long as she could remember. But as a child, she'd never noticed the decay.

Or was it perhaps her that had changed?

The heat of the midday sun penetrated the thin cotton of her blouse. The warmth blanketed her like a second skin, heavy and oppressive and she wanted to rip off her clothes and feel cool relief. There is nothing like the steamy temperatures of the hinterland, sometimes it felt like the tropics. Instead, it was northern New South Wales, but still, it was a world away from Sydney.

Back to feeling a semblance of normal, she dragged her Hermes suitcase onto the timber deck until it landed with a thud. Dropping the handle, she blew her heavy fringe out of her eyes. It flicked upwards and down again, into exactly the same spot forcing Greta to look through black strands of hair.

'Thanks, Auntie, for keeping it real.' Greta said, but she'd already disappeared. Peering inside, her eyes adjusted to the dimness and Greta saw Millie striding down the short hall. She smiled at the bobbing red straw hat, her aunt's trademark painting hat. Some called her aunt eccentric, but Greta loved her. And that is why, despite her acerbic wit and loose tongue, she'd turned up here.

Greta would cop those taunts everyday if it meant she didn't have to go home.

Home. Wherever that was now.

'Did you get my letter?' she shouted after Millie. No answer.

Indoors, she shivered as the perspiration dried on her skin. Halfway up the long drive, the left wheel of her case had broken and rolled away landing in a muddy hollow left over from recent rain. She'd had to drag the bag the remaining few hundred metres in her stiletto heels and tight skirt. Not for the first time, she wished she had something more suitable to wear.

'I guess I'll just come in then,' she sang out.

'Don't make a song and dance about it. Come in and shut the door.' Millie's voice echoed off the VJ walls.

Rushing to catch up, Greta dumped the suitcase before following Millie into the living room, or rather, the painting studio. Or even more apt, junk room. Who else used their living room as a painting studio? Only her aunt, she guessed. Greta would confess to being a neat-freak, but the mess in this room was disgusting.

And God, the smell. That smell came back like a long-lost friend. She recalled it as a child, but now it was strong, stringent and able to clog up your nostrils with one whiff. A mixture of oil paints and turps and who knew what else.

Greta spied the paint brush first. But she knew where Millie would be, where she always was. In the far corner in her chair, surrounded by easels and boards and half-completed paintings and blank canvases.

'Did you get my letter?' Greta repeated. A film of something lined her throat as she took in a breath. She zigzagged across the room.

'Hmm, no.'

'How did you know to expect me then?' Greta quizzed.

'I didn't. But I heard someone plonking up my stairs. The

whole house vibrates and it's annoying, mucks up my brush stroke. So, I answered the door.'

'Oh.'

'What do you mean, oh? What are you doing here? Have you been released?'

'Yes. It is okay if I stay awhile?'

Millie looked at her, really stared at her for the first time. Those wise old hazel eyes bored into her causing discomfort to spread through her chest. She would be kind, wouldn't she?

A brief pause.

'What will your mother say?'

Greta shrugged. 'I haven't told her yet. I'll let her know if I stay.'

'Greta, of course, you can stay. It's lovely to see you. Gosh, child, I haven't seen you, what, since when? Well before all this ruckus. When you finished school perhaps? I think your mother sent you for a week during the holidays … what, when you were eighteen?'

Greta nodded. 'Yep. She sent me here for schoolies, remember?' She laughed at the memory. Her mother had sent her to the small coastal town to avoid the scandal and risqué behaviour of the Gold Coast.

The pair exchanged a smile. It had been a fabulous week of partying with Millie who'd joined in all of the action. That's who she was and exactly the reason Greta had come.

'Did I teach you bad habits?' The tone turned serious. 'It's important to be able to moderate our behaviour.' She let the words hang.

'I've just arrived, can we save the lectures for later?'

The reply was a vocal sound of displeasure. 'I'm sure we agree that I'm hardly the lecturing type. But I'm also not stupid. Anyway, I'm working. Settle in, do what you must. You know where the spare room is.'

Millie lifted a cigarette to her lips and dragged. The plumes of smoke drifted up to hover at the ceiling. Another smell to add into the mix. When would she give up that revolting habit?

Greta placed her hand to Millie's shoulder and peered at the canvas she worked on. 'It's beautiful,' Greta whispered as she drank in the artwork and leaned closer. A pastel green vase held a posy of daisies and next to it sat two mint jars and a plate of grapes. All shades of green with a backdrop of a red and blue tablecloth. 'I've missed seeing your paintings. Missed you, too.'

Millie squashed out the butt of her cigarette and rose to embrace her. Greta squeezed into the hug, clutching too hard to the soft folds of skin around her aunt's middle. For the first time in months, she felt safe. Gratitude washed over her and her limbs loosened, the tension releasing. Greta held in the tears threatening to stream down her cheeks.

Pulling back, Millie's hat tipped sideways, the flower on the side sitting askew. 'That's enough now. It's wonderful to have you here. Settle in and we'll catch up later.'

Millie sat and raised her paintbrush and it landed with a flourish and a twist of her wrist in one perfect stroke. Greta recognised the satisfaction streaked across her seventy-six-year-old face. One of triumph and perfection. She'd seen that look on Millie's face many times. Hadn't seen it recently though. Had it really been eight years since she'd visited? It can't have been … and yet it might. She'd been busy.

Millie hadn't changed. Perhaps the wrinkles next to her eyes and mouth had deepened, her shoulders more rounded. Maybe an extra kilo or two? Her auburn hair had always been streaked grey and now, from what Greta could see spilling from the trim of her hat, the colour appeared the same. It could be that she'd gone back in time.

Now that would be a blessing: a chance to right her wrongs,

make different choices, start over again. She wished. There was no getting out of what she'd done. She sighed.

Nonetheless, that's how it felt returning here. As if time had stagnated. But Greta hadn't. She'd lived a whole lifetime, fucked up and lived to tell the tale.

Millie was back in the zone, a place difficult to pull her out of. Even in an emergency.

From the entry, Greta trudged towards the narrow staircase at the rear of the room that led to the upstairs bedrooms. Her high heels click clacked on the polished floors. Would they make a dent? Somehow, she didn't think Millie would care.

Her bag clunked onto each step making a dreadful clatter. A loud tsk drifted up the stairs each time it landed. Only ten to go. This was a better workout than she'd had in the last six months. At the top Greta paused, out of breath. Walking a square of ten metres wide daily didn't allow one to gain marathon fitness. As for the gym, she hadn't been able to face it recently, either. Might have had something to do with her exercise pals.

With one last tug, she opened the door of the room she'd always stayed in and shoved the case inside. And she had stayed a lot, when she was younger, anyway. The suitcase caught on something and she overbalanced, landing flat over arse with her hair falling around her face.

'Um, hello.' The voice was deep and husky. Greta shook the hair from her eyes and a man came into view who, from her angle, appeared to be a giant. His too-long hair was mussed with tufts sticking out, like her old boss used to look when he raked his hands through his hair whilst yelling at her. He had matching facial hair three days past a shave, ripped jeans with holes too large to be fashionable and displaying hairy kneecaps and broad shoulders crammed into a deep blue collared shirt unbuttoned at the top but splattered with a riot of colour. And there was that goddam awful smell again. She stifled her gag.

'Who are you?' he asked.

'Who are you?' she said.

'I asked first.'

Greta dropped her head and made to get up. He rushed forward and grasped her arm. His grip was strong, and his fingers covered the circumference of her pathetic bicep. Greta shook it off. 'I don't need help.'

Standing at her full height, he didn't appear quite the giant, but he was tall and wide; his presence filling the small room.

'I'm Millie's niece.'

'Niece? I didn't know she had a niece.'

'Well, she does and it's me. And this is my room.' Greta looked around and déjà vu hit. This room resembled the living room. 'You're an artist, too?'

'Um, I guess.' He nodded.

'You guess? I'm saying the easel and the paints and the brushes might be a clue. Plus, that smell. Don't you worry that you'll overdose on those chemicals? Man, it's strong.'

He shrugged. 'I can't smell it.'

'Yep. Well that confirms it, you've lost your brain cells already inhaling that stuff.'

He took a step back and crossed his arms. 'What are you doing here?'

'Well, I was planning to stay here, in *my* room.' A territorial urge rose within her to claim her old space back. Her journey to the past had provided familiarity and treasured memories. She hadn't realised how desperately she was clinging onto everything being the same. But that was stupid, *nothing* about her life was the same.

'Oh,' he said and paused. 'I wasn't expecting you—'

'Clearly,' she interrupted him.

'... but I can clear out. It'll just take me a bit.' He looked around, his brows drawing together and his face tightening. The crammed area was like the living room, but also not. Millie's studio, while cluttered, held delight. This room was dark not by nature but with its contents. A black canvas leaned against one wall; a cluster of messy pieces were on the floor, some with explosions of paint in all colours: reds, blues, and oranges that resembled a child's finger painting. Standing against the bed in the corner was a portrait with a contorted face with sharp edges and evil eyes. In a row on the top bookshelf were human skulls. And of course, the usual tubes with caked paint at the lid and lots of tins. What sort of artist was this guy and how could Millie possibly tolerate it? But what did she know? She couldn't even draw a stick figure. She and her aunt did not share this talent.

At his crestfallen glance around the room, she softened. 'Don't worry, I'll take the other room and crash there.'

'You staying long?' he stared at her with bluish-green eyes. A ripple of something shot through her chest, snagging her heart.

Who was this guy? And why was such a damn good-looking man—albeit in a messy, unkempt sort of just rolled out of bed way— in the spare room? Surely Millie didn't have a toy boy? This guy had to be around her age, perhaps heading more towards thirty. She wasn't there, yet.

'I'm not sure.'

'Okay, well, welcome.' He held her gaze.

Greta turned away. It didn't matter what a knockout he was. There were other things on her mind. Like the headache throbbing at her temples. The pulsing moved to behind her eyes and her vision blurred. Her legs ached from being on her feet too long and her arms from tugging her worldly possessions around in the broken bag. She resisted kicking it, wanting to take out her frustration for this situation and the one she'd caused all those months ago. She dreamed of a soak in a hot tub and to wash away the grime and sweat of today and the past six months. She prayed there was a stash of bubble bath.

That, and then she'd sleep for a week, safe and comfortable, even if it wasn't her own bed.

'I'm Brodie, by the way,' he said in a voice now dripping with honey.

'Greta, Greta Johnson' she muttered hardly audible as she pulled the door shut.

CHAPTER 2

*B*rodie Quade had a spoonful of breakfast cereal half-way to his mouth when Greta entered the dining room. He shut his mouth and chewed.

'Good morning, darling. What a sleep. I expected you downstairs last night, but you didn't show. Lucky, though, because I painted through to the wee hours. I wouldn't have been much company.' Millie lowered her newspaper and addressed her niece.

Brodie's gaze flicked between the two.

Greta mumbled something indiscernible and he glanced at Millie to check if she'd understood.

'Still not a morning person?' Millie chuckled.

'I didn't sleep well and really need a coffee. I'll be all right, then.'

'I've not long made one, I'll fetch you a cup.' Brodie jumped up, leaving his cereal to get mushy. He hated when it went soft.

She squinted at him then, her lips moved as if to speak and then went tight-lipped.

Millie's niece sure was pretty. Except her chocolate brown eyes were hidden under a face of make-up.

'Are you going somewhere?' he asked before thinking his question through.

'No, why?'

He shrugged. 'You're all dressed up.'

Greta looked down at her clothes and Brodie's glance followed.

'Um, I don't have much else in my wardrobe at present.'

Were her cream pants linen? Her top was nice and sat ruffled at her neck in waves. Her neat, square bobbed hair sat straight and slick, like she'd sat in a salon and had it ironed. He knew about these things from his mum and sister. If this is what she wore to breakfast he couldn't imagine what she'd wear somewhere special.

Brodie shrugged and made no further comment. Greta took a seat at the table.

'Who is he?' he heard her ask Millie as he drifted out; he didn't wait for the reply.

Returning with the coffee he placed the steaming mug in front of Greta and hesitated.

'Thanks,' she said but her nose scrunched up. He took his seat across from Millie who was back reading her paper and didn't seem at all concerned with her niece's distemper. He stirred his cornflakes that were now a globby mess. He pushed the bowl aside to take a sip of his coffee when Greta's spurted from her mouth.

'Instant?' She turned on him like he'd dished up poison.

'Well, it's Moccona,' he responded and watched as the brown stain bled into the tablecloth.

'I've been dreaming of an espresso for months...' she held her head in her hands before rising so fast the chair scraped on the floorboards. The hot drink slurped over the edge of the mug as she grabbed it and left the room.

Within seconds she returned. 'Millie, where's your coffee machine?'

Millie peeked over the top of the paper. 'When have I ever had a coffee machine? That's what the coffee shops are for.'

Breakfast at Millie's wasn't normally this interesting. Usually Brodie would lumber up early, barely awake with uncombed hair and yesterday's clothes. They wouldn't talk until Millie had read the paper and he'd eaten. Occasionally, they'd discuss breaking news or local issues but usually only about their painting goals for the day. She'd give him tips on technique or they'd spar about the approach to whatever respective painting they were working on. Given their stark differences in style, the conversations were often heated.

Greta hung her head and leaned it against the doorframe before disappearing again. This time he couldn't resist a smirk. That is, until he jumped at the sound of a cupboard door slamming. Millie wasn't fazed.

Greta came back and sat down in her chair, held the mug and sipped the drink without grimacing. A red lip imprint appeared on the rim.

'Tastes all right, doesn't it?'

She didn't respond.

Millie piped up. 'You'll just have to go into town, love and get one of your fancy espressos.'

'I don't have any money.' The words were a whisper.

Brodie rattled around in his pocket for his wallet. 'Hey, no worries. I can spot you a fiver.' He extracted the pink note and offered to her.

She looked down at it but didn't take it.

'Really, I don't mind. You can buy me a coffee another time.'

Greta stared at the money and her face crumpled. Confused,

Brodie looked over at Millie. Why was she crying? He hated it when girls cried. It was only a fiver for a coffee. He couldn't imagine she needed it so desperately.

Millie took her time lowering the newspaper, folding it, and placing it beside her plate. 'It's going to take some time to adjust after being in jail.'

Greta bowed her head, two hands cradling the china cup but she didn't drink.

Jail?

'Don't worry I was locked up once, too,' he said and placed his hand on her forearm.

She heard him and shifted forward on the seat, forcing his hand to drop. 'How long?'

'What? Oh, how long was I in jail? Well, it's a funny story. My mates and I had too much to drink one Friday night and the pub refused to serve us. We were clever though and got hold of a few beers and were walking home like. We were singing and it sounded good. But someone complained about the noise and the coppers, we knew them, too, thought we needed to sleep it off and they put us in the slammer overnight. Best sleep I'd had in a long time.'

'Overnight?' The words rolled off her tongue.

'Yeah. It was okay. No harm done. The police didn't charge us with anything.' Her look seared into him and he stopped talking. He had a strange sense this wasn't going well when he'd only been trying to make her feel better.

'Overnight?' she repeated.

Huh? Had he said the wrong thing?

'I have spent the last six months in the women's prison for embezzlement.' Her voice rose an octave.

'Embezzlement. Geez, okay, holy shit. That sounds serious.' Je-sus! He didn't know what that was, but it sounded like some hard-core shit.

'Millie,' she pleaded with her aunt, her expression forlorn, her eyes brimming with tears.

'Greta, please, Brodie is my guest here, too.'

'What happened to not being the lecturing sort?'

'Well, if you'd been in touch over the years, you'd know more about what I've been up to. I mentor young artists, and Brodie is my current protegee,' she smiled at him across the table. 'He's using the space upstairs as a studio. We paint together most days.'

Greta seemed to consider this information and ran her eyes over the length of his torso. Usually he didn't care less what he looked like. What did it matter? Most of his clothes became ruined from the paints anyway. So, no need to take care. But he guessed, today, he didn't look acceptable by usual standards. His shirt sleeves were rolled up to his elbows and hanging loose from his waist with shorts of faded brown. Thongs adorned his feet and he pulled them back under the chair to hide them.

'I'm sorry, I'm not myself,' she glanced at the note and he held it up again. 'I don't want to borrow your money because I'm not sure when I'll be able to pay you back. But I really want that coffee. I promise I'm good for it.' Greta's gaze remained on the money.

This crazy, over-done city girl looked at him with hooded eyes that held such depth of sadness he would have given her the five bucks regardless. Prison must have been a real hellhole for her.

'Of course.' Brodie thrust it into her hands. She wrapped her fingers around it and placed the note into her pocket. 'Thank you.' His heart did a funny little giddy-up in his chest.

Placing the mug down, she stood and moved away from the table. 'Best put some sneakers on, those won't cut it on the walk to town.' Glancing at her feet adorned in sparkly high wedges, she sighed and headed upstairs instead of the door. Moments later she rushed out.

'Millie, does she know how far it is into town?'

Millie titled her head to the side. 'I get the feeling Greta isn't ready to be told things yet. Some things need to be learned, don't they?'

'I should have lent her my bicycle …'

'Let's get on with things. What are you working on today, Brodie?'

WHAT WAS WRONG WITH HER? IT'S TRUE HER LIFE HAD TURNED to shit. She had done some stupid things and boy; she'd paid for it. But when had she turned into a bitch?

Well, perhaps when she was convicted of a crime and sent to prison? Yep, that might do it.

How could she have been so stupid? She'd asked herself that question a million times. And there were varied answers. None of them satisfactory. The day she'd signed away millions of dollars to the boyfriend she'd loved and trusted without reading the detail. So dumb. Or really, it wasn't only that…it went right back to the beginning and the day she fell in love with Charlie Clarke.

Greta paused on Millie's driveway. Tiny birds fluttered in her chest and rammed against her rib cage. Closing her eyes, she turned her face towards the blazing sun. The brightness seared into her closed lids and the pounding receded.

She vowed to do better; had to do better. This was her chance. A little time to recover and get her life back on track and she'd be okay. Could return to her normal life. She needed to get her shit together and despite her rocky start, she was convinced this was the place to do it.

Unbidden tears slid down her cheeks and she wiped them away with the sleeve of her cardigan and kept walking towards the main road. Reality check — she was out and walking next to a rainforest in a green and moist hinterland beneath a cloudless sky.

The rays of the sun bit her skin, but she ignored the burn. Only one day after release and she was adjusting. A double shot latte would place everything back into perspective. She could already taste its creaminess. Then she'd get a job. Without checking her bank balance, she knew it was nil. Even if Millie didn't charge her rent, she was skint. Without money, she couldn't pay her debts and more importantly, commence the road to redemption.

CHAPTER 3

Tiny bumps erupted across Greta's skin as she entered the copse of trees bordering Banyan Creek cottage. The bundle in her arms grew heavy and she cradled it tighter; her cashmere sweater making a useful sling. Breathing in the animal scent, she forgot about her aching feet and enjoyed the gentle thrum purring under her hands.

Damn it. The trip to town was supposed to have her skipping home on a cloud of success, not exhausted and still pissed off with the world. Even the coffee had been mediocre.

Where were all the jobs in this town and how could she not have secured one?

'Ahoy there!' A voice rang out.

Ahoy there? Really? Who said that? She shaded her eyes from the sun encroaching through the branches of trees leading to the deck.

Greta spotted her aunt and Brodie who sat in reclining chairs sipping drinks.

Before she'd reached the bottom step, he shouted, 'how was your coffee?'

This guy was full on, or full of beans as her mother might say. She had no choice but to run with it.

'Good.'

'That's good,' he replied.

'You didn't tell me there was only one coffee shop in town.'

'Nah, there must be more. Lucas Heads is a tourist spot with loads of visitors. You mustn't have seen 'em.'

She collapsed into the only spare chair carefully protecting her package.

'What have you got there, love?' her aunt asked.

Greta unfolded the garment and Brodie moved closer.

'A cat! And kittens!' he exclaimed.

'They were abandoned on the road, near the driveway. I couldn't leave them. They might get hit by a car or die of starvation ...,' she looked at Millie. 'You don't mind, do you?'

'Still love animals then?' Millie turned to Brodie then. 'As a child Greta was always bringing home stray animals much to my sister's consternation and looking after the school's pet mice or guinea pigs. And she longed for a pet. Something her mother steadfastly refused.'

Greta agreed.

'Of course, I don't mind if you're caring for them. But will they get on with my little Lola?' At the mention of her name, the pug dog wandered onto the deck, stretching out its back.

The mother cat tensed, its fur standing up. The kittens snuggled in close unaware of the potential threat. Greta stroked her coat and turned the mother cat away so she couldn't see the dog. Lola found the only spot on the deck with a patch of sun and rested languorously; if she'd noticed the cat, she didn't seem to care.

'Lola looks pretty relaxed about the company, but the cat might need to get used to her,' Greta said.

'How many little kitties in there?' Brodie leaned in to pick one up. The mother hissed and swiped at him with her paw. He laughed and backed off.

'Only three. I think there should be more because cats usually have large litters, don't they? Perhaps some have already died. But I'll save these ones.'

Memories of her rotten day receded. And of that wretched long walk. She wouldn't attempt that trek into town again anytime soon.

Brodie left the deck but came back with a box. 'Here you can use this. I guess you'll have some spare blankets somewhere, Millie?'

'Of course, but is this what you want, Greta? There's a wonderful wildlife sanctuary close-by; they'll care for them. Don't you have enough on your plate at the moment?'

The smile dropped from Greta's lips. 'I have nothing else to do.'

'Not right this minute, but you will. How did you go on your job hunt?'

'Terrible. There's a couple of mortgage broker type places in town but they aren't hiring and there's only two banks. I don't want to work in a bank, but I could. I need a job.'

Brodie jumped in. 'What line of work you in then?'

'Finance. I manage people's investments.'

'Greta,' Millie turned sideways in her chair to face her. 'Are you sure you want to return to that sort of work? It's the perfect time to consider a fresh start. And what about your obligation to tell them what happened? Surely they won't hire you after that?'

Greta took her time to answer. Brodie shuffled his feet back and forth on the deck breaking the silence with the annoying sound.

'Would you like a drink?' he eventually asked.

'Yes. Yes, I would. A glass of white wine, please. That's another luxury I've been dreaming of.'

Brodie glanced at Millie who nodded curtly. Greta didn't understand the exchange. Why did Brodie need Millie's permission to serve her a glass of wine? Millie held a stout glass of clear liquid, too. Gin? Vodka? Her aunt loved a drink. Millie was that family member who'd always brought the drink to the party and was the first one to finish it. She'd always been the life of any social gathering.

Greta considered her answer while Brodie returned with a stemmed glass with the condensation rolling off the surface. She smiled, took a sip and relished the cool liquid as it slid down her throat.

'I have no skills, Millie. What else can I do?'

'Of course you do. You can do anything. Haven't you lost the heart for investing, anyway?'

Her aunt sipped her drink. The slice of lemon floated to the top as Millie placed her glass back on the low table between them.

'Do you mean will I be dumb enough to get taken advantage of again?'

'I have no concerns about your intelligence, but yes, won't it be difficult in that environment? You should think about it.'

'I won't be that stupid ever again.' Greta's body trembled. 'I've lost everything and have to start from scratch. My apartment, my car, my belongings except for the stuff that didn't have any value and no one wanted. I have a mountain of debt. I need money. I need a job and finance pays well.'

'Exactly. Are you listening to yourself? You need money. You have, what is it? A million dollars in restitution.'

Brodie burst into a fit of coughing and downed the remainder of his beer.

'It's more than a million …'

'Tell me you're strong enough to survive in that industry

when there's so much at stake. The pressure, the stress, would it be worth it?'

'It sounds to me like you think I'll be stung again. I won't.'

'What's changed?'

'I've changed. Everything has changed. I've been in prison, Millie! It was the worst experience of my life: degrading, disgusting, horrific.'

'Plus, no coffee or alcohol,' Brodie said.

'Are you trying to be funny?'

'Me? What no, just pointing out the facts, like you said. There are reasons not to go back, right? I don't know much about finance but what is it that you used to do exactly and why can't you again?'

Greta paused. She didn't have any obligation to tell this guy. But she had to get used to telling her story, didn't she?

'When people have large sums of money, for example, retirees with their superannuation, or people who earn a lot and want to invest it, they'd go to a financial advisor. That was me. I'd advise them on ideal investments and ones that would secure them a good return. They'd accept my advice and I'd manage their investment and get paid dividends.'

She paused. That was all factual and correct. But there was more. 'My job was fantastic, and I was good at it. I was living a dream life; had everything I could ever want and more. But then, Charlie commenced working at my firm. I liked him and we started dating. I didn't realise he did drugs, but it became quickly obvious. I never took drugs.' She looked both Brodie and Millie in the eye when she said it to ensure they heard.

Life could be worse, she could be fighting an addiction to ice.

'His habit spiralled out of control. Charlie borrowed funds that didn't belong to him to pay his druggie debts. For a while he repaid most of it. I begged him to get help, go to rehab. But it was too late, his addiction was strong and he couldn't keep up the repayments. Soon, it wasn't just about him anymore. His dealers required payment. They didn't care how or where the money came from. At first, he begged me to help, borrow money for him. I refused. Sometimes he sought help and I thought everything would be okay, he'd get better and stop using. One day he told me about this fantastic investment opportunity and said that we should become involved. Use our savings and we'd be rich. Despite using drugs, he was a great financial advisor and I trusted his judgment. He prepared all the paperwork and I signed without checking the documents. But I signed authority for release of my client's money and he stole it, too.'

Greta looked away, into the distance, across the vast yard and through the canopy of treetops. The sun was setting on the horizon casting them in a golden glow.

'He stole the money but I was responsible for entrusting my client's details and protecting their security. I didn't. It's my fault those people lost their life savings. I had no idea until clients wanted to change their investments or draw down funds and I realised something was wrong. It was a nightmare. Long story short, I got caught up in his mess even though I didn't actually do the stealing.' She paused. 'I was convicted of embezzlement of over $2.5 million dollars, lost my job and was ordered to pay it all back.'

Greta still nursed the cats and the mother rolled over and pushed her little kittens into the crook of her arm. She balanced them and collected her thoughts.

'He got caught too, yeah?' Brodie asked.

'Yes. Last time I saw him was in court. He'd already started to detox and looked dreadful. He was ordered to attend rehab along with other orders. I haven't seen or spoken to him since.'

'You made a mistake. People make mistakes.' Brodie said. 'There's a lot worse people than you.'

'You sure did, getting mixed up with that Charlie fellow,' her aunt added.

'Yeah, a huge mistake. But I was responsible for my client's money and should never have let him have access to those private details. I didn't steal,' she said the words forcefully. 'Not that it matters. Intention doesn't seem to count. I'm paying for my mistake, though. I have nothing. No money, no job and nowhere to go.'

'Hey, it isn't that bad. Millie here will look after you.'

'Don't be nice to me. I stuffed up big time. I'm a criminal. I've embarrassed my family, my friends …'

'Yep, you have. But you've also done the time. And you're sorry?' It was a question.

She would offer up the usual platitudes, expressions of regret. But wasn't she a victim, too? Of love and stupidity? Yep, she was a victim. Life wasn't fair. But she only had herself to blame. But she was sorry, for everything and just a little bit sorry for herself, too.

'Yes, I'm sorry. Which is why I'm going to pay back every cent I owe those innocent people.'

'Well, in my books that makes you a good person then. Plus, you like cats.' Brodie showed off a wide grin. Everything about him was over-sized. He was like one of those quintessential male softies, large and menacing-looking but gooey on the inside. Greta wondered what one of his cuddles would feel like.

'Thank you.' Greta swallowed the remnants of her drink. 'Will you grab me a blanket, Brodie and then I'll settle these guys in their box and get us another drink.'

'Nothing for me darling. I'm on soda water.'

'What? It's Friday afternoon. Why aren't you drinking?' Greta couldn't contain her surprise.

'I'm getting old, can't drink as much as I used to and now it makes the paint blur, and we can't have that.' Millie offered a weak smile and Greta didn't quite believe her.

Brodie returned with a tattered old rug and as they arranged it in the box, their hands brushed. Greta pulled back at the rush of warmth and glanced at him under her lashes but he didn't notice. His attention was captured by the tiny kittens he held in his large hand and one at a time placed into their new home. Greta followed with the mother cat.

'I know a job you can get, start straight away,' he said to her.

'Really? That would be fabulous! Do you know someone at the bank?'

'No, nothing like that. Cleaning out the caravans and cottages at the local holiday park. I know the owners are looking for someone.'

Brodie was funny. Except she didn't laugh. Instead, shivers raced up her spine and a memory returned painfully clear.

The prison toilets.

Stupidly, she'd volunteered to clean them as part of her duties. Thought it would be a quiet place away from the menacing inmates who never left you alone. Ribbed you with their vicious tongue at every turn, poked and prodded you until you were desperate to retaliate. But no, the toilets were quiet all right; too quiet. And out of the way. The perfect spot to be cornered. It only took seconds.

Sweat droplets formed on her brow and her stomach churned with the wine she'd drunk. The blackness threatened…

'Um, ah. No, sorry. I'm not a cleaner. I need something else.' Greta remembered her manners. 'But thanks anyway.'

She stood and shook away those images of prison and brought herself back to the present. 'Can't mess up these hands anymore, my nails are already shot.' She faked a laugh to conceal her trembling hand. She grasped it and held it tight in front of her. 'I'll get a position. The bank said a woman is going on maternity leave at the end of the month. Didn't seem to have a lot of detail though, sounded vague. I'll have to scout out what else is around.'

Greta went to take a large gulp of her wine but it was empty.

When she looked over at the pair, Millie stared at Brodie, her brow creased in a frown. He seemed to be determinedly not noticing. But then he jumped up.

'Right, I'm off. Got stuff to do. Thank you, Millie, for another fabulous day. I've cleaned all the brushes and the room and opened all the windows. Catch you next week.'

Greta watched him walk around the back of the cottage and return with a rusty bicycle. It squeaked as he sat on the torn leather seat.

'Greta,' her aunt said and shook her head before getting up and returning indoors. Baffled, Greta nursed one of the baby kittens extra tight.

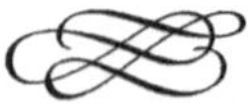

CHAPTER 4

'What you been doing with yourself lately? Haven't seen ya much,' asked Sam. 'You haven't been wasting your time with that painting shit, have you?'

Brodie shrugged. 'Doing this and that.'

'What do we want?' A person on a loudspeaker screamed.

The crowd responded. 'Climate change!'

Brodie leaned into his friend, shouting over the din. 'Good turn out this arvo.'

Sam nodded before they were caught up in the swell of movement and the protesters held their placards high and stormed down the Esplanade of Lucas Heads, walking until they reached the pub.

Brodie was sure Sam was only protesting for the catch up at the end of the march when they'd down a few beers. If he asked, Sam probably couldn't tell you the action he'd like the current leaders to take on climate change. But that was all right, Brodie reckoned, he was here supporting the cause.

Brodie loved the gathering at the end too, it gave him a chance to chat with the *real* activists. The members of the group who knew exactly what the politicians should do and how. Last night he'd been reading the latest report about the threat to the northern rivers area from rising water levels and temperatures that impacted on the native wildlife and increased risk of bushfires. He felt for their local farmers. And for the future.

No one could trust the government. They avoided the big decisions and didn't take risks due to worrying about their rich voting electorates and probably lining their own pockets from associations with oil and gas companies, and worse, overseas investors. Foreigners were buying up the country, too.

At the pub he stuck his hand in his jeans pocket and scanned the group for a target. Brodie wanted his fingers wrapped around an ice-cold beer whilst he blew off talking to someone who cared as much as him. He appreciated this activist bunch and felt at home amongst them.

It was crazy. He was an activist; spent time walking the pavement, writing letters and listening to local concerns. He was one of them, but it seemed he had difficulty calling himself anything whether it be artist, creative, or climate change supporter. It didn't matter though, did it, if he called himself a greenie or simply got on and helped? There were other ways to spread the message and that's what he'd focus on.

'Hi, love. How was your day?' Back at home, Brodie's mother planted a kiss on his forehead as if he was a child.

'Fine. How was yours? You look tired.'

Niamh Quade smiled and patted him on the arm. 'A busy day at the park being a Friday. We've got five new families in for the weekend and one checked out after being here all week.'

He nodded. 'Okay, what cabin number? I'll get onto the

cleaning after dinner so it's ready in the morning for a last-minute booking.'

'Thanks, love, that'd be great. Cabin two. I purchased fresh cleaning supplies the other day and it's in the storeroom ready to go.'

Summer months, whether school holidays or not, were always hectic at the Holiday Park. It was a wonderful place to grow up. He'd spent his entire youth running around barefoot and playing with visitors. There was so much room on the large block of land with the beach directly across a narrow road and on the other side, a lake, so when they tired of the beach, they'd paddle in its cooler waters.

Paradise.

'Uncle B!' screamed his nephew Tommie. The little boy raced into the kitchen and stood, waiting, gazing up at him with big, round eyes. Brodie swung him high above his head before catapulting him roughly around the room. Regardless of what sort of day he'd had, seeing four-year old Tommie and his baby sister Kristabelle never failed to lift his spirits.

'Did you go to the rally tonight?' his sister, Leonie, asked as she entered.

'Of course.'

'Did the pollies turn up this time? They said they were …'

'Nope. Just means we'll be back again next week if they aren't going to pay attention. Eventually they have to–'

There was brief commotion as the remainder of his family arrived. Leonie and her husband, Mark, had moved to nearby town. But with the two littlies, they returned to visit as often as possible.

'How's the trade?' he asked his brother, Derek, the youngest of the tribe.

'Yeah, good. We've just about finished building a brand-new house up on the hill, on the road running out of town. You should see the money being pumped into the place. Not a cent spared.'

'It's the new generation, isn't it?' His father, Henry, offered with a hint of melancholy. 'Those that can't afford Bronte Bay make home here in Lucas Heads, lifting our housing prices and everything else along with it.'

'That can be a good thing, right, Dad?' said Leonie as she served the children portions of spaghetti Bolognese.

'Of course, darling. Moderation in everything though. If that sort of money hits town, it can leave the rest of us behind. Then suddenly visitors don't want to spend their weekend in a simple beach shack like we offer, but rather, they'll want to stay in a swanky new resort. That'll be the next thing, mark my words.'

His mother waited until he'd finished and said grace. 'Lord, thank you for this meal, for the family beside us and the love between us, Amen'. The words raised the hairs on the back of his neck, but he bowed his head all the same and remained quiet out of love and respect for his Mum. He peered up through his lashes at his Dad, wanting a nod, smirk, anything, but he avoided his eye. Nonetheless, Brodie knew he felt the same.

'How's your piece coming along?' Mum asked before she'd taken the first bite of her meal.

The room went quiet. He wished his mother wouldn't do this. Always show such interest. No, not interest, he loved her interest, but express it publicly, even if they were his family.

Derek guffawed. 'How's the creativity flowing, bro? Did you manage to make those globs of paint on the cardboard resemble something that no one else will recognise?'

That was why.

He loved his family with all their foibles and flaws and unique characteristics. But he wished they would try to understand. Or if they couldn't understand his desire to create meaningful pieces of art, to at least shut up about it and not taunt him.

But his mother didn't let up. She was genuinely interested and encouraged him at every turn by buying paints and equipment she couldn't afford; listening to him explain the purpose of a painting when she didn't understand; offering ideas even if they weren't helpful.

'It's coming along. I've roughed in the underpainting and next week hopefully, I'll do the fat over lean.' He loved using these art terms that no one else but his Mum understood.

'I can't wait to see it.'

'What's this one about then,' his sister asked.

'Immigration.'

'Best thing the government ever did was shut those borders,' Mark piped up. It created a political discussion around the dinner table that in equal measure made him feel sick and embarrassed.

'Hamid at the servo, he came over on a boat,' Brodie started, 'has cigarette butt scars along each leg reminding him every day of what he fled. He's doing a fantastic job at building up the mechanical side of the business and does a real good service.'

Tommie threw his fork across the table. Kristabelle fussed and Derek downed his beer.

'Mum, Flannery's are having a sale this weekend. Will you come and help me choose summer clothes for the kids?' Leonie asked.

The conversation moved on. One day, Brodie hoped his words would change their attitudes, even a little bit.

'Thanks for dinner, Mum. I'll get on with the cleaning.' He stood and lifted Tommie under the arms and wrestled him to the ground one last time.

'Brodie, do you have to?' His sister whined. 'I'll never settle him for bed.'

He roughed up the boy's hair and the pair exchanged a wicked grin. 'That's the job of a naughty uncle.'

Hours later, Brodie crashed onto his bed, the smell of ammonia lingering on his fingers. His body might ache from the physical work, but his mind was restless. Laying prone on the mattress in the van he called home, he searched for his sketchbook.

He didn't draw often. Only when there was a fire in his belly caused by a demonstration and he'd belt out an aggressive idea for a painting. One that would right the injustices in the world. He might use harsh and too-deep strokes but the end result could usually advance into something real and most often these were his best work. Tonight he had other images in mind.

Retrieving the sketchbook from the kitchen bench, he propped up his pillows to lean against. He yanked the flimsy cotton curtain across the window above his bed. It was a small van, only a few metres long. Long enough. His mattress filled the entire width at one end, his kitchen in the middle and amenities squashed at the rear.

His fingers danced across the page. Not angry tonight because he captured something different. He sank into his happy place where thoughts were released, images created and the outside world faded away. His body relaxed, shoulders dropping and nothing else mattered except lead on paper.

For the next hour he didn't move. He heard people wandering around outside, coming and going to the shower block, or returning home from dinner. Eventually the world grew quiet until all he heard was the rhythmic crash of the waves onto the beach and the subsequent silence as the sea rolled towards the shore before being sucked back out to start all over again.

Brodie stopped his stroke and dropped the pad when his fingers ached. He fisted and uncurled his knuckles a couple of times. Outside the sky was midnight black with a sparkle of stars.

No moon tonight. Picking up the notebook, he stared at the image of Greta Johnson. Her blunt, cropped hair made her face appear square. That hair sure was a statement. Probably fitted in perfectly in swishy Sydney. He imagined there'd be times she'd hide behind that hair. Despite the level of sadness he'd observed in her eyes, the ones he'd drawn delved deep into him, challenging and daring. Expressive. He couldn't wait to see what else they delivered. This image was her serious face. To be fair he hadn't observed too many smiles yet, but he loved her intense gaze. She was a thinker, like him. Well, he thought so but he hardly knew her.

This image only focused on her face, nothing else, except the slightest hint of an elongated neck. With a shiver, he imagined suckling the nape of that creamy, pale skin.

Without bothering to tidy up, he lay flat, the drawing beside him and fell into a dreamless sleep.

CHAPTER 5

No dull throb. It was the first time since release Greta had woken that her temples didn't pulse. She opened her eyes and blinked a few times to be sure. Nothing. Not even a slight hum. Unlike those first two nights where her sleep was disturbed by nightmares, she couldn't recall waking last night in a cold sweat. Wow, could this be the turning point?

Without the hammering to her head, she might avoid the urge to attack anyone in her sights like a wild animal before that first cup of coffee. Today might actually be a good day.

Maybe today everything that had felt so far out of kilter would fit back into place and make sense. So far every task presented as a challenge: the amount of space, her freedom, the lack of routine, choosing food. Who'd have thought she couldn't adapt to change?

Desperate not to let fear suffocate her, she focused on the mother cat and her kittens that second night. Their mewls and whines were loud enough to drift under the laundry door and up the stairs. Not wanting to disturb Millie, Greta had jumped at each sound. The kittens had their mother for support, but Greta had run a solitary finger down each of their backs in comfort until they curled back into her spine. Last night they'd been more settled, like she had.

As usual, Millie sat at the dining table having breakfast when she came down. Did the woman sleep? Clearly, she didn't have any trouble with routine. Greta went around behind her chair and kissed her on the cheek. 'Morning, Aunt Millie.'

'Good morning, love. You look so much better today. I'm pleased.'

'I feel a bit better. Would you like another tea?'

'Yes please.'

'I'll put the kettle on and check the cats. I didn't hear them all night so I hope they're all right.'

'I heard them scratching around before so I'm sure they're fine.'

Muffled chuckles came from behind the laundry door as Greta pushed it open. Brodie lay on his side on the linoleum floor next to the cardboard box, one kitten climbing over his head and one in each hand. The mother sat back licking her fur, her purr loud.

Greta laughed. 'What are you doing?'

'Oh, hi, Greta. Thought I'd check on them. They are looking so healthy and rested. You've done a great job caring for them.'

Her heart swelled in her chest. 'Thank you. I've loved looking after them, except that first night they were restless, and I had to check them a few times.'

'Yes, little kitties will be like that. They must have had some fun overnight because when I arrived their water was spilt. I've cleaned it up and refilled their kibble. How soon do you think we can let them out, with their mother of course?'

'I can clean up their mess but thank you. But you know what, I've never owned a cat, so I'm not sure when it's safe for them to go outside. I'll have to Google it.'

Greta stopped then, remembered her phone and computer. She hadn't unpacked them since she'd arrived. Hadn't turned her phone on since she'd left Sydney. She shuddered at the thought. What would she find? Ignored messages? Nothing? She didn't feel like reconnecting with reality. It was nice isolating from the big bad world but she guessed that couldn't last.

'Is there internet here?'

'Yeah, but it's patchy.'

'Okay, I'll have to try and do some cat research later.' She moved away and towards the kitchen but stopped. 'Do you know anything about cats?'

'Me, nah. My mum might though, I can ask her.'

Greta nodded.

Without asking, Greta made an instant coffee for Brodie and a pot of tea—she hadn't made a pot of tea ever—for her and Millie and had placed it on the table when the house shook. They glanced at each other when the knock sounded on the door.

Brodie shrugged. 'I'll get it.'

There was an exchange of greetings and Brodie returned to the dining room with a woman in tow.

'Greta, someone here to see you.'

'Me?'

'Good morning, Greta. My name is Charlene Harris and I'm from Corrective Services. I've left messages on your mobile and sent various emails, but you haven't responded.'

The woman carried a folder of material in one hand and held a tan leather brief case in the other. She wore a ballet bun pulled back so severely her eyes lifted towards her forehead. Her eyes appeared overly large through the thick-rimmed glasses she wore.

'Oh, shit, sorry. I haven't checked my messages.'

Millie kicked her under the table.

'Ow,' she squeaked and received a glare from her aunt. She dare not look at Brodie.

'Yes, well. It's a requirement that I visit so can you please check it more regularly in the future?'

'Yes, of course. I'm sorry.' She stood. 'Are we, should we, do we need to talk?' she fumbled.

'Yes, we do but I also need to meet and talk with the people you live with, so given you're all gathered together perhaps we should get on with that?'

'Sorry, Millie. Is that okay? I wasn't aware of the visit.'

'Of course.' Her aunt rose and introduced herself and shook Charlene's hand. 'Please take a seat and have some tea.' Greta bustled around locating another fine china cup and poured the parole officer a drink. Who'd have thought those words would ever roll off her tongue? Suddenly, she really needed that coffee.

Charlene turned towards Brodie. 'And you are?'

'Um, I don't live here …'

'You almost do,' Greta interjected. 'He's always here.'

Her aunt intervened. 'What Greta means is that this is Brodie Quade and he's an art student. He works here most days.'

'Lovely. So the two of you live here and the two of you work from home.' Charlene scribbled some notes but then stopped, pen held aloft.

'Oh my goodness. I've just realised. You are *the* Millicent Osborne, the artist.' Her intonation rose at the end of the sentence.

Millie nodded.

Charlene's face lit up when she smiled for the first time. She glanced around but turned back quickly, obviously not spotting the current work in progress or any other priceless pieces on display. Her aunt did not hang her own artwork on her walls. Did any artist? It must have been an unspoken code. Greta didn't know but poor Charlene would not spy a masterpiece today. She wondered if it would help her cause to show off Millie's studio. It might if she was an art fan. Or gift her something? A little discarded corner of a canvas even? Because let's face it, she needed all the help she could get.

Greta sat back as Charlene gushed about an exhibition she'd attended years before. A solo in Millie's honour at the Art Gallery of New South Wales.

'Are you having another show soon?' she asked.

Momentarily off the hook and grateful, Greta sank back into the chair, not brave enough to lift her cup of tea in case the woman remembered her presence.

'I am actually. I'm holding an exhibit towards the end of the year and will be introducing my very talented protege here,' she said swinging her hand in Brodie's direction.

What? Greta said up tall in her chair and flicked looks between Brodie and Millie. Huh, they'd never mentioned an exhibition. But of course, Millie would be preparing for a show, that's what she did. Brodie didn't agree.

He laughed self-consciously. 'Oh, she's funny, isn't she, Charlene? Millie is right, she is working hard at present on twenty or more pieces that she will exhibit *solo*.' Brodie emphasised the word.

'Tsk,' Millie said shaking her head. 'The boy underestimates his talent. Even if it is not my sort of art, he does modernist abstract paintings, he is technically brilliant and has an incredible ability to express himself through his work.'

'I look forward to seeing your paintings,' Charlene said and turned away, back towards Greta.

Bugger.

'So, Greta, you are surrounded by motivated and talented people. Are they inspiring you?'

Was that a question, really? Inspiring her to what? She didn't paint … she paused too long and Charlene continued.

'It's only been a few days but what have you done to organise work, a permanent place to live and your reintegration into the community?'

'Wow, gosh. I've been focusing on getting a good night's sleep and remembering how to live.'

Millie kicked her under the table again. This time she didn't respond but felt the throb in her shin.

'Sorry, joking of course.' Greta cleared her throat buying time. The cat meowed.

'I've spent a bit of time thinking about projects to fill my time and that are worthwhile. I'm already caring for a set of abandoned kittens and their sick mother. I found them last Friday and will restore them to health.' Her aunt and Brodie exchanged a glance. She jumped up and retrieved the box and carried it out to demonstrate.

'Projects are good …'

Greta didn't let Charlene finish and instead shoved the box of cats in her face only for Charlene to recoil. *Shit.* Greta glanced out the window and caught a glimpse of the overgrown and neglected garden.

'Yes, I agree. I need to keep busy, so I've also been thinking of revitalising my aunt's mess of a garden because she simply doesn't have the time. So I'll pick out the weeds and plant some fresh varieties—'

'Do you have a lot of experience with gardening?' Charlene asked.

'Um, no, but it's like a fresh start and a time for new beginnings.' Greta picked up the mother cat and nursed her for support; she discarded the box onto the floor, keeping the kittens nearby.

Charlene nodded and wrote notes in her spiral-bound pad.

'How will you fund caring for the cats and plants for the garden?'

A simple question. What was her answer?

'I have a job.'

All heads turned towards her then.

'Oh, that's wonderful news. Tell me about it.'

'A temporary position at the caravan park. They require someone to clean the vans and cottages after residents check out. I'll do that while I continue searching for another position. There are only two banks and a couple of mortgage brokers in town –'

Charlene placed her notebook down, removed the glasses from her nose and twirled them between her pointer finger and thumb. 'You do understand, don't you, Greta, that you are permanently forbidden from engaging in practice in any capacity in the finance industry?'

Greta dry swallowed.

'Forever.' Charlene confirmed to avoid any doubt.

Brodie coughed. Did he have a nervous tic? He seemed incapable of keeping simple bodily functions to a minimum when Greta was under stress. Or did she simply notice them more at those times?

'I forgot.'

Charlene nodded officiously. 'Okay, well, a timely reminder. You are not permitted to undertake any work in that profession ever again. So, as you say, time for new beginnings. Perhaps you can retrain?'

Her parole officer parroted on with ideas of courses to study and other alternative work options and pulled numerous pamphlets and brochures from her bag.

'And another timely reminder that you have three months to commence restitution payments or you'll be hauled back into prison.'

Bile burned at the back of Greta's throat. She couldn't even swallow to chase the taste away.

'Regardless of how much you earn in this temporary position, make sure you start your contributions straight away. In these circumstances it is not a case of too little too late. Every small amount alerts the court to the fact you're trying. The cleaning won't pay much though. Ensure you continue your job search for something permanent so you can make regular and more sizeable payments and keep yourself out of jail.'

A time-bomb ticked in her head.

'Right. I'm back for another visit in a fortnight. I look forward to your progress with work, the cats and the garden, of course. On the next occasion, I'll obtain the details of your employer at the park and speak with them as well. You should investigate and make some other plans for work. Your aunt confirms she is happy to support you until you are self-sufficient. But we want that time to come sooner rather than later.'

Millie showed Charlene out while Greta sat at the table and listened to the door click shut.

Greta didn't wait for Millie to return. Taking the steps two at a time, she raced upstairs and retrieved her phone and computer. With cords trailing behind her, she rushed back downstairs. She took the last gulp of tea that had gone cold and went into the front room. She'd call it a study but it was more a living area or perhaps once, it might have been a parlour. This room was welcoming with pale green walls and curtains from floor to ceiling pulled wide open to allow the morning sun to stream in and warm the space. It had two floral armchairs for wiling away hours with a book and a cool drink. The shelves were lined with bric a brac, photo frames and vases filled with flowers. The room was calm and pretty, not at all like Millie.

Greta located a power point and plugged in her phone and laptop. No more hiding, or avoidance. She couldn't pretend she didn't exist in the world.

While the devices powered up, she stood in front of the bay window overlooking the front garden, the one she was miraculously going to replant and looked at the vista down the drive towards the road. She couldn't focus on the beauty of her surrounds as a sudden ache formed in her chest. A return to prison teased her and her body turned to jelly; the prospect was still too real.

Who was this woman that stared back in the windowpane? She didn't know anymore. She looked ridiculous if she was being honest. Out on this sprawling property, with no one for miles, her hair was straightened, her lips smudged red and she wore designer gear that didn't suit. Not anymore anyway. Any feeling of restfulness disappeared and now, she saw the dark and puffy bags of skin under her eyes, the sunken cheeks and set jaw. The ache returned again and spread to her temples.

What did Charlene think of her? A crim who needed rehabilitation pretending to be something else. How did she present to her aunt? Millie always looked at her with sympathy, that certain sad expression that her niece was lost and would hopefully soon be found.

Greta rubbed the back of her hand across her mouth to wipe away traces of her Chanel lipstick. God, what did Brodie think of her? Why did she insist on putting on bright red lipstick? She knew the answer – a pretence, that she really was who she used to be; a drive to reconnect with that person.

How stupid! That person was dead. And frankly, even in her discombobulated state, that version of herself was well gone. But that was the trouble, wasn't it? If she wasn't that person, who was she?

She buried her head in her hands and groaned. Brodie must think her a right royal city twat.

Sitting in the bay window seat, Greta picked up one of many postcards that lined the sill. This card was an image of the Arc de

Triomphe with tiny people at its base and a blue sky that mesmerised. She lifted it closer to her face to discover it wasn't a photo but a print with fine and technical detail. Gosh, how she'd love to visit the city of love, wander the Champs-Élysées, eat baguettes and sip espresso; walk to the top of the Eiffel Tower. Most likely she'd need to put that dream to bed. How could she ever? She'd be in debt for eons yet. That was her punishment and what she deserved.

'I love that city,' Millie stood in front of her before sitting down and picking up another postcard. A Monet painting, the famous pond at his home in Giverny.

'Have you visited these places on your cards?'

Millie nodded. 'Yes. I spent the most glorious summer in France, I'll never forget it.'

'You lived there?'

'Yes, in my twenties. It was the most exciting adventure. I stayed with friends all over the country, mostly in Paris but out in the countryside for spells as well. I met the most amazing people, creative and alive and interesting and I painted and drew almost every day.'

'Where are those paintings now?'

'Many were sold in exhibitions, some are in galleries, others I gifted. A few were not quite good enough and probably ended up in a bin somewhere.'

'If you created your own works, why did you buy these?'

'I buy a postcard from each place I visit. It's such a lovely memento. And even though I don't travel half as much now, when I do, I take a few of my postcards with me and place them next to my bed, it feels like home then.'

'That's a nice thing to do.'

'That's something *you* need to do now, Greta. Find out who you are, what you like, what you represent. I love collecting beautiful things – other people's rubbish oft times – but my little treasures, and postcards are part of that. But that's a trivial little example. You need to discover the substance of who you are,' Millie emphasised the words and brushed a tear away from her cheek.

'I thought I knew, Millie. I worked hard, was successful in my job, was well-respected, had a good life and could look after myself.' Greta plumped up the base of her bob hair with one hand to ignore the hitch in her voice.

Millie placed the card back on the sill. Glanced at the others, memories flitting across her face. 'Work is important for many reasons, it provides us with an income and allows us to live. Fills our time and if we are lucky we gain a lot of satisfaction from doing it. I could never say you shouldn't devote yourself to your work. I've done exactly that my entire life, sacrificing at my choice – a husband, a family. But it's given me so much more than I ever committed to it. And I hope that it has also provided something to others, objects of beauty to be admired. I'm not like that young Brodie. He tries to make a statement, send a message. I only wish people to look at my work and fall in love with it, the scene, the setting, the image.'

'I helped people make money. Sometimes it was important, you know retirees who wanted to secure their future, make a small profit on the funds they'd saved to live a good quality of life.'

Millie nodded.

'Sounds lame when I say it out loud.'

'I guess someone has to do it, but is that someone you?' Millie smiled. 'You know what? You don't even have to think about that anymore because it's no longer an option. New choices and experiences is the only way forward. So you have an interest in gardening?' Millie's eyes sparkled and Greta burst out laughing and it loosened something within, like a knot dissolving.

'Oh my God! I don't know why I said that. I'm such an idiot!'

'Well, gardening can be very cathartic. Soothes the soul, they say. And frankly, I know that woman was pushing you, but what's the rush? The time is now for you to sort out the future and my dear, to get it right. Muck it up and you'll be heading down the wrong path again.'

'No, Millie you're wrong. It's urgent, I have to start paying back my debt within three months or I'll return to prison. I have to get a job. And the pittance I'll earn at the caravan park probably won't help. What a disaster.'

Millie went to say something but stopped. Then started again. 'Don't be too harsh. Some people do certain types of work because they can, because they enjoy it or simply because they have to for survival. Three months is plenty of time. Long-term, it doesn't matter what you do, as long as it's your choice and makes you happy.'

Greta's phone dinged three times in quick succession.

They both broke into grins and Millie placed her hand over hers. 'Guarantee your mother has left a dozen messages. Don't avoid her, she'll worry.'

'I won't.'

'Now, I'm going to spend my day getting lost in my own world. The world of my easel and paints and the glorious images I'm creating at the moment.'

'Is there a theme to your next exhibition?' Greta didn't know much about art.

'Yes, a broad theme. Images of this house, the local area, some landscapes and hillsides, but also capturing where those grassy knolls meet the wind-swept beach and sit alongside each other. I'll give you a sneak peek later.' Millie kissed her check and left the room.

CHAPTER 6

Greta scanned the floor to ceiling bookshelves in the parlour. When did Millie have time to read? Moving closer, Greta discovered many were art manuals and glossy coffee table books. Artists she knew? But there were loads of novels too. After reading the titles on a few spines she extracted a book from the shelf.

'Have you read that one?'

Greta's gut churned. She didn't turn, but a shadow fell across the bookcase.

Turning the book over, she read the title. *The Great Gatsby.* She shook her head.

'You?' she asked turning around to find Brodie standing in front of the bay window.

'Nah, too high-brow for me. I'm reading a ripper at the moment. A whodunnit.'

'Crime?'

Brodie nodded. Her muscles loosened a little.

'I think this is too high-brow for me, too.'

'You? Nah, don't be silly. You could knock it over, no problem.'

'I'm not, um, a very good reader.'

He started at her blankly. 'You can't read?'

'No! I can read, but not very well. I'm dyslexic.'

'Okay. Is that where you mix your letters up?'

'Yeah, the letters jumble and I get confused and it takes me ages to read even a sentence. I've had all the training and stuff but you have to get used to it. It can't be fixed, but I'm sure I can try harder.'

'Well, I'm sure the institution of school didn't assist.' She gazed at him quizzically before he continued. 'Yeah, but man, that sounds tough. Don't be too hard on yourself. It's like a gym workout that you know you should do but it hurts like buggery, so you stop. I get it.'

'Given this is a time to rediscover things, maybe I'll challenge myself to read more books, all these books.' She swept her arms wide.

'I admire your pluck but don't get too far ahead of yourself. Why don't you start off with one book and not that one.' He tossed Gatsby back and his eyes roamed the shelves. 'What about this one?'

'A story about Rosie? I don't know whether you're taking the piss or being genuine but I'll give it a go.'

'All right. Your afternoon of reading is set, but first, should you meet your new employer given that Charlene is going to check up on you and all?'

'What, now?'

'Yep, no time like the present. You'll need to be ready for the next clean.'

'Okay, let's do it.'

∼

'How far away is the caravan park?' Greta asked once they were outside the cottage.

'It's a few kilometres but I've got my bike.'

'I need to get my shit sorted. I hadn't thought about transport living here. I need a car but can't afford one. Whilst it might be wonderful for my health, walking kilometres every day to get anywhere isn't an option Another problem to deal with.'

'Greta, give yourself a break. It's early days. But for now, I'll give you a lift, I've gotta come anyway, show you the way.'

Brodie could tell she was beating herself up, again. Her head hung low and she didn't respond.

He retrieved his bike, patted the frame and indicated for her to hop on.

'It's not exactly a speed racer, is it?' she said and cracked her first smile. Her tone sprinkled with lightness.

'I don't know what that means, but I'm assuming you're dishing out on my trusty old bicycle. I'll have you know it's reliable and has done a great job in getting me around. And it will you today, too.'

Brodie observed the bike through someone else's eyes, saw the rust near the rear wheel, tyres that were flat and the torn leather seat that bit into his backside when he rode.

'It's not exactly a Malvern Star, but it'll do,' he said the words out loud.

Her grin dropped and she nodded. 'Thank you for the lift. You're making a habit of saving me.'

Brodie held the bike steady and inhaled as she sat between his arms, his hands in position on the handlebars. Her head was so close he smelled her hair. He didn't know the fragrances but it smelled fresh and clean, like a peach. Or a tree in blossom that would make his sinus go crazy. He heard his heart thudding in his ears and he focused all his energy on balancing the bike and circling the pedals.

The moment they moved she burst out in a loud infectious giggle. He smiled. 'Please don't crash,' Greta squealed.

Her hair flicked into his face, her shirt billowed and occasionally she'd turn backwards and smile. He could feel her sadness lift and blow away in their wake.

Brodie took the long route up and down the hills of the hinterland back streets, past the majestic houses on acreage; glided past the bushland bordering the town, along the main drag with its shops and restaurants facing the beach where the salt sprayed their faces and stung their skin. Greta'd never know because she wasn't familiar with the way of the land yet. And he wanted to savour having her between his arms, in his care with her voice drifting back to him for a little longer. It wasn't far and too soon he turned into the reception area of the park and his arms were empty. An unexpected longing gripped him and he wanted to pull her into an embrace.

It was killing Brodie not to help with the cleaning. He hadn't realised that one family had stayed an additional night after the weekend and checked out today. That left cabin five dirty. He'd only intended to show Greta around, not put her to work straight away.

He'd offered to do the cleaning and she could watch and learn, but she'd refused.

Was insulted, actually.

She knew how to clean, she'd told him and picked up the bucket and mops and brooms and walked inside the cabin. Seconds later, he'd heard the low rumble of music and saw her figure flit across the window and back.

To carve out some time he ducked into his parents' house for a snack. Dad was drinking a coffee at the dining table, the newspaper spread in front of him.

'Heya, Dad, how're ya doing?' he slapped him on the back in greeting.

'Good, son,' his father said, and continued. 'Derek's concreting mate needs a hand, three or four days work. Good money. Think you can help out?'

These were often the way his conversations were with his father. Asking about paid work, his next contract or intentions. It was never a direction, always a suggestion that someone needed his help. Brodie interpreted the statements as a need to pull his weight, get a real job and do something productive with his life. Well, other than art, anyways.

The offer was timely though. His only pocket money was the cleaning work from the park and now Greta was doing that.

'Yeah, sure, the cash would be good.'

'Right then, I'll let Derek know and he'll get you the details.'

Conversation over, Dad headed back outside and Brodie heard the mower start up.

Over his corned beef sandwich, Brodie's thoughts drifted to his unfinished painting. He wondered when he'd get back to it. Last week he'd been on track and he couldn't wait to continue and knew he'd be a funny sort of anxious until he worked on it again. He slumped in the chair.

Over the next few days he'd be creating something of a different kind; his hands would still be dirty, the end result not quite as creative. Perhaps he could use the time to think over what he'd tackle next? Not a bad plan. In the meantime, he could sketch up a few ideas while he waited for Greta to finish.

Walking back towards his van, he wandered past cabin five. The music no longer played so he paused at the door, listening. Nothing. Then a hiccup. An item dropped. A frisson of discomfort swept through him.

Brodie opened the door and glanced around the living space. The floors were clean and the chairs placed neatly back under the table in the kitchen. The benches were free of crumbs and the strong scent of bleach hung in the air. A noise came from the bathroom to his left.

He heard the gush of running water and quickened his pace. Entering, he sidestepped to avoid the cleaning equipment sprawled across the tiles.

'Whoa! Are you all right?' Greta lay prone in the white porcelain bathtub, her head beneath the tap getting soaked.

Sobbing, she looked up through a wet fringe, strands of hair sticking to her face. Water droplets clung to her long dark lashes.

Brodie turned off the tap and Greta cried louder. 'What's the matter?'

'I'm so sorry,' she mumbled.

'What for?'

She didn't respond and Brodie held out his hand. Greta peered around the spout and seconds passed. She sniffled, shifted and placed her fingers in his before he pulled her up and out of the tub.

Greta's bare feet skated on the wet bathroom tiles and Brodie jerked forward to grip her arms to prevent them both from tumbling. They bumped into each other but were unable to maintain their balance and crashed to the ground.

'Are you okay?' he asked but Greta remained silent. Until catching him by surprise, she threw her head back and released a peal of laughter. The sound rippled through the silence of the room. Greta's eyes crinkled with amusement and he couldn't help but chuckle too.

'I'm sitting in a puddle,' he said.

Greta nodded, 'I'm saturated,' and she pulled her t-shirt away from her skin.

'What happened?' he asked again.

'I was scrubbing the tiles in the corner and lost my balance and slipped. Stupid really,' she shrugged.

'Are you crying because you're hurt or because the bath isn't finished?' he grinned too wide, still trying to work out what was going on because so far nothing made sense.

Greta covered her eyes with her hands. 'Oh my God, I'm such an idiot. I'm not hurt, I felt stupid because I can't even clean a bath.'

He reached out and ran his finger along the edge and when it came up clean, said, 'Seems pretty good to me.'

Greta released her hands and smiled weakly and wiped the back of her hand against her runny nose. Brodie untangled their arms and legs and stood. He helped her up for the second time in a matter of moments. Standing, water dripped onto the floor. Brodie ignored how wet he was and pulled her in close and held her tight. Greta didn't resist and placed her cheek against his chest and snuggled in. Brodie exhaled a breath as he clung to her.

Too soon, she pulled away. 'You okay, now?' and he looked down into her face. 'The bathroom is immaculate. You've done a great job, please don't worry.'

Those sad brown eyes peered at up him and his insides melted. He loved having her close, feeling as if he was protecting her. Why was he always compelled to make sure she was okay?

'It's not about the cleaning. It's me. The shock of the slip overwhelmed me and I tried to picture my future, tomorrow even and I couldn't. Everything is uncertain and it feels shit.'

'I hardly know you, but you seem like a really nice girl who's had a tough time. You're so hard on yourself. You stuffed up. Everyone does. It doesn't mean you're a failure. You've achieved so much already. You don't have to be anywhere, do anything amazing. Maybe you need to soak in the sea air for a while. Look at me, I live here, at the park, working odd jobs, getting by, not really achieving much ...'

Greta pulled back and looked at him and wiped her face with

the bottom of her shirt. 'That's not true. You're an artist. Millie *loves* you and she's a harsh critic, so you must be all right. Particularly with all that modern stuff you do.'

Brodie nodded, only wanting to feel the warmth of her body again.

Fat tear drops rolled down her pale cheeks but Greta talked through her sobs.

'I'm so sorry. I'm such a mess. I can't seem to function outside of a cell anymore but thinking about being back inside makes me want to vomit. I keep thinking about those four walls…the prisoners, the guards, the rules, the violence.'

Her body tensed. Brodie reached for her again, but her hands covered her face.

'Do you know what's worse? I deserved it. I am guilty. How could I have been so stupid? I broke the law and didn't even know it because I trusted other people to do the right thing. People suffered because of my ignorance.' As if saying the words out loud motivated her, Greta wiped away her tears and stood up taller, took a deep breath. 'Brodie, I'm going to pay those people back, every cent. I promise and I will make something of my life. Okay?'

'That's my girl!' and he shoulder bumped her. 'And in the process you need to learn to forgive yourself too, you can't do anything if you're feeling rubbish all the time.'

Those big round eyes stared at him again. Man…

'I'll try,' she nodded, appearing ready to move on and say no more. 'I'm sorry I've made you all wet.' Then she jerked away from him, the moment over. 'I've got to clean this up so I can keep this job.'

She went to move but Brodie stopped her. 'How about you strip off those wet clothes, use one of these towels,' he indicated to the shelf, 'pop them in the dryer. I'll make you a cuppa and clean up here.'

Brodie had to do something. Her saturated T-shirt clung to her and outlined the perfect, round shape of her breasts. He diverted his eyes but some uncontrollable force kept drawing them back. The breaths he inhaled didn't quite reach his lungs.

As if she could read his mind, she held the towel up to cover her chest. He was both disappointed and relieved simultaneously. Greta nodded.

Maybe he should jump in that cold shower and cool himself off, too.

'Brodie?' she queried as he turned away. 'You live here?'

Greta took her steaming mug outside and sat on the timber steps leading to the cabin. It faced the lake on one side and while she couldn't see it, the ocean lay across the road, behind the local surf club. The roll, hiss and thunder of the waves crashing against the shore filled the air and she focused on the sound as she sipped her tea.

God, he must think her an idiot. Crying and blubbering like a baby.

Another wave in, out. Over the years she'd tried many relaxation techniques. Always when pushed to the limit with work pressures. She breathed in and out and focused on her immediate environment. In addition to the waves, she heard a trio of birds in the trees lining the road talk to each other before they flew away. A door opening and closing, murmured voices, car engines. Her heart rate slowed and slowly she drifted back to the present and away from the blackness that threatened.

Problem was she wasn't used to being out of control. She'd always been a meticulous planner. Of course, now she didn't have a schedule but she needed one, everyone needed purpose, didn't they?

Greta picked up a pebble and tossed it onto the paved road.

She knew all this, had only talked about it with Millie this morning. But she guessed a schedule was different to finding your passion. That's what Millie had done. But what if you didn't have a passion? She loved animals but that may not lead to a future direction. Study would be too hard with her disability. She threw another rock, bigger this time. Maybe something would simply evolve if she had faith in the universe. She smiled; quack thinking now that she was in the heartlands of the hippies.

She'd taken the last sip of tea when Brodie appeared around the side of the cabin rolling a bicycle next to him. Not his bike. A bright yellow antique bicycle with large wheels and a basket with a flower.

Greta stood. 'What's this? Has someone borrowed yours?'

He grinned making his face light up. Greta was getting a sense life for Brodie may not be a barrel of laughs, but you'd never know it. He presented as the happiest bloke around but sometimes she detected the shadow in the corner of his eyes.

'It's yours. Found it in the shed. Used to be my sister's but she hasn't used it in yonks.' He pushed it towards her.

Greta stepped forward but didn't take it. 'I don't need your charity.' His grin dropped. 'And you don't need a cleaner here, do you? If this is where you live, is the cleaning your job?'

'This is not charity. It's helping a friend. At the moment, whether you like it or not, you are on your own and need some help.'

Greta flinched.

'Okay, wrong choice of words. If you accept gestures of kindness, then life will be easier. And usually, when people are back on their feet, that's when they help someone else out who needs it. Paying it forward and like. You know what I mean?'

'What about the job?'

'My parents own this park. I do the cleaning if there isn't anyone else available. They do need someone. Someone they can rely upon and who does a good job. Don't do it because you're desperate. Or because you have to show Charlene you've found employment. Don't muck my parents around. They are good and hardworking people and deserve better.'

Greta shrank to two inches tall. 'I'm sorry, Brodie. I'm such a bitch. It's like I have to relearn the usual subtleties of life.'

'Like being kind to people and accepting help? I guess there wasn't a lot of that in prison.'

She shook her head. 'I won't let your parents down. I need the job. I'll do it well, I promise. And thank you for the bike. I'll look after it until I can get one of my own and return it schmicko.'

She grasped the handles and their hands brushed. 'You're too kind to me,' she said as she left her hand in place. The touch of her skin upon his created a delightfully warm and tingly sensation on the spot. It wasn't a zap of electricity, it was so much better than that. Comforting, inviting and safe and it sent a thrill straight up her spine.

He glanced at their hands and then at her. He'd lost that impish grin and she fought to keep her other hand by her side. She wanted to reach out and rake her fingers through his too-long facial hair. For a fleeting moment she imagined holding the nape of his neck as his face moved in close to kiss her.

'Do you want to follow me back to Millie's?' His voice was husky, low without the hint of joviality it usually held.

'No, I can find my way back.'

'This is yours,' he held out a small bundle of notes. 'Your first pay.'

A flush of embarrassment crept up her neck and her chest and head exploded with heat. She quickly stuffed it in her back pocket.

As she rode away, Brodie's gaze burned her back.

CHAPTER 7

Greta was almost to the shed before she noticed the shiny metallic blue convertible Porsche parked in the drive. A funny pang of something hit in her the chest as she remembered the black Mercedes she had once owned.

It wasn't envy. She didn't admire the sleek curves and white upholstery of the convertible. Nostalgia for an experience she'd once had? Maybe.

She moved past the car and stowed the bicycle out of the weather. Humming beneath her breath, she walked to the front of the house and came face to face with Charlie Clarke.

Bile crept up her throat and she swallowed it back, the sour taste burning on its way down.

'What the hell are you doing here?' she said when she could speak and stood, feet hip-width apart, hands on her hips.

'That's not a very nice way to greet me.' The usual dazzling smile, all teeth and lips greeted her as he rose off the bottom step. And together with his pin-striped suit and too-shiny leather shoes, he was an assault to her senses.

Charlie circled his arms around her middle and pulled her in close before landing a full, wet kiss on her mouth. 'It's so good to see you.'

Greta stepped back and wiped her hand across her mouth. One fist clenched by her side as she fought the urge to clock him in the nose. Hard.

This couldn't be happening. Was he really here? In the middle of bloody nowhere. It was a violation of her privacy, of her sanctuary. Of everything.

She turned around quickly as panic gripped her. Charlene could turn up at any moment. It was a breach of her parole conditions to associate with him or any other criminal for that matter. But what did a breach mean? Could she be sent back to prison? Fear spiralled up her spine like a cluster of spiders. She had to get rid of him.

Blinking her eyes shut, she opened them again but Charlie still stood before her. She shook her head. He belonged to a different time and place. This man had ruined her life and had no right to assume anything; no right to touch her, kiss her. He looked exactly the same. How could he not be irretrievably changed, like she was?

Plus, he'd been deafeningly silent these last six months. Not a message, a telephone call, a letter; not one word.

'Where have you been?'

Charlie laughed. The sound stabbed into her heart. He joked?

'Same place as you, honey. Except in the male wing at Her Majesty's service.'

Greta searched for his discomfort in referring to the aberration in both of their lives. Not a single drop of sweat appeared on his brow and there was no pause in his speech.

Bastard.

'When did you get out?'

'A few days ago.'

Around the same time as her? How unfair! He was sentenced first but to a longer term.

'How did you find me?'

'Asked around …'

A figure moved to her right. Her aunt stood on the deck, facing down upon them like a priest in a pulpit. Her face was creased with worry, her lines deep and her usually sparkly eyes, sombre.

A thread of dread unfurled in Greta's stomach. She couldn't allow Charlie to creep under her veneer, what would happen if she did? Faced with him, her confidence waivered and her mind scattered to a million different places and yet at the same time, was blank.

'Are you coming in then?'

Charlie glanced at Millie. A faint flicker of uncertainty crossed his features. Perhaps they'd already exchanged words.

'Let's go for a drive,' he said instead.

A war battled in her head and Greta didn't know what to do. She didn't owe Charlie anything but something held her back from sending him away.

Her hand felt heavy and she looked down. She'd forgotten about the bottle of wine she'd bought as a gift for Millie. Without responding to Charlie she moved towards the house and placed the wine on the stairs. The words were out before she could stop them. 'It'll be okay, Millie. I'll go for a drive and send Charlie on his way. See you soon.'

Her aunt pulled her house cardigan in close around her body and moved away before slamming the door shut.

Greta hopped into the passenger seat of the car and felt transported back in time, to a different life. And with absolute clarity, it made her guts churn.

~

Bastard. She said the word over and over in her head. It was the only word that summed up Charlie.

She should have sent him packing when she'd first laid eyes on him. Instead, she'd been weak and held onto the hope that he'd apologise. Well, truthfully, she'd wanted the full scene: grovelling, tears, regret and even begging. She sure didn't get that and didn't get the apology either. That's what she wanted and the reason she'd gone with him.

Some part of her needed him to say the words; she might have forgiven him then and been able to move on with her life. If only he'd confessed he'd made a mistake and was sorry for his actions.

That wasn't so stupid was it? *Hell yes,* it was. She must have been dreaming. If the man was desperate enough to steal his client's money and then those of his girlfriend and ruin her in the process, why had she even considered he'd be remorseful?

Stupid. Stupid. Stupid. Again.

Greta took another slug of the wine from the bottle she carried. The cool liquid did nothing to dampen the anger swirling within and making her chest tighten. She paused, breathed in and out right down to the base of her lungs until her heart stopped racing. If she didn't, she'd be lost to the darkness and Charlie was not worth going there for. She was mad, but she was more disappointed at herself. She had to learn to be smarter and make better choices. But that wasn't any help to her now as she trudged home alone in the dark.

As she drew near the cottage, she saw it was illuminated in light and soft chatter drifted out through the open windows.

Entering, she headed towards the dining room. Inside a dozen guests sat at the table drinking and smoking and engaging in animated conversation. The low rumble of jazz music played in the background.

Distraction and a good time was exactly what she needed. 'Cheers,' she sang out and held up her bottle.

BRODIE TURNED AT HER VOICE AND HIS HEART JUMPED INTO HIS throat. Thank God she was safe. Greta'd been gone for hours and he was starting to doubt she'd return. Millie hadn't voiced her opinion, but he knew she'd been worried too.

She stood with her arms held up in a V shape, a bottle of wine dangling precariously from one hand. Her T-shirt hung out of her shorts, her usually dead straight hair was tousled and those eyes that usually looked good enough to drown himself in, were glassy.

Greta was drunk.

He darted around the table to reach her side and tried to swipe for the bottle but she was too quick.

'Don't snatch. Ask me if you'd like a drink,' she spoke too loudly.

'Where's Millie,' she asked, her head turning each which way as she searched the room. 'Millie!' she screeched and strode across the room. Along the way she turned the volume down on the old-fashioned record player and switched on her phone. Music blared from the one speaker making an uncomfortable doofing noise. It followed her as she walked towards Millie. Reaching the table Greta picked up a free tumbler and poured some wine and handed it to Millie.

'I don't want any, thank you, dear,' Millie said and blew her cigarette smoke out the corner of her mouth.

'Ah, c'mon. You're having a party. Where's the fun aunt I used to know?'

Millie's guests seated at the table exchanged glances. They were all drinking, some port, others whiskey.

Greta offered the glass, slopping the contents over its edges.

'Perhaps you didn't hear me, Greta dear, I said no.'

Greta's hand hung in mid-air before Brodie reached over and attempted to take the cup. Her arm swerved out of his way spilling yet more wine. 'No. If Millie is going to be a party pooper, I'll have it.'

'It would appear, darling, as if you've had plenty.'

Lola appeared of nowhere and growled at Greta, her teeth barred. There was no sign of the cats.

Greta leaned down to seemingly placate the dog and overbalanced. Lola leapt away and Brodie shot forward to grip her arm and pull her upwards.

'Let's get you something to eat. Millie made the most delicious roast chicken and vegetables.'

'Some water, too, I think, Brodie,' Millie interjected and her friends laughed.

Greta snatched her arm out of his grip. 'I'm fine. I don't need you Mr Perfect looking after me. Perhaps I don't want to be saved, don't deserve to be cared for. Why don't you go find some other damsel in distress to help?' She moved too quickly and backed into a chair. It toppled with a clatter to the ground. Greta paused and then collapsed dramatically to her knees.

Brodie counted to ten before placing a hand on her shoulder. He felt her shudder before she rose, languorously stretching out her limbs, like one of the kittens. She stood on wobbly legs and gazed up at him before turning on a brilliant and broad smile. A twinkle returned to her eyes. The sparkle of a girl up to mischief.

Greta reached up and placed her arms around his neck, locking him into place. She leaned in, her head resting against his chest. He braced himself for her next move, or the next cutting words off her sarcastic tongue. Instead, she was silent before a gurgle rumbled out of her throat and a hand flew to cover her mouth. Too late, Greta vomited down the front of his white t-shirt.

The book flew across the room where it hit the artichoke green wall at the exact moment that Millie entered the study.

'Not enjoying it, then?' she asked, all innocence.

Greta didn't respond.

'Still have trouble reading?'

She nodded. 'It's always worse when I'm feeling average.'

'Unwell from overindulging or feeling low?' Her aunt joined her in the facing teal armchair. Her aunt and her green shades, she couldn't get enough.

'I do feel wretched but vomiting most of the night has cleared me out, now I'm sculling water to rehydrate. But fatigue makes my vision blurry and I can't focus.'

'It's wonderful you're reading again. Keep it up, little bits at a time is the key. I remember saying that to you as a child. You'd get so frustrated. Some things haven't changed. But you'll get there. Of that I'm absolutely certain.'

Millie wasn't wearing her painting hat yet but was in a flamboyant multi-coloured floral dress with her greying hair pulled back in a bun. A few random wisps framed her face. Greta thought she looked older, but she was getting on, so of course, she would. Hadn't lost any of her positivity though.

'Why don't you drink anymore?'

'Well, you said it yourself. I drank too much when I was young, it kept my shyness at bay. The exhibitions were so daunting in the early days. Everyone wanted a piece of me and then either wanted me to dissect the painting for them, or they'd do it for me and tell me exactly what they thought. A shot of sherry before I left calmed me down. But it becomes a habit, you see. And then it was a shot before I left, during the show and more when I arrived home. And that didn't include the wine drunk with dinner. It became a problem, Greta. When you lose control of something, it's an addiction. I had to stop. Even now, I still crave it. Want to feel the cool stem of a glass in my hand and laugh with good company and nibble on cheese. Alcohol and I are not friends and at the detriment of my art, it had to go.'

'I would never have called you shy, Millie, but I'm sorry. I didn't realise. I've been insensitive about it, trying to force drinks on you.'

'I'm a big girl, learned to look after myself a long time ago.' Millie patted her knee and continued. 'What happened with Charlie? You were gone for hours and we were worried.'

'We?'

'Brodie and I.'

'Oh,' Greta nodded. 'Alcohol is not your friend. Well, Charlie has a demon and it's called ice. It's what caused this trouble and he remains gripped. Incredible because in prison he detoxed and attended rehabilitation. But the moment he's released, he's taking again.' She shook her head.

The gut-wrenching swirl of anger she'd experienced when

he'd asked her for money to buy drugs re-surfaced. How could he after the hurt they'd caused?

'One thing I've discovered, is that you have to really want something otherwise, it's too hard to give up. I could have lost my career, that's what alcohol was doing to me and my career was too important, my art is everything. It sounds like despite being convicted, embezzling funds and a stint in prison, he hasn't hit rock bottom yet. When he does, things might change. You can't force him. You know what else it tells me? That you are so much better than him, in many, many ways. You feel dreadful remorse, Greta and that speaks volumes. You're struggling at the moment, but without remorse, how can you move on? If you aren't sorry for what you did, there's no hope for change.'

Greta let the tears roll down her cheeks and didn't wipe them away. She flashed a smile of thanks at her aunt but the corners of her mouth hardly turned up. 'But Millie, I just can't seem to do anything right. I'm so embarrassed about my behaviour last night,' she hung her head in her hands, 'I'm sorry I acted like that in front of your friends, but there's worse …'

The door opened and a man entered. 'Oh, there you are. I've made some tea and toast. Can put some coffee on too, if you'd like?'

This question was directed at Greta.

'Fred, this is my niece, Greta.'

Greta acknowledged him but kept glancing at Millie waiting for an explanation to follow. Her aunt felt her glare.

'Oh, Greta. I'm allowed to have friends, aren't I?' Millie wore a mischievous smile and she turned it upon Fred who returned it double fold. He was an elderly man, same age range as her aunt, she guessed, white hair with an air of confidence about him. He looked a little bit like an eccentric professor.

'I'll be in the dining room when you're ready.'

Well, the old devil. Greta couldn't wait to tell her mother; she'd save that up for later to surprise and horrify her mother in equal measure.

Millie moved her feet under the chair and knocked something. She leaned down.

'What's this?' she said as she extracted a container slightly larger than a shoebox. The colour drained from her face.

'Greta, what's this doing here?' Her tone was clipped, gone was the softness of moments ago.

'Um, I'm not sure. I had to move it out of the way to get the book from the shelf.'

With an ashen complexion, Millie sat the box on her lap and lifted the lid, held it away so that Greta couldn't see. She didn't remove anything and snapped it shut.

'This is special to me, please don't touch it.' She rose and placed it on a low shelf with a sliding door and clipped it shut after it was locked inside. 'After tea, Fred and I are going to sit by the creek and sketch. Come and join us later if you wish.'

Saved by the bell as they say. Greta had been about to confess that she'd lost her first pay.

Well she prayed she'd lost it.

Opening her purse this morning it had been empty. She vividly recalled the colourful notes she'd placed in there after being paid by Brodie. And before heading off with Charlie.

Yes, she bought alcohol and hot, greasy chips. But they weren't expensive.

Every time she thought about that empty wallet, her mouth turned sour and she tasted the vomit she'd spewed during the night.

Where had her money gone?

But she knew.

Charlie Clarke had swindled her again and she only had herself to blame.

When he'd asked for money, she'd snapped. He hadn't

witnessed this sort of vitriol from her before and his attitude had gone from flippant to begging as his chance slipped away. He'd tried hard but soon realised it was pointless and she wasn't budging. Then he'd yelled and with each word spittle flew from his mouth and his face turned puce. She wasted no time getting out of the car.

And that was after he'd kissed her.

Yes, she'd wanted him to beg, but not for money, for her forgiveness. He'd said he was broke, implored he was desperate. Yes, poor but driving a new car; poor but wearing designer clothes.

She'd been played. So many regrets from last night; thinking about it made her nauseous again.

Damn it, she should be proud of herself. She hadn't given in to Charlie; not given him what he wanted. But he'd taken it anyway.

So she didn't feel proud, only stupid.

Greta needed that money. She hadn't put aside even one dollar to contribute to her restitution. Idiot! She should have left some money behind, saved it, hidden it.

Cell doors slamming, voices yelling obscenities, the relentless cold temperature and the acrid smell of body odour rushed into her head all at once. A light sheen of sweat covered her forehead. She had to stay out of that place. Had to. It was not an option.

Fuck!

Yeah, well done, Greta, you stood up to him, showed him what for.

Damn it, she was a fool.

With no purpose, and no cleaning required she was at loose end. She'd go mad, had to do something. After cleaning out the kitty litter and playing with the cats for at least thirty minutes, she stared out the window. The garden!

She still hadn't Googled cat care but she dragged their bed outside and placed it near the first patch of garden. They could do with some sun, right? Who knew, but she'd keep an eye on them anyway.

One idea would be to research gardens. Or did Millie have some books on the topic? Probably. Because she had no idea. In her twenty-six years, she'd never owned a garden. A couple of indoor potted plants had survived in her apartment but she couldn't even remember where they were now.

Brushing those thoughts aside, Greta gazed at the wreck of a yard. And there was a lot of land. No doubt it would have been beautiful once but was now suffering from lack of attention, like the cottage. The two garden beds in front of her had simple timber edging and sat in squares symmetrical to each other and aligned with the house. Greta imagined flowers blooming in a range of colours instead of the wild patch of weeds that grew there now. Stretching beyond the plots was an expanse of lush grass in desperate need of a trim. It led to a forest of eucalypt trees that spanned the width of the property and eventually ended at the creek. A few random boulders were scattered around the lawn, giving it a prehistoric feel. Standing at this point, catching the gentle breeze that swept up the slight incline where the cottage sat at the peak, Greta was struck by its beauty. It was a wonderful vantage for what could be an idyllic backyard. At this height your eyes caught the tops of the leafy trees and beyond was a glimpse of a glittering blue ocean. A perfect Australian landscape captured in one lens.

Ideas ricocheted around her head, but she figured the photographs she remembered from glossy magazines with round shaped hedges, shrubbery and water features would be out of her budget; given her budget was zero. Regardless of investment, she wanted to create something special for Millie. A gift of thanks for taking her in, thanks for, well, everything. Believing in her, being the one relative that always had, even when she was small. In return, she'd make a fantastic garden, she would.

But Millie wasn't a neat and tidy sort of gal, so it couldn't look like one of those gardens out of a magazine. It needed to stay a little bit ramshackle, busy with lots of plants and colour. Her aunt loved colour. Okay, that was a start. She knew where to head, well sort of.

The beds already housed some lovely plants that could be saved. Donning a broad-brimmed hat she found in the hallway, and a shovel and pitchfork in case she needed it, Greta attacked the brambles.

Her shirt became damp from sweat. It sure was back-breaking work: all that bending and kneeling and tossing. But in no time, she cleared a patch. Yes, this was a good idea, she could see progress and watch the garden develop.

Little buds of something sprouted in her chest at this miniscule achievement. Leaning down she pulled out one overgrown prickly weed and had to tug harder, its roots buried deep. With two hands, she bent back when Brodie skidded down the drive on his bicycle, scraping to a stop, flicking pebbles from the path in her direction. She glanced sideways to see him arrive and the weed gave way and she toppled, landing on her backside.

'Ow,' she said and used her palms to rise back up. 'That was a tough one.'

Brodie stood beside her, blocking the boiling sun. The sweat immediately cooled on her moist skin and she shivered.

His hands clenched on the handlebars of his bike and a newspaper was tucked under his arm.

'Is everything okay? Did I do a bad job cleaning? Are your parents mad?'

'Greta, not everything terrible that happens in the world is your fault.'

Okay, that felt like a slap to her face. Not undeservedly so. 'Yes, you're right, sorry. What's happened?'

'A refugee killed himself last night at one of the Australian detention centres. He'd been incarcerated for months with no contact with his family or friends and no assurances by the Australian government that he would be accepted into Australia.'

'Did you know him?'

'No.'

Greta frowned. 'So why are you so upset?'

He turned on her then; got off his bike and threw it to the ground and held the paper up and slapped it back down against his thigh before discarding it on the ground. 'We cannot treat people like that. Do you know where this man came from?'

Greta shook her head and her curly, loose hair fanned outwards. She needed a hair tie.

'Bahrain. He spoke out against the President and was imprisoned there for many days before he was finally released without charge. Then he became involved in a youth political group who were wanted by the government. He knew they were after him and he fled to Australia.'

Greta listened, still confused. 'Why can't he say what he likes?'

'There's no freedom of speech in that country like we have here. All he wanted was to be safe and we've killed him.'

Brodie paced. Stepped over her pile of discarded weeds and the second pile of plants to be saved. He muttered to himself as he walked. Greta had never seen him this worked up.

'You didn't kill him, Brodie. You shouldn't feel guilty…'

'We, the Australian people, our government allowed it to happen. We are all responsible. I need to think about what I can do to help.' He paused in front of the next bed she was working on and started ripping out anything green. In a few short shifts, half the garden was gone. She let him go on for a few minutes, his arms moving violently with heavy heaving breaths. When she couldn't bear it any longer, Greta placed her hand on one of his muscular arms.

CHAPTER 9

 he touched him mid-movement and their arms jerked
back together and the weed with its intricate array of
roots and bulbs of dirt, smacked her in the face.

'I'm so sorry!'

Four hands scrabbled at her face, wiping dirt out of her eyes
but it clung to the sweaty surface of her skin. Brodie grasped her
flailing hands and pinned them down by her side. She opened
one eye and grit slid into the corner and she blinked furiously.

'Don't move,' he instructed.

Okay, not like she had much choice. Lids squeezed shut, she
spat out bits of garden bed, and from far away heard a tap
gushing water, its pipes creaking with the effort.

A solitary finger under her chin titled her face upwards. A
damp cloth swept across one eyebrow and lowered to her lid.
Greta's breath stalled in her chest and her nerve endings went on
high alert. Brodie and his body, all hulking man of him, stood
very near. So close she heard his breaths, felt his movements.
Then his warm, sweet breath brushed her skin while sweeping

caresses moved across her cheeks and around her jaw line capturing any residual dirt.

'For someone with such large hands, you are incredibly gentle.'

She opened her eyes and stared straight into Brodie's hazel ones. They were flecked today, not able to choose between being blue or green. She liked the contrast.

Only inches separated their bodies. One movement and they'd touch. Except his closeness rendered her paralysed. Her tongue darted across her lips; her mouth suddenly dry. When she swallowed, dirt was the only taste.

With his gaze pinned to her, he rinsed the cloth in a small bucket next to him. The water was murky like the creek after a storm. Squeezing the excess liquid with one hand, he started at her forehead, down her nose and the narrow crevices beside it, in broader sweeps across her cheek and brushing only the very corners of her lips with tiny, delicate touches. His eyes flicked between her gaze and the cloth. When the cloth landed on her upper chest exposed in her skimpy white singlet, her heartbeat accelerated so fast she worried it'd jump right out of her chest. But Brodie didn't stop. The cloth traced the edges of the shirt and granules filtered down her top. It tickled but she didn't laugh. She swallowed again and his hand halted, held unsteady.

Greta placed her fingertips to his broad hips. He paused, lowered his hands next to his body. Time around them stopped and the world seemed to tilt.

He slopped the cloth into the bucket where it slapped the water. Birds chirped in the nearby trees and her arms and chest itched from grass cuttings. A hint of breeze blew.

She inched forward wanting those lips on hers, now.

His head dipped and she rose on tiptoes to meet him; their lips connected, at first it was soft, then harder, his tongue forcing her mouth open to explore. Sensations exploded and she closed her eyes to saviour the taste. He drew back, once, not losing their touch, then kissed her again. His lips were full, wet and covered her entire mouth. His hand slid around her back and applied slight pressure. Her hips met the bulk of him, angling forward to touch his pelvis. The feel of him lit a fire in her belly. Her hand climbed up his spine, craning to reach the nape of his neck. In between hot breaths she wanted to rake her hands through his hair. She couldn't reach, though, and instead pulled him in closer.

And more and more, she couldn't get enough. She wanted to climb into his skin, until they were one. Bodies together, the outline of his jeans and buckle dug into her skin; she didn't care. He was close and his body hot. Argh! Was it possible to melt? She was disappearing. Lost in the moment, she groaned, guttural and low. The sound encouraged him, his force upon her mouth heavier and urgent. He was hungry but not rough. Gasping for air they tilted their heads in the other direction and she tasted him again. Salt and dirt and earth.

Hitting a crescendo, her tummy exploded with fireworks before he pulled away. His chest heaved with deep breaths, a broad grin on his face. The moment could have been awkward, but not with Brodie. Greta panted, her mouth open, already dreaming of more.

'Wow,' he said.

His smile was infectious and she grinned in return. 'Yeah, wow.'

'I like you with this curly hair and no lipstick.' His hand braced each side of her waist, locking her in place. Was he worried she'd run? He should be.

Greta bit into the melted cheese of her toastie and it dribbled down her chin. It was the smallest of details she'd missed. The toasted sandwiches in prison had too thick cheese slices that never melted but the bread was burnt. And she always seemed to get the butt end of the tomato.

Not today, the cheese was evenly sliced and it was delicious. She sat on the front stairs to the cottage, that incredible panoramic view of Millie's land stretching in each direction. Not long after they'd kissed—*kissed!* —Brodie said he'd had a brainwave and needed to work on the idea immediately. He'd described the concept as eating him up on the inside; his fingers had twitched as he'd said it, desperate to create some magic. Her aunt wasn't as expressive about her pieces, but Greta knew inspiration struck in a similar vein. In the past, often mid-sentence, Millie would pull out a scrap of paper, a serviette even, and start to scribble. When satisfied she'd crumple it up and place it in her dress pocket. Brodie didn't do that but he bounced on his toes and she recognised in him that same need. That was the passion she lacked. Maybe she'd find it here in these hills. She laughed, remembering the old theme song to the Hillbilly show her mother had watched at home.

If she was going to find herself, once she would have rolled her eyes at the phrase, it had to be possible here, didn't it? The scene was picture perfect. Secluded, quiet, tranquil. Surrounded by verdant, rolling hills, bushy knolls, copses of trees with bird song and animal life.

Her heart skipped a beat. Where were the cats? She jumped up and raced over to the box. In the moment, she'd forgotten about them. But there the three kittens lay asleep, one in each corner of the box and the mother cat, laying back, looking like she was having a well-deserved rest. The animal rolled over onto its back, legs stretched waiting for a scratch and a tickle. Greta indulged her before sitting back on the stairs.

She couldn't concentrate. Brodie had kissed her. Her insides still quivered. Remembering the touch of his lips upon hers sent a bolt of pleasure through her body. The exact opposite reaction she'd had to Charlie yesterday. The two men were different. What did that mean? How could she have been attracted to sleek and suave Charlie with bucket loads of ambition and confidence but also to sweet, passionate Brodie who cared deeply about others and the world they lived in. Such contrasts. That didn't make sense to her, but she was a different person now, as Millie had said.

Brodie was a good person. Is that why she was attracted to him – to help make herself a better person? Surely, it was more than that?

Despite the magical kiss, she didn't want to over-think it. Her focus was on the future. Was Brodie in that future? She dampened down the warmth spreading through her tummy and picked up the paper he'd left behind.

He'd been worked up about the news of the refugee in the paper. Greta flicked it open and there the news article sat on the front page. Argh, just like she was front page news only those few short months ago. Thinking of the expose on her caused a sharp shooting pain to crack across her chest. *Today's paper is not about you, Greta, focus on this news.*

The title was large and bold, easy to read. She remembered her lawyer father ranting about Manus Island and detention centres once, she'd zoned out, bored. But now, her eyes zeroed in on the fine print and she read each line. It wasn't a long piece but as she read her pulse rate increased and beat out of her neck and upon reading the last words she crumpled the paper into a furious ball and squished it until her palms hurt.

She couldn't pretend to understand the politics behind what had happened, but at a human level, she knew, like stealing people's money, that how this man had been treated was wrong. Greta wanted to know more and couldn't wait to talk to Brodie about it again over dinner.

The sunlight was fading fast and it was time to call it a day.

'Hello there,' Millie said as she and Fred wandered up and stood next to her with their pads and pencils and fold away chairs. Her aunt's 'friend' was still here then. Well, she deserved some fun, with all the time she spent lost in her own worlds.

Her back spasmed and Greta stretched.

'Have you been at it all day?' her aunt asked.

'Yep. Got heaps done, too.'

'You sure have. I haven't seen the beds of these gardens for years. It was a bit of a mess, wasn't it?' Millie surveyed the piles. 'Are you going to use those as cuttings?'

'Hmm, yes. I think they can be saved and replanted, don't you?'

'Looks like it, love. But you'll need to keep them hydrated to stay alive.'

Greta stared back with a blank expression.

'Put them in some water or lay them in wet towels or soak them at least.'

'Oh, right! Of course. I'll do that now.' There was so much she didn't know.

'We're heading in to heat up the lasagne Fred made this morning. See you in five minutes.'

Walking inside she was greeted by raised voices and found Mr Quade in the living area.

'Hi, Mr Quade.'

He turned towards her then. Millie came forward and stood beside him. 'Henry, I'm sure it's the case he simply lost track of time.'

'You're very kind, Millie. But you know it's not that. He had a commitment today, people were relying on him and he didn't show. And I had to make up excuses. Again.'

'I agree, it's not good enough. I wasn't here this morning

when he arrived, not that I knew about this job anyway …' Millie shrugged.

'He's painting. A new piece. He's quite agitated about it, raced inside …' Greta wasn't sure if this was helping or not. True though.

Mr Quade looked at the ground and shook his head, defeated. Without uttering a word he walked towards the door, let it close behind him and was gone.

Inside at the dining table, they waited for Brodie. He was a permanent feature at the house, and no one, including Greta now, questioned his presence. Millie expected him for meals, and tonight, Greta did, too.

'I'll run and up and tell him dinner is ready,' Greta said, and she moved to get up.

'No, leave him, Greta. If he's working on something, he won't want to be interrupted.'

'But he has to eat.' And he'll want to see me, she thought, but didn't say.

'Yes, he does, but when he's ready.' Millie and Fred both picked up their cutlery and started eating. Greta noticed there was no wine served tonight.

The pleasure from the day disappeared. She hadn't realised how much she wanted to see Brodie, maybe even relive their kiss. He was in her thoughts between each tug of a weed and when dust particles landed on her cheek and she wiped them away. Her mind immediately went back to his caress on the same spot. Damn him and his moral high ground. Couldn't the painting wait until tomorrow? He'd still be working on it then anyways.

Dinner, usually an enjoyable event at Millie's house with robust conversation and laughs, was short and perfunctory. As soon as the last mouthful was swallowed, Fred stood declaring an early night. Greta yawned. Millie said she would clean up so Greta headed to her room too.

She paused outside Brodie's studio. She heard murmurs, the scrape of a chair, a sigh and a lid being unscrewed. Brodie worked on, oblivious to the world. It seemed he had forgotten her. Had forgotten their kiss.

In her room, she realised she'd left her phone in the study, charging. She could also retrieve the book, give it another go. It was amazing the confidence she felt after successfully completing that short newspaper article. Reading might also help her sleep.

She crept downstairs through the dim and deadly quiet cottage, like it was midnight except it was only eight o'clock. The door to the parlour was ajar and a sole beam of light shone through the crack.

Greta peeked inside, scanning the room. He aunt sat on the sofa, the box from earlier beside her, its contents spread on her lap. Millie fingered something gently with her thumb but in the light, Greta couldn't make it out. Or the few other tiny objects scattered on her lap. But she could see her aunt's face illuminated by the lamp. Her eyes were distant, lost in another time. Her gaze intense as if she wished the object could talk, or perhaps reveal something important? Greta could sense her aunt's loss as if it was a real-life living thing. Longing permeated off her, radiating in waves. The hairs at the back of Greta's neck stood. Millie was an open book, well, she'd always thought so. She told you what she thought, kept her emotions in check but felt them strongly and always appeared so sure of herself. As if she'd worked out everything that needed working out, long ago.

Not tonight. She was lost to another place. Her aunt kept something back. What was her secret and why was she keeping it hidden?

CHAPTER 10

*B*rodie rubbed his eyes with the palms of his hands. His lids scraped like sandpaper on his eyeballs. He closed them for a moment and the relief was instant. The sun streamed into the room; the day had begun hours ago. He'd promised then that he'd stop, rest, but he couldn't, he had to finish.

Adrenalin had kept him upright for the last twenty-four hours but it was quickly seeping away. The excitement, the hope and promise of new art, gone. He loved those initial feelings: ideas swirling in his head, the desperation to put brush to colour to canvas. It was such a sublime place to exist where in his mind everything he created was exquisite. He pictured how he wanted it to look, the colours, the contours, the technical lines. Always so vivid. And the urge to get on with it not able to be stymied.

When that rush ended, his body ached, his limbs heavy. His mind was sketchy, too, like he imagined he'd feel after running a marathon. He hadn't pulled an all-nighter for ages because no idea had compelled him enough but this one, this refugee painting was a living breathing, visceral thing.

Standing back, hands on hips, he looked at the three canvases and a knot formed in his chest. Voices filled his head.

'You're a naughty boy, wicked.'

'Such a frivolous waste of time.'

'This ugly picture is the work of the devil.'

Brodie flinched. He heard the voices; felt the laceration burning after the whipping of the cane. Instinctively, he rubbed the back of his thigh.

It's true, they weren't good enough. He balled his fists to keep them steady, to prevent them ripping the paintings in half, or worse, into tiny shreds that could never be recovered. He'd do it, too. Even if they weren't perfect, that didn't mean they should be destroyed, he reasoned with himself. Always these same feelings. He pulled in some deep breaths encouraging the moment to pass.

He continued to stare at the paintings and the emotions churned through him like a tsunami. How could they be better? In the ideas phase, the vision of the dead refugee had consumed him and that portrait, of his dead face had formed hard and fast. The contours of his face came with little effort. Then he'd worked backwards and portrayed the fellow as happy, trying to recreate times of his childhood. And the third, really it was the second in the series, a tall strong man who emanated fear. About to board a boat to what he imagined was paradise and safety only to quickly realise it was not.

There was longstanding argument in the arts about cultural appropriation. Those comments hit Brodie now as he glanced at his work. How dare he portray someone he didn't know? What right did he have to imagine what this fellow thought, felt or imagined? His inner voice spoke up and reminded him of the purpose of the work, and defended it because what better way to send a message about the treatment of our refugees?

Or, maybe, he'd simply created more pieces for his own

collection. The ones no one ever saw, his assortment was grow-ing, he had quite a number of them.

But for now, Brodie needed sleep. Plus the paintings needed to rest and dry. He'd mull them over some more, talk with Millie and ascertain what she thought. He'd always been a terrible judge of his own work. He turned all three canvases around to face the wall.

Rinsing his brushes and tidying the room, a recollection of raised voices came back to him. He'd not paid any attention at the time as he was so engrossed in his work. Millie had frequently said his demonic method, zoning out the entire world when he worked wasn't healthy, but how else did he approach it? He tried to think back. Where those voices yesterday? What was today? He checked his wristwatch. It was heading towards eight o'clock.

Oh shit!

No time for sleep. Brushes forgotten, he dropped them in the sink. It was Wednesday. Yesterday was Tuesday and the voice downstairs was his father. He'd forgotten about the concreting job. He hadn't forgotten about kissing Greta, that sweet sensation had popped into his mind many times throughout the early morning hours and spurred him on, and kept him focused.

But the job, bugger! His dad and brother would be furious. If he raced out now, he'd get there in time for today's shift.

Taking two steps at a time, he rushed downstairs. Greta and Millie were at the dining room table eating breakfast. The room was bright with morning sunlight and the scene looked so civilised after the darkness of both the night and the sinister world he'd occupied the last twenty-four hours. He blinked a few times to reorient himself and moved towards Greta and placed a kiss upon her forehead. She beamed up at him. He acknowl-edged Millie with a nod.

'You've been painting all night, then?' she asked.

'Yep.'

'How are you feeling about what you've produced?' She didn't ask what he had created, only how he felt about it. This woman knew him well.

'They're rubbish.'

The empathy on Millie's face almost broke him. 'What do you think about this one?' she asked and pointed to a pencil sketch displayed at the end of the table. She was testing him.

'Is this what you did yesterday at the creek?'

Millie nodded.

'It's beautiful. Eerie, stark, dark, not like your usual pieces.' He moved in closer to examine it. 'The detail is incredible.'

'What makes it beautiful?' She tossed various other questions at him, so that it felt like he was being interrogated about his own work and not hers. She knew he wouldn't talk about his own piece, not yet anyway, but she was smart. Brodie went along with it.

'Can we see yours?' Greta asked innocently.

She had no idea.

It was hard to refuse that blinding smile and twinkling eyes, but he would. 'No, it's not finished.'

'Okay, but Millie hasn't finished hers either and she's showing us. Actually, she can't stop talking about it this morning.'

'It's still mulling around in my head and needs more work. I'm trying to figure out how to improve it.'

'Take today to think about it but I want us to talk it through, okay?' Millie waited for his agreement. He didn't provide it, but both of them knew it would happen.

'Holy shit! I keep forgetting. I have to go, promised Dad that I'd help the blokes with some concreting. Proper paid work.' He directed that comment at Millie, knew she'd understand.

Greta sat up taller. 'Oh yeah, he was here, upset, you'd better go,' she said, ushering him away with her hand, 'go and we'll see you later.' She smiled and it momentarily stalled him. Her hair was curly again today, not that dreadfully straight do she seemed to like that made her face appear severe. Her face was fresh, like she'd slept well and her cheeks had a little flush of pink to them. He waved his hand and left.

HER AUNT GAVE HER A LOOK. HOW DID SHE MANAGE TO CONVEY so much without words? Damn, Millie Osborne was good.

Greta ignored it. 'Where's Fred this morning?' she asked flashing a cheeky grin.

'He's gone home.'

'When shall we see him again?'

Millie shrugged. 'When you do, I guess.'

Greta stared at Millie's sketch. 'It really is beautiful, Millie. Is Brodie no good, is that why he won't show his art?'

Millie turned sharply. 'Don't listen to him. The boy has enormous talent with an inability to believe in himself.'

Her gaze wandered back to her piece. Millie needed to spend more time with it, Greta could read the signs. 'I'm going to get a coffee in town. I'll take the bike and scout out more jobs. Maybe have a look at a few plants.'

Greta wasn't sure if Millie even registered her leaving.

Artists, they were a funny bunch.

But she had more serious issues on her mind.

GRETA SIPPED HER COFFEE AT THE OUTDOOR TABLES OF THE café and watched a lady post a sign to the glass wall of the local independent supermarket. It read WANTED in capital letters like a notice for a runaway criminal.

Casual worker required to cover busy lunchtime period each day.

It was the first job she'd seen advertised in Lucas Heads and something resembling hope bubbled up inside of her. So far all the available positions were in surrounding towns and they weren't an option for her. She couldn't ride her bicycle ten kilometres or more, to work each day and couldn't afford a car. But if she got desperate enough, she might have to. Bigger towns, more work. The adage was true. This gorgeous bayside town that bustled with people, didn't bustle with employment opportunities.

She'd bit her tongue this morning and pushed down the urge to ask the barista for a job as she'd made her coffee. What was it about cold-calling? She'd been happy to do it relentlessly when she had a service to sell and the potential to make money. Now, she was too embarrassed to ask for a job. It felt like begging. As if she was desperate. But the hollow pit in the base of her stomach demonstrated she was getting desperate, and fast.

A supermarket though? She was better than that. She should wait. A better opportunity would arise but ….she needed money fast and needed to deposit some funds towards her restitution.

Could she serve groceries with a smile?

Even as a teenager she hadn't lined up like her friends to work at the big chain stores. She'd taken the retail route and sold fashion at one of those hip sort of shops she'd not be seen dead in now, mainly because the clothes suited teens with bodies to match.

Hard reality pressed down upon her. She could play the bitter card, or she could accept her options were limited, no non-existent. A little old lady's voice whispered in her ear. She knew what she had to do.

It wasn't about what she wanted anymore.

Greta gulped the last of her coffee, threw the take-away cup in the nearest recycling bin and ventured inside. It was a modern supermarket with a deli at the front selling pre-made meals and takeaway. Hot foods were kept warm in an oven, cold salads and meats next door and a large offering of cakes and slices. A bit of a one-stop shop.

She approached the lady behind the counter who'd displayed the advert and offered her a warm smile.

Forty-five minutes later she walked out an employee. Her enquiry had been before the rush and Kathleen, the manager had taken her straight in for an impromptu interview, sized her up for the appropriate black pants uniform with old fashioned stripped apron and given her the 101 on working in the supermarket.

When asked in the interview about recent employment history, various theories entered Greta's mind to explain the gap, ranging from the farcical to the possible. Sky diving accident? A redundancy? Nervous breakdown? She didn't have to tell, did she? In the end, she'd told the truth. She wasn't a liar, despite what people might think. Kathleen had gazed at her and they'd fought a battle of wills until her new boss turned away. Kathleen took notes and nodded but made no further comment. Imagine if she couldn't secure a lowly supermarket job because of her past?

But she'd nabbed the job and been introduced to the girl behind the till who exited the store at the same time she did.

'Hi there!'

'So, you'll be covering my lunch and then we'll do the rush together. Not that it's much of a rush, but for 'round here, we get a queue at lunchtime.' The girl laughed.

Greta thought she looked younger than her, maybe early twenties. She had bright red hair and was lanky and tall, with a scattering of freckles across her nose and cheeks.

'I'm Jasmine,' she said.

Greta introduced herself.

'I'm on my break now and going to grab some fish and chips. Want to come and sit with me on the beach?'

Greta fingered the corner of the twenty-dollar note in her pocket. Salty hot chips were tempting and her mouth salivated. But she wanted to make a start in the garden and had planned to purchase a few pots.

She vowed not to buy lunch and almost said no. But when was the last occasion she'd spoken to a friend? Someone her own age? She couldn't remember. Greta used to have a great group of girls from high school and they'd catch up regularly. She'd caught up for a coffee with one of them not that long ago, but before the shit had hit the fan. So, clearly, well over six months ago.

It hadn't helped that not long after she started work her hours blew out and she couldn't make it to catch the early movie, didn't have time for lunch and drinks were no longer served at the hour she turned up. Then Charlie arrived and she spent her life outside of work with him. Until eventually, the invitations stopped coming.

Reflection was a wonderful thing. She'd made many mistakes.

An ache shot through her chest for lost friendships and lost priorities. Along with her growing list of things to improve her life, she made a mental note to reach out, how, she wasn't quite sure.

But in the here and now, other than her aunt and Brodie she hadn't met any locals. That was impossible locking herself away at the cottage day after day. It was a day of new beginnings, fresh starts and trying to be the better person. A good a time as any to start.

Plus, her biggest worry was over. She had another job.

'Sure. I won't eat, but I'll sit with you.'

'Okay, then, let's go, I only have thirty minutes.'

Jasmine introduced her to the best chippie in town and Greta stored that information away for later. She would get those hot chips, soon.

The main street of town, where the supermarket was located,

faced the water. A patrolled beach stretched a few miles in each direction before the cove ended and another started. She'd put on her list to walk these coves as far as she could one day. It was a beautiful coastline. It reminded her of the soapie, *Summer Bay*. Lucas Heads would be a place she'd long to visit if she was stuck in her office in Sydney and here she was. Greta made a vow to enjoy it.

Jasmine was bubbly and laughed at the end of each sentence even if it wasn't funny. A smile on her face even as she ate. She offered Greta a few chips and some to the seagulls that gathered around them. If Greta had been worried about filling gaps in the conversation, she shouldn't have been. The girl barely took breath but Greta learned all about her upbringing in the small town. She knew her aunt, who didn't? And Brodie of course.

'And what's brought you here? It's a long way from the bright lights of Sydney.'

A whole range of excuses formed but didn't come out. She opened her mouth to speak and closed it. The sea air and the gentle breeze almost loosened her tongue. But this was a very different situation to her job interview. A fortress of distrust like a castle's walls was built around Greta and it wasn't being demolished today. There was no way she'd be revealing her dirty secret.

Jasmine glanced at her watch and jumped up. Relief washed over Greta.

'I have to get back to work. It was great meeting you. I'll see you tomorrow.'

Greta watched Jasmine's departing back and jubilation replaced the panic of only moments ago.

She had another job! The words *it's only a supermarket* sprang up and she squashed them back down. It was only a food store, but it was a regular gig with income. Albeit small. How did people survive on these wages? She'd taken her generous income for granted, but she'd worked bloody hard for that money. Now her only focus was to commence regular payments to her debt. And stay out of jail. A better paying job would make things easier, though. Maybe she needed to be back in the city where incomes were higher? She pushed those thoughts away too. Picturing the Sydney traffic, the queues, noise and pollution. Plus, her old haunts and the prison. It would be too real, and she wasn't ready for that.

The nursery was on the way home. She'd stop and fill her basket with a few purchases to give her a head start on the garden beds. Greta hoped Millie would be about when she arrived home so she could share her news.

CHAPTER 11

'Millie!' Greta shouted out as she pushed open the front door and walked through to the studio.

Empty.

The cats wandered out; the mother curled her body around Greta's legs, her head caressing the bare skin of her ankles. Did animals count as friends? If she had to rely upon them, she was in trouble. The kittens ignored her anyway, they were only interested in playing. Nonetheless she loved these little beggars and bent down to give them all a tickle across the ears. 'It's so good to see you,' she said. And thankfully, Millie hadn't mentioned giving away the kittens. Greta wasn't sure she'd tolerate another loss.

At the disturbance, Lola meandered out too. But the little dog only had time for her master and upon detecting it wasn't Millie, she walked out to the front deck and lay in the sun.

A feeling of pride bubbled up in Greta's chest and spread like a blossoming flower, all light and fluffy and delicious. She was proud of herself for talking with Jasmine today. It was a start.

After only a few hot chips, her stomach rumbled. She'd make herself some lunch and then try and figure out where everyone was. Craning her neck, she couldn't hear any noise from upstairs, so Brodie hadn't returned either.

A note fluttered on the table. Millie advising in her loopy cursive that she was out at an appointment and would be back soon.

The house that always rumbled with creaks and the clanking noises of normal life, rang out silent. She was grateful for the whistle of the kettle and the domestic sounds of making a sandwich. Greta hadn't been home alone before; not alone for over six months. The only solitude in prison was lying in your bunk after lights out. Greta shuddered at the recollection of the clunk of the latch into place each night. Once she'd craved quiet-time but now it came in too great an abundance.

She checked social media. The Wi-Fi connection patched in and out but she only wanted to trawl through the accounts of her friends. Photographs flashed up on the screen: new men, houses, a baby. Wow, she'd well and truly lost touch. Together her old group of friends posed at picnics, rock concerts, exercising. Memories of the past flashed up but it was pointless reminiscing. At the time she could have turned to them, it was her felt-like-she-was-going-to-die embarrassment that had prevented her. Reality check: these people had moved on. And who'd want to be friends with a crim anyway? Another mistake, another regret for her to live with. The list was growing.

'Okay, enough wallowing, kitty cats, let's do some planting.'

Twenty bucks didn't buy much—who knew—so it didn't take long to place the four plants into the empty beds. Greta sat back on her haunches and her heart sank lower in her chest. The gardens were still bare. She was pulling off her gloves when she remembered the cuttings she'd saved. They might rescue her project, well one garden bed anyway. Her mood was dipping fast so she jumped up and walked towards the shed. She couldn't help but imagine brand new pavers on the path and a timber seat or maybe a table on the front lawn. It'd make a beautiful entrance to the cottage. None of which she could afford. Everything was about money or was it simply all she thought about these days? In the past she could have attended the local nursery and spent hundreds of dollars on plants and flowers and equipment without a blink of her long eyelashes. Not anymore.

That's okay, she'd do what she could today. There's always tomorrow.

Wandering back inside to clean the dirt from under her fingernails, Greta planned dinner. Hopefully Brodie might make an appearance, but even if he didn't, her aunt had cooked each night and it was her turn. The pantry was full of an assortment of tinned goods and fresh produce in the fridge. When did Millie do the shopping?

Greta checked the time, too early to cook. It was more like wine o'clock but she wouldn't indulge today. Next project? She'd read a chapter of her book in the front room so that when Brodie returned she could report her progress. Dreading the thought, she bargained with herself that she'd only tackle one chapter. Sometimes starting was the hard part.

After a few pages, the words blurred, and Greta couldn't recall anything she'd read. At hearing the chirp of a bird, she gazed out the window. Mother cat nudged the door open and entered before curling up on the rug.

Greta's eyes drifted over to the bookshelf. All the available space taken up with ornaments, books and magazines. On the top shelf a bundle sat slightly skewed and hanging precariously close to the edge. It was a parcel tied with a faded red ribbon. Greta recalled her aunt's box and her odd reaction the other day. Strange because her aunt was not possessive about her belongings. Everything was to be used or admired and Millie graciously shared. Greta's eyes diverted down low to where Millie had placed the container. The sliding door to the bottom shelf was shut. The message was clear.

But what was the package at the top?

Like a child with no self-control over a sweet treat, Greta reached up high and retrieved the bundle. It was heavy and bulky and she needed to ensure it didn't fall off the high shelf, didn't she?

Letters.

She flicked through the pile of fifty or so envelopes adorned with green, orange and lilac stamps. Purple ones had the Eiffel Tower on their front and the orange ones were the head of someone famous, no doubt. As she leaned in, she read French words. Letters from France! Millie said she adored France; these must be a memento of her time there. Perhaps they were letters with artist friends or other women she'd met on her travels.

Without the slightest consideration for her aunt's privacy, Greta pulled out one envelope and extracted a sole sheaf of paper.

Dearest,

Oh ma Cherie, I can hardly bear it! When are you due back in Paris? It's so dull here without you.

My daily coffee at Le Bonne Fleur isn't the same without your company. How quickly we become creatures of habit. On days I can't convince Henri to join me, instead of savouring my espresso and people watching and gaining inspiration like we did every morning together, I sip my coffee and get on with my day. It all feels such a rush and makes me feel quite discombobulated.

I'm throwing myself into my work which is a positive thing with you being away in the country. I think you'll notice the progress I've made on these pieces. I'm claiming it my greatest collection of French works yet. I miss your insight about just the right way to tackle the angle and light on the finished pieces. I'm really stretching myself for this collection, I have taken a few different approaches. As you've often told me, it's good to experiment. But of course, it's a risk and I'm staking a lot on it, hoping the critics will be pleased. Don't listen to them I hear you shout! But after the success of my last show how can I not worry? Damn the pressure we creatives put on ourselves. But that's where you come in, you balance out all the bullshit. I'm sure you'll tell me what you think with your usual wit and brutal honesty upon your return. God forbid if you think they're rubbish.

I miss our strolls around the Ile de la Citie during the day, sitting in the park, bird watching and listening to the Notre Dame bells chime each night as we lay in our bed. Plus your warm body next to mine… I feel my muse has deserted me. When will she return?

Life here in gay Paris continues without you. But my love, how is Dieppe? Have you fallen in love with the harbour with its glistening water and sailing boats? Will you paint anything but? You absolutely must paint the chateau and perhaps a landscape of the clifftops with its idyllic pebble beach. The castle museum has the most incredible collection of impressionist paintings. Some of your favourites will feature, of course. It is a wonderful spot. But I do hope it won't keep you enchanted for too long. Oh, and of course, how is your friend, Marguerite? Is she well and sketching too? Write and tell me all about your work.

Now I must scurry, Albert's exhibition is opening tonight at the gallery and it can't be that I am late!

Best, Reggie.

At the base of the letter was a hand drawn sketch, a tiny caricature of Millie. Greta's hand clutched her chest and she felt its rhythmic beating. What a beautiful thing to do. And it captured her aunt in a calm moment of repose. Greta couldn't help her mind racing to perhaps after lovemaking. Who knew? Who was this Reggie fellow? And for him to write to Millie after they'd spent time together. Romantic time, clearly. A lump formed in Greta's throat. Perhaps her aunt had a special someone? Where was he now?

Millie had always been the spinster of the family. A title she wore with pride. Married to her work was always her response. In her brief stay so far, Greta had met Fred, perhaps the current beau, but this fellow Reggie was the past. So her aunt had experienced love? For some inexplicable reason, this filled Greta with joy.

Reggie signed his letter with a swirl and a flourish, very neat for a gentleman.

Greta thumbed through to the bottom of the pile. Her heart beat erratically as she came across a smaller, separate bundle of envelopes. She wanted to hear her aunt's voice, her reply, her expressions of love to this man. Could she be so lucky to have her letters, too? It might answer the questions swirling in her head.

Her aunt's script was on the first yellowed envelope affixed with a faded stamp and her excitement lifted. Greta raced to turn it over. Empty. The next couple had no letters either.

Of course she wouldn't have Millie's letters to Reggie. He'd have them and they might be tied up with a similar red ribbon and kept somewhere safe.

Damn. She'd just have to keep reading Reggie's letters.

DEAREST,

Oh yes, I know you say I carry on! You've only been gone seven days but I am lost without you.

I'm ever so pleased your arrival into Dieppe was without incident. The train ride comfortable. You must have been so happy to see Marguerite. The evening you spent at the local tavern sounds fun. What a delight to drink too much and sleep late the next day. I have to say I'm not at all surprised overindulging didn't stop you from perching yourselves at the harbour the next day, in amongst the action as you describe it. I cannot wait to see what paintings you deliver from that scene — so much inspiration: the fishing boats, the shore, tourist groups, boat keepers and the landscape itself are all moments in time. I am not surprised you are fascinated by it. You will not tire of that beauty.

I'm sorry to hear that Marguerite suffered with a nasty head cold and didn't venture out the following day. But you mustn't lay idle with so much on offer. Sitting at the clifftop sounds delightful. I hope your sketches are useful for more painting inspiration. Of course Marguerite was improved on your chicken broth. I wish you were here to make me some!

I agree the countryside, and Dieppe in particular, does not quite have the buzz of the city. Nonetheless, I feel quite whimsy hearing your tales. As usual I wander the art galleries and watch the vast array of people. Being in the country is good for the soul, so I'm sure you feel quite invigorated and inspired.

I'll pass your wishes to Albert, such a bother you missed his debut! It went well. Missing you.

Reggie

These letters were better than any novel Greta could read. She wanted to devour the pile and learn more about her aunt's lover. Why hadn't she asked about her life? Convention, she guessed. It was never talked about. She opened the next one, this time a mocha cream coloured envelope with slight embellishment. Greta swore there was a scent from the wax-thin paper. The sloping cursive bounced off the page.

DEAREST,

Well, as I feared, I'm lacking inspiration. The time has passed so slowly and my current collection is finished, alas, without your input, and my mind simply cannot, will not turn to a new idea. Where art thou my muse?

To cheer myself well and truly up I resorted to …

. . .

THE WALLS SHOOK. GRETA GLANCED UP AS A KNOCK LANDED ON the door. *No!* Before she'd risen from the sofa chair, a 'yoo hoo' sang out.

Her mother? No …

Frazzled, Greta stuffed the letter back in its envelope and placed the package back on the shelf more haphazardly than she'd found it.

When the happy cheerios kept sounding, Greta knew it was without a doubt, Grace Johnson.

She swung open the door.

'Greta!' Her mother lunged in for a hug. 'It's wonderful to see you. I'm annoyed you didn't come home.'

Greta returned the embrace and was still connected to her mother's shoulder as she talked over her head. Greta pulled away.

'I've explained this Mum, on the phone. I needed to get away, have a break.'

'Well, dear, it seemed like you had a break, from real life anyway and you need to get back into the swing of things. I've come to help you pack and take you home. I'm not taking no for an answer.'

CHAPTER 12

Greta reached for the wine bottle that was almost finished; she'd had three glasses to her mother's one. She hoped Millie had another stash, because at this rate, Greta would need another bottle, and fast.

Greta nursed one kitten and Lola sat at her feet. The mother cat was at the base of Grace's chair but her mother ignored her. Were the animals frightened of the voracious force that was Grace Johnson? Greta sure was. They'd sat on the deck for the last hour and for that entire time her mother hadn't caught a breath.

'I think you should go into teaching.'

That caught her attention. 'Teaching? Mum, you're kidding right? I can't spell and have trouble reading.'

'But you've overcome those difficulties and maybe not an English teacher. What about home economics?'

Greta rolled her eyes. Her mother was intent on fixing her life. Rebuilding it back to a satisfactory and un-embarrassing status. It seemed the only way to do that was a career. She'd covered nursing – like her, perhaps midwifery – and other health-based philosophies – physiotherapy, or that new age osteopathy, maybe podiatry, she'd mentioned law, like her father, but quickly dismissed it, thank goodness for small mercies.

'What about a counsellor then?'

Greta wrapped her fingers around her glass to prevent throttling her mother. She turned at the sound of a car rumbling down the drive and heaved a sigh of relief.

The car pulled to a stop and Brodie jumped out of the driver's seat and raced around to help Millie out of the passenger side. The animals scat and Greta jumped up. Anything to get away from her mother.

'Grace?' Millie said as she approached the stairs. 'I wasn't expecting you. Has the Johnson family lost their manners? First Greta arrives unannounced, a delightful surprise nonetheless, and now you.'

Millie didn't add that it was a delightful surprise that her younger sister had arrived unexpectedly.

'Don't be stroppy, Mil. I've come to take Greta home, that's where she belongs.'

Her aunt glanced in her direction. Greta noticed the dark and full pillows of sagging skin under her eyes. The blackness of those bags exaggerated next to her translucent skin. Her lips were set in a tight, narrow line.

Where had she been?

Millie reached for the handrail and paused with one foot on the bottom stair with Brodie directly behind, as if to catch her if she fell. Little sparklers popped in Greta's chest as she drank in the sight of him. He was one big strapping man and right now, she wanted to be squished in those strong arms.

Her mother barrelled down the stairs and kissed her sister's cheek. 'Still wearing that silly hat, I see.'

'And you're still a smart arse.'

Exhausted or not, she was still as quick as a whip. Her mother and Millie were more than ten years apart in age. Greta sometimes forgot they were sisters, they often acted more like mother-daughter. Her mother had loads of energy, an annoying skip in her step and the body to match. Grace was tall, slim with unblemished skin. She was never mistaken for the older sister. Whereas Millie was her truest form and age in all its glory. That wasn't the only difference. Millie was often accused of being a daydreamer and following crazy creative pursuits. That was until she'd cracked it and her art made a living and she surpassed the income of those around her. By comparison, her mother's only creativity was a visit to a gallery or an occasional night at the opera. Instead, she lived a life of service, nursing in the oncology ward at a Sydney hospital. Grace was a no nonsense, practical woman, bordering on conservative and not in anyway alternative; to her, creative pursuits didn't make sense. She must have cringed leaving the sights of Sydney behind for the relaxed and less restrictive northern New South Wales highlands.

'Come in and have a drink and help me convince Greta to come home. We miss her.'

Millie sighed and climbed the stairs.

The sisters entered the house and Brodie came up beside Greta and planted a kiss to her cheek. That wasn't what she wanted, but she guessed it'd have to do.

'Staying for dinner? I'm cooking.'

'Well, I'll have to, then.' As they moved together indoors, he snaked his strong arms around her middle and cradled her. Her insides squealed with delight.

'I'll have to wash up, I'm filthy. I worked on the concreting today. It's a shit of a job, sorry for the language.'

Greta laughed. His honesty was refreshing after the berating she'd received all afternoon from her mother. 'I'll have a beer ready in the kitchen. You'll need it with my mother here.'

'She seems nice.'

'You're too polite, Brodie Quade,' and she turned in his arms and faced him, forced his arms to capture her in a hug. Her hands sat at the top of his backside, her groin precariously close to his waist. The action felt natural, but she flushed bright red, wicked thoughts going wild in her brain. He glanced down and smiled a mischievous grin. Forget what he was thinking, she wanted to pull him aside right then and there, spend a few minutes alone, but he extracted himself and moved away to the bathroom.

She brushed down the front of her cotton dress now covered with grey silt. He was right when he said he was dirty.

'Holy mother of Jesus,' she heard her mother exclaim. 'Millie, this is a pigsty, honestly, you should know better.'

Greta caught up with her mother as she stood in the doorway to the studio.

'This is my workspace, Grace. It inspires me.' Millie stood a shoulder-width away from her.

'Your brain must be one cluttered place then. I couldn't think straight in here. I can get right in and tidy it up for you, no problem. Let me do it, now.'

'You touch anything in there and I'll chop your fingers off.' Millie grasped Mum's arm and pulled her away towards the kitchen.

'How's Matthew?'

The distraction worked well, and her mother babbled on with how busy her father was at the law firm, the incredible hours he worked and how they didn't spend enough time together with her shift work. Blah. Blah. Blah.

She loved her mother, she really did. But there was a reason she didn't go home.

Greta stirred the pot bubbling on the stove and peered back over her shoulder. Millie sat at the table, a magazine of some sort open in front of her. 'Where's Mum?'

'Not sure, love.'

A sinking sense of dread entered her stomach. Racing away, she took the stairs two at a time and rushed into her bedroom and pushed the door open with such force it slammed against the wall.

'Mum, get out!' Greta surprised herself at how loud she yelled.

Her mother's hands ceased their folding and held one of her T-shirts clutched close to her chest.

'I love you, but you are not listening.' Greta sat on the bed and curled her feet under her. She pushed the half-packed suitcase to the side and it fell to the floor with a crash.

'Greta, there's no need for that.'

'I'm not coming home with you.'

Her mother's lips turned down and she collapsed onto the bed next to her. Her hand crept across the faded cream bedspread and she linked her pinkie finger around hers.

That made her calm the hell down.

'I'm sorry, Mum.' She avoided her eye, focused on her words instead. The fingers on her free hand picking at loose threads in the fabric. 'I'm lost, completely lost. What happened, it's broken me. How do you come back from something like that? That's what I'm trying to work out. I'm embarrassed, I've totally stuffed up and it's hard to admit. But even if I can get over what I've done, I don't know who I am anymore.' What she didn't mention was scared. Greta had never been so petrified.

'But I do know that I want, need, to stay here, with Millie. Even in this short time, I've made some ground. I feel stronger, more focused. I have two jobs that are helping me start my repayments. Things are working out, sort of.'

Her mother had done well to keep quiet that long. 'I can help you, support you.' Her eyes pleaded with her.

'You can't pay my debt.' Pause. 'I understand you can

support me, but Sydney doesn't feel right. Plus, I need to sort myself out.'

'You're not taking drugs are you and worried about temptation?'

'What! No. I never took them, you know that.'

Her mother's body curled in on itself.

'My entire life in Sydney was my work, the places I went were linked to my job, the people I hung out with, the people I worked for, my customers lived around the corner. Everything in Sydney screams financial advisor and the life I previously led. I'm not that person anymore. Instead I'm a criminal and there's no escape. I need a fresh start.'

'I promise I won't ...'

'You want to fix me, but I need to fix myself,' Greta glared at her.

'Okay, I admit to having a little trouble sitting back. I want to steer you in the right direction, that's all, to avoid this happening again. I obviously didn't help you enough before, give you support. I should have seen the signs –'

'Mum, you think this is your fault?'

'Well, no. I didn't steal anyone's money.'

Greta winced.

'But a good mother knows something is wrong with her child. I wasn't paying attention, thought you had it all worked out, were doing well. We worried about you so much when you were small. All that bullying because you couldn't read and write like the other kids. I wasn't sure what would happen to you. But Greta, you made it work. You succeeded, did so well. Your dad and I were so proud. All those hardships and you got through. Had money, was independent ...'

'Such a success story...' Her mother didn't detect the sarcasm.

'Greta, how could you let it happen?'

She flung her hands in the air, palms up. 'Mum, you know the answer to that. I mean other than being stupid, in the wrong place at the wrong time, being too trusting…what else do I say to that?'

'I still don't understand why you didn't come to us. We could have helped and what about Charlie's parents?'

'What? You would have lent drug-addict Charlie money to pay his debts if I'd told you? Hardly. That's a bit optimistic, isn't it? And plus, an adult child doesn't keep running back to her Mummy and Daddy, does she? And it was his problem and he had to sort it out.'

'Let us help you now.'

Greta shook her head.

'What can Millie offer that I can't?' Her mother's voice cracked.

'It's not that she's doing anything, but that's the point. She listens and doesn't try to fix it, fix me.'

Greta let that sink in. It hurt her mother, that was obvious. Loud banging echoed through the wall. Brodie? He better not have started painting. Dinner was almost ready.

She reached over and grasped both her mother's hands. 'Can you let me do this on my own, my way?'

Her mother's feeble nod was not convincing.

'Mum?' Her tone was stern.

A heavy sigh. 'Yes, yes, okay. But if you're going to stay, can Dad and I come to visit one weekend? He's desperate to see you. We miss you.'

'Of course you can. I miss you guys, too.' Her mother pulled her in for a fierce hug that only a mother bear can offer. Greta jumped up, 'I've got to save dinner, otherwise we won't be eating tonight.' She pointed her finger. 'Don't touch my stuff, okay?'

'The local art gallery is holding its annual competition soon,' Millie said.

Brodie slurped his soup and didn't respond.

'Brodie! Earth to Brodie. Are you going to enter your recent pieces into the local art comp?' Greta repeated. 'You still haven't showed us.'

'What? No.'

'No. What do you mean, why?' Greta's eyebrows arched.

'Ah, now I understand. You're a student are you, Brodie, is that where you fit in?' Grace asked.

'A student of life?' His laughter was hollow. 'Sorry, yes. Millie lets me work out of a space upstairs and we talk about art.'

'So profound, Brodie. I hope we do a lot more than that. Otherwise, I'll have to trade you in for a better version.' Millie commented.

'Still doing that, Mil? Taking in lost souls, offering them hope. God, you've been sponsoring aspiring artists for years. Have any become famous?'

Brodie glanced between Millie and Grace. If this was a family spat, he didn't want to be involved.

'Famous?' Millie scoffed. 'That is not the benchmark of a talented artist. I nurture them, encourage them, challenge if necessary.' She glanced at Brodie then.

He glanced away.

'But whilst he's here working on his talent, he could be out contributing to the community and making some money.'

'Geez, Grace, not this again…'

'You sound like my parents,' he interjected, trying to keep his voice light while his throat was constricting.

'It's true, though, isn't it? Where do you live, Brodie? You must have to pay rent?'

'I live in a van in my parent's holiday park.'

'So, no rent. Makes life easy. Surely your parents could be

making money on that van if you weren't living there? All I'm trying to say is that there are consequences to our actions.'

'There are occasions I really crave a drink, and right now in my dearest sister's company is one of them.' Millie mused.

'Would you like some more bread, Mum?'

'Why are we eating soup, Greta? It's thirty degrees out.'

'Because it's a recipe I can make.'

'Well, that's another thing to add to the list then, cooking classes.'

Brodie saw Greta roll her eyes and smirk at Millie. They were clearly used to the bickering.

'Are you still buying those expensive paintings and giving them away?'

'You're so tiring, Grace. What you mean of course, is am I still acquiring priceless pieces of art to add to and contribute to our burgeoning art industry in Australia? The answer is hell, yes. We have some of the most fabulous pieces of art in this country because of me.' Millie dropped her cutlery on her plate and it clanged.

'What about the one from years ago? I can't remember what it was called but it cost you a fortune. And was rather ugly, to boot. By some fellow, Reginald, or other?'

Brodie sat back, the name didn't mean anything to him, but Greta's head popped up. Brodie watched her consider Millie with interest.

'Yes, that was one of my most magnificent buys. What a scoop.'

'I can't believe you paid hundreds of thousands of dollars for a painting, then gave it away. Is it at the local gallery?'

'No, but that's where my next exhibit is being held. I haven't done a local show for ages and they deserve it. It's easy to prattle off to the big smoke with its fancy buildings and galleries and pretend you're *famous,* but really, this show is much more meaningful.' She paused and turned to face Brodie. 'Now is as good a time as any. I was going to ask Brodie, will you exhibit some works with me?'

The table fell silent and Brodie kept his head down. He wanted to pretend he hadn't heard the question. But he wasn't rude.

'You're kidding, aren't you, Millie?'

'Not in the slightest. The next step is for you to exhibit some of your work.'

He was shaking his head before he spoke.

'Think about it, boy. Why not?'

'Well, if you won't exhibit, why don't you enter the prize? You might win.' Greta smiled at him, all innocence.

His temples throbbed. His eyes ached. He felt like a chicken pecked in all directions. A little jab here, a poke there.

'I said no.' He pushed his chair back, it scraping along the floor making a dreadful squeal. The door banged shut after him.

'Now, that is a young man with issues,' said Grace.

CHAPTER 13

At school, she'd always been the last kid picked for a game. Anxiety had clawed at her insides at the prospect of once again being chosen last; a booby prize as the names were shouted out, but never hers. The worst part was standing alone after everyone else had moved into position, all eyes on her and the realisation she wasn't wanted.

Greta felt like that little kid right now. And she didn't like it.

The first few hours at the supermarket had been a breeze. Jasmine had greeted her with a hug and hadn't stopped talking since and Kathleen had run a brief induction. There had been nothing to read and no sums to calculate in her head. The hardest part was the small talk and even she could fake that.

Now she stood behind one of the two checkouts during rush. The crowds had doubled since the start of shift and there was a queue, but not for her register. Five people waited in Jasmine's line.

'Can I help anyone?' Silence. No movement. She glanced across to Jasmine, but she was busy packaging groceries.

Then a tourist in their beach gear rushed forward juggling three ice creams with children in tow.

Okay, phew!

She overdid her friendly spiel she was so grateful.

After she'd finished, four people still waited for Jasmine but eight pairs of eyes stared at her. When their glances connected, they turned their heads sharply, whispered to the person in front. Customers wandered past with their baskets and slowed near her register to check her out.

Greta glanced down at her uniform but it was in order excepting that her apron was too stiff and new. She brushed her hands over her face to check for leftover breakfast lining her mouth.

'Why isn't anyone coming in my line?' she whispered in Jasmine's ear when she rushed over to help load groceries into a recyclable bag.

Jasmine laughed. 'Don't worry, it's a small town. I've been serving the locals for years, they know me. Give them a chance.'

'Okay.' Not at all convinced, Greta moved back behind her cash register.

'Hoi, Mr Wilson, get in Greta's line over there, will ya? She's new and won't bite!' Jasmine sang out and Mr Wilson dutifully obeyed. Lifesaver!

'Hi Mr Wilson,' and Greta made diligent small talk.

Mr Wilson gave her a constrained smile but didn't respond to her questions about his day or the beautiful weather they were experiencing. Greta plastered that false grin to her face, but her eyelids tremored. Was she really shit at this or were the town's people mean?

A few others followed suit after Mr Wilson. One lady watched her place the twenty dollar note in the drawer and extract the change. Greta counted it into her palm and then the lady dumped it on the counter and double checked it. Satisfied, she nodded and scooped it into the pocket of her skirt.

The tourists were pleasant, adding to Greta's theory that the locals were nasty. It didn't make any sense; the people she'd met so far were lovely. What had she done wrong?

With Jasmine on her lunchbreak, people gravitated toward Kathleen manning the deli rather than her check out. Feeling despondent, she realised she'd somehow failed but didn't know how. Then a woman rushed forward. Her head was bent searching in her carry bag. When she looked up having found what she was after, she exclaimed, 'Oh. No, no, you can't serve me.' She retrieved the carton of milk from the counter but Greta's hand was already on it, holding tight, and she tugged it back. The woman did likewise. It was one of those old-style cardboard one litre sort – who still bought those anyway – and a tussle began. She didn't mean to be childish. Something inert drove her but the woman was more determined to get away than Greta was to serve her, and the customer yanked the carton so hard it slipped and deliciously white milk spilled and spread quickly across the chess-board patterned tiles.

'You stupid girl! Look what you've done!' the lady screeched.

Greta thought to get the mop and bucket, but the veracity of the shout made her stop. It was only spilled milk. Surely the woman was overreacting.

Kathleen rushed over as the woman continued her diatribe against Greta. Kathleen's calm tone reassured her it was an accident and she grasped the elbow of the customer and moved her away.

Greta's limbs were heavy as she cycled home. How had the shift gone so badly? Can she not even manage that job? It all seemed a bit incredulous to her. Could she put it down to a bad day? It made her feel shit alright, though. She didn't even stop for the coffee she'd promised herself.

The house was empty again. Millie hadn't mentioned she was going out, but Greta wasn't her keeper so her aunt didn't report to her.

She'd grown accustomed to the routine of the house with Brodie and Millie always painting. Not today, though, Brodie was concreting, bet he loved that. And who knew where Millie might be. The gardens beckoned to her, but Greta knew exactly what she'd do. Ditching her work clothes and changing into a cool summer dress, she headed for the study. She'd been dying to get back to those letters since she'd been interrupted and since the infamous Reggie had been mentioned at dinner.

Greta reached for the pile. So Millie had purchased one of his paintings a few years back and he was famous enough to warrant a place in one of Australia's galleries. Only one way to find out, she'd Google him. Not as easy as she'd thought – she didn't have any amazing search terms that might yield good results. Best she could do was – *Reginald artist.*

Hah! Hundreds of hits came up. Her eyes scanned the screen fast trying to take it all in. Images flashed up of an old man, others of paintings and sketches and lots of photographs of France.

Famous painter dies at age 57 at his home in Paris

He's dead? Her excitement evaporated like a deflating balloon. She chose an article from a prominent Australian paper and clicked on the link.

REGINALD SMART, ONE OF THE WORLD'S MOST TALENTED Impressionist painters, has been found dead in his Paris apartment in the exclusive Ile de la Citie area. Neighbours raised the alarm when they hadn't seen the reclusive painter in a number of days.

'Whilst he kept to himself, I always used to see him head out each morning at exactly the same time to have his coffee at the Le Bonne Fleur. You could set your clock by him, he was so punctual,' said Clarice his next-door neighbour in the apartment complex.

On a bitterly cold and frosty morning, the Gendarme found him reclined in a chair, the fire long gone out.

It was quite a scene, they reported later. Dozens of sketches flooded the floor at his feet, some scratched over to conceal the face, others completed. Oddly they all depicted the face of one unknown woman. The room had countless canvases, at various stages of progress, the paint long dried. Mixed in amongst the mess were empty wine bottles – a very fine red drop apparently – and various brown paper bags with an assortment of left-over meals.

In the sixties Reginald was a prolific producer of landscape works in the impressionist style of his favourites – Monet, Manet and Renoir. And all of his adopted country France. Born in England, he moved to Paris as a young artist and simply never left. Alongside of his own works, he managed a gallery and was very supportive of aspiring artists.

The article listed an array of names, many of whom benefitted from exhibitions at his gallery. One name stood out – *Millicent Osborne, Summer of 1969.* It had to be the same fellow. The article continued:

THE SIXTIES SEEMED TO BE HIS HEYDAY AS HE PRODUCED SOME OF his most famous works including Lavender Fields, French Street, Avignon and Paris Summer to name only a few. He also held endless exhibitions of artists whom he called friends more than colleagues, held the most outrageous of parties and lived a jolly good life.

The seventies were a different story. There were only a handful of showings of his own works in 1971 and 1973 but some say these were his most successful. He produced acclaimed pieces that have been labelled his most romantic and dramatic yet. Reginald held only a handful of exhibits for others during these years also. The last in 1971. Perhaps he was ill?

Doctors report he died of liver failure and had been suffering for some-time. No one would comment on exactly how long. He lived alone and seemed to keep to himself those last few years before being found dead.

Much to everyone's delight his apartment was a treasure trove. Excited art historians and curators have reported that a fine collection of finished works were in residence along with a private collection that housed some of the most famous art of our time. It's understood these pieces were gifted to him by the artists themselves. Before his death, his work was priceless, but now, everyone is struggling to value them. The French are saying it is the most exciting find ever.

Outside of painting, Reginald was a lover of Gertrude Stein's writing and during most winter days he could be found indulging in his passion for ice skating.

THE ARTICLE PROVIDED DETAILS OF HIS FUNERAL AND HAD A number of photographs of his apartment with dozens of paintings lined up against the walls. Even Greta recognised some of the more well-known.

Greta clicked out and scrolled down to another *Sydney Morning Herald* article dated 1978.

MILLICENT OSBORNE, ONE OF OUR OWN RENOWNED ARTISTS HAS donated a Reginald Smart painting to the Art Galley of New South Wales. Rumoured to be worth hundreds of thousands of dollars, Osborne refused to be drawn on the exact value.

'It doesn't matter,' she is reported to have said when asked. 'It's priceless. Reginald Smart is one of the world's best painters and up until this donation there hasn't been one owned by an Australian gallery. This was a problem that needed to be rectified. Quite honestly, it is a travesty and no one seemed to have the foresight to negotiate for a piece now that they have become available. I did and now we have one. It can be forever enjoyed by everyone.'

Osborne also refused to comment about her personal relationship with Smart. It's public knowledge that in the summer of 1969 she had an exhibition at his gallery in Paris but it's possible the two were close.

'Go find some other news that people want to read about,' she commented when pressed further.

THE ARTICLE HAD A LOVELY PHOTO OF MILLIE NEXT TO THE acquired painting and other dignitaries. Was this man the love of Millie's life or a passing summer crush? Greta didn't know but she was determined to find out.

CHAPTER 14

'Man, that was disgusting. Those people were pigs!' Greta exited the van holding her nose and gagging.

'Yeah, some can be shockers and others, like they haven't even stayed there. Weird, hey?'

Greta dumped the cleaning gear at Brodie's feet. 'Thank goodness that's over. Oh, sorry,' she paused, 'you know what I mean, right?'

Brodie detected her slight flush. He loved that her embarrassment was so obvious. It was cute. And made her easy to read.

'I mean that it's hard yakka right and gross. All that hair in the plug!' Now she shivered.

'I get it. I guess I'm used to it. Nothing fazes me anymore,' Brodie said.

'I don't think that's quite right,' she responded and sat next to him on the grass.

He ignored her comment. 'Do you still need to do the cleaning work now you've got the supermarket job?'

'Absolutely. I only do the lunch cover at the shop, so whilst I work there every day, it's only a four-hour shift.' She paused. 'Unless of course, you don't need me cleaning anymore?'

'No, no that's not it, I was checking.'

He handed her a can of lemonade and she skulled. Some dribbled down her chin and Brodie reached out and wiped the drops away with the back of his hand.

'Are you doing anything this afternoon?' he asked.

'Nah, nothing much. Maybe reading a few Man Booker prize novels …'

He laughed. 'Can I show you around a bit? I have a favourite beach. We could go for a swim?'

'I'd kill for a swim! But aren't you painting today?'

'Nah, not today. Let's go.'

'This beach is popular with the tourists and thrums with people most days. That's the only negative. And on an amazingly fine day like today, it's gonna be hectic,' Brodie said as he reverse parked his mum's car into the only available narrow spot.

Hopping out, Brodie watched Greta, waiting for her reaction. Nearer the ocean, a wind whipped up and her still curly hair blew into her face. She took in the grand mansions to the right, hugging the coastline and in prime position to soak up the view of the small cove and beach.

'Wow! It's so beautiful. Imagine owning one of those houses.'

It was an innocent comment, but Brodie heard the whimsy in her voice and the prospect of what might have been.

'Could you have owned a house like one of these in your previous life?'

Without hesitation she scoffed and his question was answered. He felt immeasurably better for asking it.

'They are between say four and six million, the ones at the top, probably more. Pretty achievable, right?'

She mock-punched him on the upper arm. 'Yep, for million-aires like us, sure.' He watched her turn more serious then.

'Do you think Millie could afford one? I mean all that talk about her donating famous pieces of art. That's big money right?'

'To be honest, I have no idea. Of course, you hear about famous dead artists and their paintings being worth millions of dollars, but most Australian artists aren't rolling in money. It's not something Millie and I ever talk about. And none of my business. She helps me out so much. And plus, I think it's because they're dead. Once you're no longer alive your art doubles in value. Strange concept isn't it?'

Gazing into the golden sun and watching swimmers at the beach, they both were lost in their thoughts until Brodie broke the spell.

'There's a lighthouse at the top of the mountain and you can reach it from the end of the beach. Let's work up a sweat and go for a walk first. I might be biased, but it's some of the most spec-tacular shore in this country.'

'Let's do it,' Greta reached for his hand and their fingers entwined.

It felt like the most natural thing in the world to be walking along one of his favourite beaches and holding Greta's hand. He grinned at her and she returned it with a smirk of her own. Neither spoke for a few hundred metres.

'What's the beach called?'

'Willow Beach. There's a hotel on the crest at the other end,' he gestured with his free hand, 'where all the rich and famous stay. Bronte Bay has become a bit of a destination in recent years. All the house prices have skyrocketed and driven the original townsfolk out. It has a history, like a lot of beach towns, of attracting people for an easier, alternative sort of lifestyle.'

'Hippies?'

He laughed. 'Yeah, hippies. They lived in communes, shared vegie patches and made stuff to sell at the markets. It was all very harmonious. But now, many can't afford to live here. It's become a real melting pot of cultures. A mixture of the uber rich and those seeking different lifestyles.'

'What do you think about that?'

'I've never lived in Bronte so it's not affected me. But thinking about something similar happening at Lucas Heads, well, my blood boils. It's idyllic, all these small coastal towns are, but they are not impervious to development. So far so good for my neck of the woods. But it has to be around the corner. Even now there are a few major developments, big companies coming to town and building three or four storey complexes. A few more of those and it could destroy my parent's business.'

He pulled on her arm and tugged her up the path. A short way along the trees cleared and a lookout provided a panoramic view of the ocean beyond.

'All the blues,' Greta commented. 'It's hard to tell where the sky stops and the ocean begins.'

'I never get tired of this view. There's something about the never-ending reach of the sea, its calm waves calling to you. Look behind, you'll see the tip of the lighthouse.'

'White?'

'Yep. Greta,' he said, pointing, 'look there.' His finger landed on a figure in the water. 'Dolphins!'

A pod of the elegant sea creatures breached the waves.

'Oh my God, they're magnificent.'

Brodie moved in close behind her and whispered into her ear. 'They sure are.' She leaned back and he snaked his arms around her middle. Greta's body curved into his and he squeezed tighter while she placed her hands over his.

All he smelled was the sea air.

'Could you paint this?'

'Yeah, but I wouldn't. This is more Millie's style. She's the one who captures beauty. I could picture what it might look like, the shades of blue she'd choose to mirror the sky and water. There'd be greens in there, perhaps at the borders, demonstrating the sea being connected to the land.' He mimicked brush strokes.

'How would you do it?'

His hand moved faster, harsher, less delicate. Large strokes almost violent. He stabbed forwards a couple of times, too. 'Does that give you an idea?'

'Um, yeah. That's how you'd do it, but what would it look like?'

'I take things further. So, oh look, there's the blowhole of a whale. And another one.' The octave of his voice rose higher with his excitement. 'I would paint a whale being pulled from the water with a spear gun in its gut and blood oozing out, spreading like a blanket across the water. Sharks circling, trying to scoop up the intestines and the smaller fish that have been attracted by the spectacle. Other boats attempting to catch a bigger kill, the greedy fisherman leaning over, desperate, saliva dripping from their mouths. Maybe dolphins at the fringe, faster, swimming away, laughing behind them as they crest the waves.'

'Holy shit. You would take this scene and turn it into that?'

'Uh huh.'

'That is one crazy messed up imagination.'

'I know it sounds bizarre. Millie is about ascetic beauty and adoring something because it's pretty. She's all over that, is an expert. I'm not trying to make something attractive. I want people to look at what I've created and question it. I want it to jump out at them and shock, or at least get them talking about it. What does it mean? Is it okay, for example, to kill whales? And maybe, just maybe someone will start to feel something and they'll act differently, or in the best-case scenario take some action.'

Greta turned then to face him. The ocean behind her, the dancing whales moving out to the horizon, the dolphins putting on a show for someone else. She gazed up at him.

'That's incredible, Brodie. Everything you do, each action, has meaning. That's a quality life. You must feel fulfilled. I'm embarrassed to look back upon my life. It didn't have any meaning. Doesn't have meaning. I'm shallow, pathetic.' She buried her face into his chest.

With a solitary finger, he lifted up her chin so that she looked at him. Her warm breath brushed his skin. 'You aren't shallow and pathetic, Greta. Some of your past actions might have been. But I've seen you with Millie, heard you talk. You got lost, yes. But I don't think you're that person.' The world around them disappeared. The voices receded, the children's squeals silenced. When he reached her lips, they were warm and welcoming.

He kissed her too hard. Gripped her face with both of his hands. They engulfed her delicate features, suffocated them. Those voices were back. They mocked him, teased. His life wasn't meaningful, images of faceless creatures laughed so hard their mouths sat open gulping in air. Useless. Ugly artwork that no one understood. His pulse throbbed fast.

Greta pulled away. 'Brodie. Brodie,' she called to him.

He opened his eyes to view her face in shadow. Her breaths matched his, two chests heaving together.

'Are you okay?' she asked.

Was he? Yes, the kiss had been magic but it was marred by the darkness, the voices in his head. It always got in the way. He focused on breathing in, out, leaned his forehead against hers, let the cool breeze settle on his skin.

Lifting his head back, he smiled, the twinkle in his eyes returned. He leaned down now with a soft, tender kiss and let it linger. 'Hell, yeah,' he whispered. Then louder as he pulled away, 'Race you to the beach. Let's cool down with a swim'.

'For an old lady, you truly are disgusting,' Greta said as the waft of Millie's cigarette smoke drifted towards her. 'You know no one smokes anymore, don't you? It's politically incorrect.'

Greta talked as she opened the heavy timber doors to the shed. It was an enormous double panelled timber framed type that always dragged along the hard ground as you yanked them open. Each time she did it, she feared the whole structure would fall down around her. But inside had a concrete panel floor and neat and tidy shelves. Wouldn't avoid, she imagined, the contents getting hot in the summer and mildew in the winter. But of course, the temperatures in the hinterland varied. The lush tropical rainforest-like bush lowered the too-warm summer heat and kept the winter so chilly it felt like the cold entered your bones.

'I don't need to even respond to that, do I darling? As if I care what others are doing and God forbid, what they thought?'

Greta chuckled. 'No, I guess not.'

'And that is exactly the place you need to be. Forget others, focus on yourself and do what is right.'

She forgot what she entered the shed for. 'But, Millie, I understand you've always done what you've wanted regardless of others, but did you want to get married, fall in love?'

The old woman took a long drag on her cigarette again and let the smoke disperse before she responded. As it drifted away, Millie coughed. And coughed, doubled over with the effort.

"Millie, are you alright?' She approached as her aunt wheezed, still bent at the middle and sucking in air. After a few moments, she straightened.

'Are you okay? You've gone terribly pale.' Greta didn't want to say it but her lips were tinged blue. Greta guided her to a flat rock where she sat.

After Millie caught her breath, she said, 'I've said this before, Greta and many times over the years. I am married to my work. It's my choice. I never wanted to be restricted, to be managed. It's quite liberating, but a concept other people appear to struggle with.'

'I respect your choices, it's not that. But isn't true love about being free to do the things you desire while being supported and encouraged and loved?'

She watched Millie pause, gaze downward towards her feet and up to take in the magnificent, clear blue sky. She took in another deep breath. Little sweat droplets ran down the inside of Greta's T-shirt. It was going to be a scorcher.

'I mean, I cannot answer that with any authority. But what I've observed, is that one person can do that, but the other becomes the supporter, the one who stands by and pats the other on the back and says 'well done' and therefore does not have the chance to pursue their own dreams. Particularly when you add children into the mix and life becomes busy and challenging.'

Millie reached out her hand to Greta who stood close. 'I'm sure it's a lovely thing to do, to spend one's life beside another whom you declare you love. I do not oppose it for anyone, but I did not want to experience the guilt at looking after children when all I ever wanted to do was paint. I shudder to imagine what that might have done to my creativity. But, my love, we are all different.'

'You don't regret anything.'

'Regrets, no. Wished some events may have ended differently, certainly. I think that's human nature. But I wouldn't do anything different. Now can you find these plants please.'

Yesterday, to her surprise, Millie had arranged delivery of a range of hard-wearing outdoor plants for the garden beds and she said, some sweet and colourful flowers to add a touch of magnifique. Greta went in search of them.

'Millie?'

'Hmm,' Millie responded from outside.

'What are these doing here?' She carried out one canvas about one metre square in size. In her other hand, she carried a second. 'The third one is inside, too.'

'That boy,' Millie muttered and shook her head. 'We've still got a lot of work to do.'

Greta stared at them and retrieved the third so that she could observe them together.

'Millie, these are, not weird, confronting is that fair to say?'

They both moved back as if doing so would make the scenes clearer. Only because they'd talked about the issue before he'd painted these, did Greta understand the face in each painting was the dead refugee. Otherwise, it could easily be mistaken for a contorted, misshapen or deformed face. The contours in two were rough, sharp and blunt. The first, even she could work out was the man in a happier state with his features less severe. More subtle, softer, but there was still an edge, a harrowed look in his eyes that drove straight into you when you stared at him. And the colour. It was all dark blacks and navy blues and deep browns.

Goose bumps erupted along her flesh and Greta rubbed her arms. Brodie had been right; his paintings were not pleasant. Did she consider them and the story they told only because he said that's what he wanted people to do or because the work itself made her question them? She wasn't sure, but immediately the issues buzzed in her head and the tragedy of the man's situation came down upon her. That's what he was hoping for. Man, he was clever.

But how do you sell this stuff? It would be considered controversial at best, maybe even political and wouldn't that cut your audience in half?

'Yes, that's true. But you cannot deny they're unique. He's a natural storyteller who happens to do it through his art.'

Greta hadn't realised she'd spoken out loud. There was one thing she did know. 'These can't stay hidden, Millie, where no one can see them, ask the difficult questions, have those conversations. It's not right.'

'I agree. But he's stubborn. He honestly thinks no one wants to see them. Brodie thinks people will be repulsed rather than drawn to them. Not perhaps in the traditional sense of beauty or because they are ascetically attractive, but they will be drawn to these and the other pieces he creates. He can't see it.'

'He needs to try.'

'That's a decision for him to make.'

A car rumbled along the drive. The purr of its engine cutting into the solitude of the silence.

Greta spotted red and blue on a white car.

The police.

<h1 style="text-align:center">CHAPTER 15</h1>

*G*reta and Millie shot a glance at each other. Greta still held one canvas and slowly lowered it to the ground. The police vehicle pulled to a stop only metres away and she forced her feet to move and placed the paintings back into the shed.

Two officers exited the car and placed their caps on their heads. Both wore formal uniforms with dour expressions.

'Greta Louise Johnson?'

If the expression losing one's stomach was possible, Greta's guts tumbled onto the dirt she stood upon. Sweat dripped from her pores and her heart rate accelerated so much her chest ached. Déjà vu images slammed into her hard.

Back then faced with the police, it had been disbelief, shock and fear of the unknown. Today, it was pure terror. She reached for the railing to hold her balance but misjudged the distance and missed its reach and lurched sideways in a funny sort of step. One of the policemen rushed forward, grasped her arm and guided her towards the stairs where she fell onto her backside with a thud.

'What's this about?' Millie spoke first.

'I'm Constable Morgan Reynolds from the Lucas Heads police station. There's been a report of a crime …'

'Yes,' Millie sounded impatient. Greta listened but the voices were muffled like she listened under water.

'Greta, did you recently acquire a job at the Collins Gourmet Supermarket?'

The supermarket? 'Yes.'

'And you've done three shifts so far?'

Greta thought and counted in her head, her brain worked in slow motion. 'I guess so.'

'Can you tell us about those shifts?'

Deep annoyance rose up through her chest then. 'What do you mean, tell you about those shifts? Why and what would you want to know? How many people I served? The tins of dog food I placed onto the shelf?'

'Greta,' Millie warned. 'Officers, before you start interrogating my niece it's best you tell us why she needs to advise about the intricacies of her shifts?'

'Greta Johnson,' the older officer said, clearly the one in charge; he wore a moustache on his upper lip that looked like it had been there since the seventies. 'You are accused of stealing money from the supermarket. Cash and some personal items are reported to have gone missing after your shift on Friday.'

Greta glanced at Millie and shook her head ever so slightly. Millie understood. An ache ripped through Greta's chest, so severe, she gripped her sides and held them tight.

'Why do you think it was me?'

'Other staff have been eliminated from our investigations. Is it true you are on parole for embezzling in excess of two million dollars?'

Something innate propelled her to stand then. The blood returned to her legs and held her firm. 'Yes, but does that mean I am now brandished a thief forever? I mean, for God's sake, those crimes involved millions of dollars. Am I going to take a few bucks from the local deli?' Despite her overt strength, her legs went weak and she sank back down again. Yeah, go Greta, that really showed them. You must be innocent.

A spark deep inside simmered, only to extinguish itself moments later. She probably looked crazy and therefore a potential criminal. Were all criminals crazy? No, she could answer that with certainty. They weren't all crazy, a mixed bunch sure, some from disadvantaged backgrounds with unfortunate experiences, and some were simply evil, others unlucky.

'Is she being charged?'

'No, but we'd like her to accompany us to the station for questioning.'

Greta rose and dragged her feet towards them, instinctively put her hands out. They laughed.

'You're not under arrest.'

Glad they found it funny.

Millie was beside her. 'It'll be okay.' A pause. 'Should I call your father?'

That did it. Greta released an anguished moan. Not again. She couldn't do this again. Shame, embarrassment, injustice, humiliation swam around inside of her; those emotions nipping at her insides, pecking, removing skin, leaving a gash. She could not go back to jail. She would not survive a second time. Barely did the first.

'Sorry. Forget your father. I'll follow you.'

Millie's face must have mirrored her own. But why did Millie feel such despair? She believed she was innocent, didn't she?

Greta was assisted into the police vehicle. As the door slammed shut, she screamed, 'you believe me, don't you, Millie?' But she couldn't hear the answer.

'ARE YOU OKAY?' BRODIE ASKED AND CAME TO SIT NEXT TO Greta on the white plastic chair in the police interview room.

Her head lay on the desk resting on her crossed arms. She breathed in and out.

'Greta?'

She lifted her head. Her skin held a grey pallor, her eyes sunken and dark. Her hands trembled.

'Brodie.' Her voice was croaky. Clearing her throat, she tried again. 'I have to sign this statement but I need to read it first...' Toward him she pushed a sole piece of paper and immediately leaned her head back on the desk. 'I can't understand it.' The words came out through a sob.

Brodie clasped her hands and held them in his own then reached for the sheet and read aloud. Greta kept her head lowered. He waited for her to jump in, correct something, but she didn't. 'Are you happy with that? Is it correct?'

'No, I'm not happy with that.' Her head jerked up. 'This is a fucking nightmare.'

'They haven't mistreated you, have they?'

'No, except for hauling my bad ass in here.'

'Okay, good,' he said and stroked the top of her hand.

'What, you're my therapist now?' She shook off his petting. 'Where's Millie? She said she'd come.'

He ignored her tone. 'When I arrived this morning she was sitting on the bottom step, sort of worn out like. Told me what had happened and asked me to come.' He looked her straight in the eyes and said, 'But I would have come anyway.'

Blinding tears rolled down her cheeks. He reached over with his sleeve, the one marred with paint splotches and dirty patches, and wiped roughly at her cheeks. 'Don't cry.'

'Why not? Everything is shit. I can't do anything right.'

'What do you mean?'

She shrugged off his strokes. 'Are you asking me if I did it? Fuck! If you don't believe me, I'm seriously screwed.'

She stood up, then sat back down. 'I cannot go back to jail.' Her head collapsed and jerked up just as quickly as it sank. 'I'll need a lawyer and I can't afford one.' Covering her face with her hands, Greta released her despair. But in the next moment, she frantically searched her handbag and yanked out every item to only disregard it as not what she looked for. With the contents spilled on the interview table, she checked each pocket. 'It has to be here …' She searched each wrapper, item of paper and card. 'I know I've got his business card here somewhere.'

'Who?'

'My lawyer. The one who helped me last time. He cost a fortune but he knows my history. That has to be a good thing right?' In frustration at not locating the card, she threw up the contents of her bag and lipsticks and lollies and her purse flew off the table.

Brodie placed his large palm over the back of her hand that still tremored. 'I do believe you. I understand this must be a crazy mistake. If you need legal help, I'll sort it out. Millie will help.'

Greta nodded then. Yes, Brodie thought, Millie would help. He, too, would do whatever it took. There were always extra shifts with his brother; tradie jobs were everywhere. Particularly with the new construction about town. It'd be all right. 'You don't need to worry about anything. I'll help, we'll get this sorted.'

'Brodie, you don't understand. I'm on parole. Any 'mistakes',' and she indicated inverted commas with her hands, 'and I return to prison. If they charge me, even if I'm claiming my innocence, that's a breach of parole and I'm back in jail.' She wailed, a deep guttural groan that split Brodie in two. Her eyes squeezed shut.

'I can't go back there, I can't −'

Constable Reynolds entered the room. He coughed lightly to get their attention. 'Greta, you're free to go.'

'What?' Her head jerked up. 'Are you for real? Why?'

'Hey, mate,' the constable slapped Brodie on the back in greeting.

'Another accused has been delivered to the police station with the stolen money in her possession and it matches the amount missing from the supermarket. There's also a witness.'

Screams echoed in from the waiting room. Before either of the men could restrain her, Greta rushed out. Brodie jumped up and followed, shoving into Greta's back as she pulled up sharp before the row of retro muted orange chairs lining the walls of the reception area. It matched the brown linoleum.

One woman was pulling another's long, sun-bleached hair and yanking so hard that the other screeched in response. Reynolds pushed past Brodie and tried to break them apart.

Brodie deliberated over whether he should help his mate. He recognised them as girls from town; he'd had a friendly drink or two with them at the pub. He considered his options too long and another officer, broader, bigger and a grey moustache on his upper lip, rushed out. Unlike lanky and young Reynolds, this guy took no nonsense and held those two screaming banshees apart. They flailed their arms about trying to land scratches when they couldn't reach.

'Jasmine?' Greta's voice was soft but clear.

The shorter of the pair turned towards Greta whose eyes widened in surprise. 'You stole the money?'

A smirk spread across Jasmine's face. 'Yeah and you would have been pinned for sure if this bitch didn't dob me in. I mean who's not going to think a previous crim with a history of theft, wouldn't do it again. I offered this one a cut but she's sore because I slept with her boyfriend...'

The reminder of Jasmine's misdemeanour tempered the

other girl's fury again and she made another lunge for her, forgetting she was locked in place by the two arms of the burly officer.

'Sherelle, calm down. You've done nothing wrong but if you keep behaving like this, we'll charge you with assault.'

'Charge her!' Jasmine yelled. 'She pulled my hair. Charge her with dobbing on a friend, too.'

'I'm not your friend!'

'That's enough, ladies. Jasmine, come with me,' Reynolds motioned for her to follow him.

'You said it was me, Jasmine? Why would you do that? I thought we were friends?'

A cackle. Jasmine came within inches of Greta's face and said, 'Why would I be friends with a slut like you?'

Brodie stepped closer, ready to pounce but Reynolds intervened and grabbed her by the upper arm and dragged her away.

MILLIE WAS ASLEEP. SHE SAT, HEAD DIPPED TO HER CHEST, purring like one of the cats. Her mouth open and exhaling a small whir after each intake of breath. Her red painting hat, today adorned by an orange and yellow marigold flower, was skewed sideways with the funny angle of her head. The cats slept at her feet, the smallest curled around one foot, the other near the leg of the chair sprawled on its back and mother and third baby, spooning on the rug nearby.

A bottle of unopened white wine was on the antique table next to her; its condensation pooling at the base. Three glasses sat empty, inviting and ready.

Greta didn't say anything and collapsed onto the sofa. Dust mites exploded into the air. Sensing the mood, mother cat stretched up onto her legs and strode over, wrapping herself around Greta's limbs. Scooping up the cat, she offered her long, broad strokes.

'Millie,' Brodie said. He leaned in, close to her ear. He'd learned the hard way once trying to wake up his Uncle Stuart; startling someone at this age could be deadly.

She roused immediately as if she'd only been on the periphery of sleep. One hand went up to right her hat, then she sat up tall and became alert. Nothing wrong with her mind, Brodie mused.

'What happened?' Fingers rubbed across her eyes, briefly, fleetingly, the only sign of her fatigue. But her words cracked, and she erupted in a dry rasping cough and gasped for breath between each hack. Millie covered her mouth with a lace handkerchief she held in her palm. Brodie watched her frail frame uncurl after the effort.

Greta was a heap, slumped into the couch, sitting low. Her hair sat out at odd angles, her face pale and her gaze distant.

'It was a mistake,' Brodie said. 'You know that local girl, Jasmine? Well, she accused Greta and concocted some cockamamie story and made Greta the prime suspect.'

Millie murmured in the right places. Brodie gave her the facts they knew.

'How did she know about your background?'

Greta shrugged. 'I thought she was my friend.' Greta sounded petulant.

'How did she find out?'

'It's this small bloody town. Gossips the bunch of them. Kathleen must have told her,' Greta burst out with venom.

Millie reached over and touched Greta's knee. 'But, in the end it was a mistake, a terribly mistimed error that has caused a fright.' She reached over to the bottle. 'I got this one out, a fantastic drop. I think we need it.'

'Millie! Give me that. I need it, not you. I'm going to drink the whole damn bottle, but not you. You shouldn't have any. I can't be responsible for you too.'

'You are not responsible for me. But you're quite right, my girl, I don't need it, but I'm bloody well going to have just one glass and enjoy it.'

Brodie felt responsible for the pair. He was up for it, though, except he felt like guzzling the bottle himself, followed by a chaser.

The wine required a corkscrew—the old-fashioned sort—and Brodie went in search of one. He returned with a motley collection of snacks: cheeses, cured meats, crackers and dried fruit.

'You are a dear.' Millie offered him that sweet saccharine smile that only an old lady can. 'What a catch! If I was younger, I'd marry you myself. I'm betting you two haven't had anything to eat?'

'Yeah, I could murder a steak.'

Millie cracked up, her joviality returned. Greta smirked.

'Heads up darling, this could have been a disaster, but it wasn't. I guess it's your first taste of the mean, outside world. Your past is going to be a rod on your back for a while. People will judge you and most likely, not trust you either.'

'Fuck them,' Greta said.

'Fuck them,' Millie and Brodie repeated.

The day drew to a close. They didn't move but instead drank, ate, talked and reminisced of old and new times. Brodie read them the day's top stories and they became outraged at the eviction of some local traditional people from their lands. The world outside grew dim.

'Let's toast to my shit day,' Greta said after her second or third drop. She held up her glass. 'I'm wallowing right now and will for the rest of the evening. But tomorrow is a new day and it'll be fine. I'm not guilty and did nothing wrong. Whatever happens can never be as bad as what I've been through, and I've survived. I'm still here, right?' She continued, "But, I'm exhausted from this self-deprecating talk. I'm going to take a sleeping tablet and sleep and sleep and sleep and dream none of this happened and wake up feeling better tomorrow.'

'Atta girl.' Millie clapped.

'You got this,' Brodie cheered. 'See you in the morning.' He clamped his hands under his legs to prevent jumping up and pulling her into an embrace. If he held her, she'd be fragile, a waif of herself. It would scare him. He'd want to give her some strength, make everything all right. Rescue her. But she was vulnerable right now and he'd leave it be, mainly because he might not be able to hold himself together.

'Brodie, I'm going to paint. Will you join me? I have pieces to finish for the exhibition.' Millie didn't need to say it was her way of calming her nerves. It was exactly what he needed too.

'I'm with you. I've got a new idea and I'm going to play with some sketching. I'll sit inside with you if that's okay?'

'I would love the company.'

Like always, a stab of wild hope fluttered in his stomach at a fresh idea. The excitement as it rolled around his mind, already forming an internal tussle. Should he do it this way or that? Which colours? Make it dramatic or timid?

'Days like today, I long to be back in Paris.' Millie muttered as she made herself comfortable in her painting seat.

'You working on French pieces?' he asked.

'I wasn't, but it's an urge I can't satisfy. I have to scratch it. Maybe I'll do one from memory, one of my favourite scenes and then I'll get back to the landscapes. It might be a bit odd to have a local landscape exhibition but have a French panorama in there, too. Do you think anyone would notice?'

'The dimwits of town would for sure and call you on it. Critique it, say you've lost it. They'd report the old reclusive artist from the hills has finally succumbed to dementia. She thinks she's painting local vistas but is confusing them with the French countryside. It could be funny,' Brodie concluded.

No more words were required. Millie escaped into her own world and Brodie into his but they were two very different places.

Brodie didn't get hungry; if his tummy rumbled he didn't notice. Millie did not break either. Occasionally he skulled from a plastic water bottle he found in the room, water probably days old but he didn't care. His only pause was to rip a page out of his book; the shrill tear the only sound in the room. Millie didn't notice. His hand cramped but he didn't stop. The first few attempts ended in the bin. The next few, on the floor. But he got the feel for what he was trying to create. The lines, shape, depth. He imagined the long painted brush strokes and knew with certainty the colours he would apply. He didn't notice when the moon sat high in the sky and started to dip. The fluorescent lights in the room continued to blaze. Millie didn't stop either. He ignored her reaching for another glass of alcohol. If she downed another few bottles he'd have intervened but they were measured sips and could only serve to fuel the passion coming out of her paintbrush.

In the early hours, he was stirred awake by Millie's coughing reverberating around the studio. He awoke to find her sipping water and catching her breath between flourishes of her wrist. Around her, on the floor, the ledge, the long table in the room, and in front of her easel, sat four paintings that hadn't been there the night before. He'd been satisfied with his many attempts at the sketch but that old woman had kept going and not slept. She was bloody crazy, and he loved her for it.

CHAPTER 16

A demonic beast lived inside her chest and drove Greta over the next few days. Told her she'd failed and to get on with real life; be an adult and act like one. Time had run out. The beast inside of her was nasty, but it almost certainly resembled something more like a rainbow unicorn with powerful hooves that kicked the inside of her ribcage, hard. Either way, a moment of stillness was an idle moment too long. Her body fizzled like a bottle of champagne; she was all frenetic energy that had to be released.

'Stop this, Greta. You have nothing to prove,' Millie urged in her soft, loving tone.

But, oh yes, she did. The garden beds were finished. It took two days to cram every plant and flower into its spot. On the first finish, she yanked them back out and started over not happy with their positioning and the asymmetrical look of the garden. Second time around was much better. Even though the urge to change it again to make it perfect, was strong. She didn't. Her body ached by then.

She scoured the local nurseries and developed a wish list for topiaries to buy to place along the path and entrance way. The list was long. The yard was far from finished.

Greta studied Millie's plant books, skipped the ridiculously long scientific names, glossed over the pictures and scanned the words for the ideal growing conditions. She sketched a plan for further improvement; it was cathartic.

'You look like a farm girl,' Millie yelled as she flew past on the ride-on mower. 'I pay someone to do that.'

'No need!' Greta yelled back.

Occasionally, she'd stop and wipe the sweat drops from her brow and take a breather. At those times she'd catch Brodie watching her. His right fingers twitching and when she noticed, he'd drop them, or stretch them in and out like unclenching a fist. A couple of times she glanced around wondering if he was formulating creative images of the surrounding scenery. Landscapes and pretty gardens weren't his thing, but what did she know? Perhaps his next project was to save the rainforests?

Kathleen rang every day. Greta refused to answer but listened to the voice messages.

I am so sorry for what happened. I would love you to come back. It's not your fault and I'm sure we can…

The voice at the end of the line cracked. A lump formed in Greta's throat and a wave of disappointment washed over her. For what could have been. Her old boss, and she was her former manager; there wasn't a chance in hell that she was going back to Collins Gourmet Supermarket. It wasn't Kathleen's fault. Or it might have been. It depended on whether Kathleen had spilled the beans on her.

The phone dinged again. She read the screen, ready to disregard the message but it wasn't Kathleen.

Charlie Clarke.

One sentence made of emoji symbols. She quickly swiped delete.

The phone rang again and Greta pressed the accept button when she saw it was Kathleen once more.

Minutes later she hung up and was pleased she'd answered. Kathleen explained that Jasmine had snuck into the office and read her personnel file. Kathleen hadn't revealed her private information. At the news, Greta's body sank with relief. The thought of someone setting her up had hurt. Kathleen was apologetic and desperate to make it up to her. Too late, it felt eerily like the end of a very short chapter in her life. She picked at the dirt under her fingernails. Greta was stoked about the garden but she needed a break from the mulch and hay. Her nose tickled.

Read? Nah, pleasure was required. The beast and unicorn were divided on that topic. *Read and you'll get smarter and won't make such bad decisions in the future.*

You need to nurture yourself and do things that give you pleasure, but reading is a good idea!

Her phone vibrated in her back pocket and she extracted it. Charlie again. She pressed the red button to disconnect and he rang again immediately. Not a chance in hell she was taking his call. Greta muted her phone.

Forgetting him, she wandered into Millie's studio. She considered the stuff: dried driftwood, dead flowers, dirty cloths, frames, china teacups and saucers. Millie's entire life was in this room. Greta picked up a miniature armadillo figurine. Where on earth did she get this? Imagining Millie in some exotic location, maybe bartering in a Marrakesh market – had Millie been to Africa? – or perhaps a quaint antique store in Notting Hill. Millie was a character who'd lived a full and diverse and colourful life. That's exactly what Greta needed to do. The question was – how to do it?

Where was Millie? She'd been MIA a lot and always seemed to slink away mysteriously. Fred? Yes, she might be with her lover.

He hadn't visited recently, though. Had she found someone new and was keeping him a secret? Oh, the intrigue!

She shuffled further into the room, stepping over items scattered on the floor and paused at one of two cluttered tables. Next, she picked up a marble figurine, but she caught a glimpse of a small odd-sized nook on the far side of the room and moved toward it

It was jampacked, too. Multiple paintings leaned against the back wall, their frames obvious. Three and four boxes sat stacked on top of each other with dust an inch thick on their lids. Piles of books towered in the corner. It was a musty, busy space.

Greta picked up the book on top of the pile and sneezed as the dust floated straight up her nose. Blowing the residue off the sides, she rubbed her fingers across the title and author. Gertrude Stein. She'd heard that name before. It was a book of poetry and she opened the front cover.

A rose is a rose is a rose is a rose, you are my rose, Millie. You know I love the readings of Gertrude Stein, you've always jested at my interest in her unusual work. But when I read her, I think of you. You are my blossoming, blood red rose. You smell divine, are beauty personified and fragile to the touch. And sometimes have a tendency to be prickly like a long, green stem lined with thorns. When I see roses I think of you. Summer has become torture for me as roses are everywhere in the city of love. As if it isn't hard enough to live here, with romance and l'armour on each street corner. However, I know you prefer the words of other poets, here is one of your favourites.

Below the inscription, signed *Reggie* was a poem he had transcribed in his neat, loopy writing.

Shall I compare thee to a summer's day?
Thou art more lovely and more temperate.
Rough winds do shake the darling buds of May,
And summer's lease hath all too short a date.
Sometime too hot the eye of heaven shines,
And often is his gold complexion dimmed;

And every fair from fair sometime declines,
By chance, or nature's changing course, untrimmed;
But thy eternal summer shall not fade,
Nor lose possession of that fair thou ow'st,
Nor shall death brag thou wand'rest in his shade,
When in eternal lines to Time thou grow'st.
So long as men can breathe, or eyes can see,
So long lives this, and this gives life to thee.

Reggie! Greta clutched the book to her chest and sighed. To be so loved. To express such love. A sudden swell of longing tugged at the edges of her heart.

She skimmed to the bottom of the page, wanting more. Nothing.

Turning the pages she hoped to find other poems, more outpouring of emotion, of vulnerability. Is this what words could do? If so, she'd not realised their power all this time.

There were no other poems because it was a book of verse. More abstract and beautiful in a less earth-tingling heart-hammering way. Hearing a noise behind her, she slammed the book shut. Adrenalin surged through her: at the love poem or guilt, she wasn't sure.

She turned and left the little alcove, once again consumed with thoughts of Millie and her mysterious friend.

BRODIE SHOOK THE TUBE TRYING TO EXTRACT THE LAST DROPLETS of strawberry-pink oil paint. Dry. This colour was vital. The muted ambers, cerise, russet and salmon shades were essential for the portrait. This painting was special, he knew it. Usually the excitement wore off if a piece didn't quite work. And sometimes it was as simple as one wrong stroke. But his entire body tingled; since the early sketches, through to the first brush stroke right up until the last he'd just completed. Was this the one? The best he'd done.

In Millie's studio, he searched for her spare tubes. His fingers itched to get back.

'Hey.' He looked up into the eyes of Distraction.

'Greta.' His voice immediately dropped an octave. Became husky and unsure in her presence.

'You've been busy.'

He nodded. 'Yep, this new piece is consuming me.'

'Any point asking to see it?' She smiled at him so that her eyes twinkled.

He shook his head. 'Whatcha doing?'

'I had this crazy idea of cleaning. Obvious place to start right?' Greta indicated around her and laughed as his lips turned downward and his eyes opened as wide as saucers. 'I know. I know. Stupid idea. I promise I haven't touched anything. But I didn't realise there was a room back there.' She pointed.

'Even worse,' he said. 'Millie keeps her most precious things in there. Move a particle of dust and she'll know.'

He moved closer to her, drawn like a magnetic current. Facing her, he placed his arms around her shoulders. 'I've missed you.'

She sank into his embrace. 'Me too. But you artist types are a bit obsessed. You lot are difficult company to keep.'

Ouch, the barb cut deep. He'd been accused of this a thousand times before. Greta meant it jovially. But without fail, it caused prickles to raise up the back of his neck. 'Maybe it's time I took a break.'

'Really?'

He watched her hopes rise like a flower budding into bloom. No chance of backing down now. Millie was out of the paint colour he needed anyway. Time to stop. He could make a trip to the art store later. And the layer he'd just applied could dry.

Being pulled away from his art when he wasn't quite ready usually caused a sick feeling to sit in his stomach. A taste of bile that he couldn't get rid of until he returned, back to the holy grail, his first love. He was similar to Millie like that. But was it worth sacrificing everything for? He had so far. But what about the woman standing in front of him? What did she mean? He didn't know but he thought he owed it to himself to find out.

'What should we do?' he asked. 'Go for a coffee, the beach, shopping?' At that suggestion he scowled.

'Not a fan of shopping then?' she tickled him lightly on his ribs.

He dodged her aim.

'No. But I'd do it for you.' His eyes sought out hers and drank in every part of her. Her messy hair was pulled back in a loose ponytail. No make-up, T-shirt hanging out of baggy denim shorts that were, well short. She caught his glare; he watched her eyes drop to his lips. She nipped a corner of her mouth with her teeth and Brodie's skin prickled with pleasure. He puffed out his T-shirt to dampen the heat emanating off his chest.

'I don't want to go into town or anywhere public. I want to stay here. Can we go for a walk to the creek?'

He didn't trust his voice but managed to squeak, 'Sure.'

'I just want to grab something, I'll be a second.' Greta rushed away.

There was no need for security on the secluded property, so they wandered off leaving the doors and windows open. The midday sun stung their bare arms. But only a few metres from the house, the rainforest began. Large eucalypt trees shaded the path and the temperature dipped. Leaves squelched under their feet as the ground became moist. Brodie reached for Greta's hand.

After only a short walk, they arrived at the creek. More of a pond really.

'I can't believe I haven't been down here yet. It's so beautiful.' Greta stood back, mouth open and hands on hips looking at the circular pool of water, the culmination of a shaded, gurgling creek. A mixture of boulders and pebbles lined the edge where they stood leading to patches of reeds lining the banks. It was quiet, secluded and perfect.

'What a waste. I need to get my shit together,' Greta said and moved over to a rock and sat down, removed her shoes and dipped her toes in the water.

'It's divine!'

'It's nice to see you relaxed and happy.'

Her smile was dazzling, one of the ones that lit up her entire face and made her eyes sparkle. Greta did not give them away easily.

'Do you read poetry?'

'Poetry? Well, sure I have, but not like regularly.'

Pulling a book out of her rucksack, she held it up. 'I don't know why I didn't think of this before. Poems are shorter, often lines of only a few words and snappy to read. Easier for me. Plus,' she looked up, 'some of them are fabulous.'

'Fabulous?'

She stared at him then and he felt her undressing him with her eyes.

'What I mean is romantic. I found one this morning. Can I read it to you?'

Greta read a sonnet from Shakespeare that he knew but had never paid attention to before. Out of her mouth, it was the most beautiful thing he'd ever heard.

Greta read another, lost in a world of rhyme and fantasy. His turn. He pulled the book out of her grip, turned the pages, skimming until he found the perfect one.

She walks in beauty,
Like the night

Of cloudless climes
And starry skies.
'That one was by Lord Byron.'
'Beautiful.'

His gaze fell to the creamy expanse of her neck. Just one flicker and he'd be staring at the tip of her breasts. Her chest rose and fell in quick breaths. For once, Greta didn't fill the silence with words, or laugh as he'd learned was one of her nervous mechanisms to cover up discomfort. He shifted and their thighs touched. A bolt of pleasure spiralled through him at the pressure of their bodies straddled side by side.

Never had he been this transfixed by a woman. He'd met many attractive women, but this was more than mere looks and pretty hair and a slim body. It was a connection he couldn't explain. A sense of being drawn inexplicably to her. An understanding. Of wanting to know more. Of his heart lurching into gear when he was in her presence. Or as his brother, Derek might say, 'they got each other.'

Being this close was overwhelming in the best kind of way. He shuffled closer. As if he could resist. Nothing would hold him back. He placed his hands on cheeks that were warm to the touch. He enjoyed the feel of her for a moment, kissed her with his eyes. Then a stream of sunlight escaped through the canopy of trees and captured her in a golden halo.

His mind returned to his portrait. Angles, imagery and yellow light.

Greta moved forward on the rock and he leaned in and their lips met. It was urgent, exploratory, tongues clashing. His lips moved down her neck and along her jaw and collar bone until he traced his way back up to her soft, open mouth. Those lips welcomed him back and he felt her need stir. She placed one hand to his chest and one on his thigh. His skin burned at her touch.

Talking through the kiss, their lips resting close to each other, she whispered, 'Let's go for a swim.'

He rested his forehead against hers, still holding her hands, wanting her near. 'In our clothes?'

She paused. 'No.'

Their eyes communicated. His hands went down to the rim of her shirt and lifted it over her head. He took her all in. Her slim shoulders, the white pure skin and torso. She did the same but once his chest was bare, she traced her fingers through the smattering of his chest hair. Touched his nipples and dipped down dangerously close to the hem of his shorts. They kissed again, deeply, breath-stealing so they gasped for more. It was a taste he wanted to experience again and again. He stood and lifted her gently with him. Looking for signs that he should stop but not detecting any, he untied the belt around her shorts. The material dropped to the ground. Brodie swallowed. But Greta was whip quick. She wasn't being left behind and undid his button and slowly, deliberately, slid down the zip of his shorts. His body came to attention; her eyes went wide. One hand lingered there, and she smiled. In a rush they ripped off their underwear. He reached for her hand and they ran for the water together. The cold temperature did nothing to dampen their desire and in the water, her skin on his, the liquid moving between them, he almost lost control. Instead, he held her close, too tight and felt her breasts against his chest dipping in the gleaming water and her slippery and wet legs snake around him and he was lost.

CHAPTER 17

Brodie stayed at Millie's that night. But not with her. He painted into the wee hours until Greta heard him sneak out—not so quietly—at around three am. Not his fault, sleep evaded her and her body remained jittery. Would she have slept better if his tall and strong body had snuggled around hers? Who knew? She'd resisted the temptation to drag him into her bed.

The morning sun crept into her room and she was unable to rest her listless limbs so she tossed the covers back and got up and went for a walk. The short-blade grass edging the drive glistened with dew. A deliciously light breeze caressed her skin and the sun's rays didn't yet hold any warmth. Forcing herself to pause, she closed her eyes, breathed in and allowed tranquillity to descend. She was still failing to appreciate the beauty of her surroundings, particularly after spending time at the creek yesterday. The glorious beach was only a kilometre away, with the lush forests, animal wildlife and the greenery. Greta needed to utilise the power of its healing.

Usually, she'd walk at a brisk pace, working up a sweat and burning as many calories as possible. Today, she strode with purpose. Her steps weren't slow but nor were they fast. At this pace she noticed every small detail: the orange faded letterbox with junk mail poking out; the galahs high up in the gum trees; the bellow of a cow in a nearby paddock and the gentle rumble of cars on the road.

Heading in a different direction to that she'd walked before, she spotted a small train of people heading up a long snaking driveway to a house hidden well-back on acreage. The high fence and heavy trees spanning the front meant if she'd kept her gaze straight ahead, she'd have missed it. Curiosity piqued and she followed.

It wasn't uncommon in these parts with large blocks and hobby farms for people to sell produce at their properties. Usually half the price of the stores and much better quality. Greta presumed this crowd had found the best spot for local, fresh fruit and veg. She'd pick up something for breakfast.

Upon approach, she realised the group was mostly women holding the hands of children. Halfway along the drive she came across a welcoming blue and white sign that said *Beach Haven*. Maybe it was a café that served good coffee?

Greta rounded a corner and stumbled across scattered tables in the sizeable yard, shaded by trees, somewhat like a garden party but something told her this was not a celebration. The women and children were eating and drinking in small clusters and appeared subdued with their heads lowered. Even the children were quiet. Greta inhaled that familiar bitter aroma.

'Hello, dear,' a lady serving drinks at one table addressed her. 'Have your come for breakfast?'

'Breakfast?' Greta queried.

The lady would have been her mother's age, she guessed and she looked behind Greta to detect if she was alone. 'Are you all right? Do you need assistance?'

Greta paid more attention to the garden now. It was an old,

one-level home of plain red brick with a wide concrete veranda spanning each side of the square perimeter. The tables were cheap white plastic, with mis-matched chairs in a variety of colours. Greta turned back towards the lady and noticed for the first time she wore a name badge that read Ellen.

'I'm sorry, Ellen, what is this place? I was walking past and saw the queue.'

Ellen smiled. 'Well, come on in then,' and she moved around the table and placed her arm through Greta's and held her elbow. 'We are a women's shelter. But we offer breakfast everyday and usually get a sizeable turnout. Some of these women are guests and others visit regularly.'

'What do you do here?' Greta felt ignorant but needed to know.

Ellen didn't seem to mind and explained that they temporarily housed women and children fleeing violence and helped them secure long-term accommodation, find employment and any other services they required, often medical treatment.

Greta was digesting this when Ellen was called away to assist someone. 'Have a look around, everyone's welcome,' she shouted as she strode away.

At the far corner of the yard, Greta spied a young woman sitting alone with vacant chairs at her table. Pouring herself an instant coffee from the urn, she headed that way.

'Hello, I'm Greta, do you mind if I sit here?'

The young girl nodded. She had pure white hair like uncoloured fairy floss and in the morning sun her skin was pale porcelain. She cradled her own hot drink and had a plate of fruit in front of her. She hummed loud enough for Greta to hear.

'That's a beautiful tune,' she said and the girl smiled. 'Do you like to sing?'

'I love to sing,' and Greta heard the excitement in her voice. 'It's the only thing I'm good at.'

'I'm sure that's not true,' Greta responded. 'What is your favourite type of music? Pop? Hip hop?'

'Opera.'

'Opera, wow, that's impressive. I'm not sure I know any opera.'

Without inhibition the girl broke out into a song with words that Greta didn't understand and took such deep breaths the air must have come straight from her lungs.

'That's incredible,' Greta gushed and those around them broke into applause. 'But I couldn't understand the words.'

'It was Italian. Opera is usually performed in foreign languages.'

'So beautiful,' Greta agreed. 'Is your Mum here with you? What's your name?'

The girl paused and then shook her head before saying 'Skye.'

'That's a lovely name. It suits you.'

A hand landed to Greta's shoulder and another woman bearing a name badge appeared to her right. 'I see you've met our very talented Skye, she has the most wonderful voice and keeps us entertained,' the woman offered a broad smile but her eyes were guarded. 'I'm the director of *Beach Haven*,' and she reached out her hand to shake. 'Robyn. Are you here to help?'

Greta blushed. 'Gosh, I'm so sorry for barging in. I was intrigued because it's such a sleepy hamlet around here and to see a group of people gathered together was unusual. I'll go.' Greta rose and Robyn placed her hand to her arm.

'Don't be silly. You're welcome.'

'Would you like me to get you some breakfast?' Skye offered.

'Well, sure, if that's okay.' Skye wandered off and Robyn leaned in close. 'Skye has recently lost her mother and she's staying with us for a while. She's a great kid.'

'What about her dad?'

'No father that we know of.'

'So all of these women need assistance?'

Robyn nodded. 'Yes, most are fleeing domestic violence and this is a safe place for them. We have counsellors on site.'

Skye came back and offered Greta a plate of pastries and fresh fruit. 'This looks delicious, thanks, Skye.'

'We're really short-handed. I don't know you Greta, but if you have any spare time, we'd love your help.' With that she smiled at Skye and got up and wandered over to another table and comforted a woman who appeared to be in tears.

'So, Skye, tell me a bit more about this opera stuff. How did you learn it?'

An hour later she arrived home to find Millie on the deck drinking her morning cup of tea. She cradled Lola in her lap like a baby.

'Millie?' she asked as she plonked herself in the chair next to her. 'Did you know about *Beach Haven*?'

'The women's refuge? Yes, of course. They do wonderful work.'

'I stumbled across it today. I couldn't sleep and went out for an early walk. There was a queue of women and I went in as if it was a country fair,' Greta tittered an embarrassed laugh. 'So stupid but I'm glad I did. I met this young girl in the most awful of circumstances. Her name is Skye and she's an orphan having lost her mother,' Greta shivered. 'She's beautiful, like a china doll and she sings opera, can you imagine?'

Millie shook her head.

A car approached down the driveway. Greta held her breath. Who would it be? The police? Charlie? Would he return and demand they speak? Quickly Greta realised it was Charlene

Harris. At first she flinched with dread, but then she exhaled with relief. Could have been worse.

The pair didn't move and allowed Charlene to exit her vehicle and move towards the porch.

'Hello again, Ms Osborne, so lovely to see you. What are you working on?'

What? Charlene greeted Millie first. Well, at least she wasn't centre of attention. Greta turned towards Millie whose mind appeared to be ticking over.

'I tell you what, Charlene. You have your visit with Greta and I'll give you a special tour. I never show my pieces before they're ready for exhibit so this is especially for you.' Millie gave the woman a sly 'we're in this together' grin that Charlene soaked up.

The woman beamed and Greta rolled her eyes.

Turning towards Greta, Charlene's entire demeanour changed. 'Greta,' She sat on the single wicker chair across from her and extracted a pile of papers from her over-sized handbag.

Shit. She knew. Of course she knew. Did Greta think she could hide recent events? No, but maybe a kinder introduction…

'There's something we have to discuss . . .'

'Yes, I'm aware of the incident—'

Charlene kept talking. '. . . there are other claims being investigated that implicate you—'

'What?' Greta stood up.

'Please, Ms Johnson, sit down.' It was her teacher-stern voice. 'I'll explain.' And she waited for Greta to sit. Then she nodded approval at her compliance. Greta didn't dare look at Millie.

'Five other complainants have lost their superannuation funds to the extent of $800,000.'

Greta felt the sting and taste of bile as it rode up her throat and raced to the railing and vomited over the edge. She stayed still until the dry retching stopped. Wiping her mouth with her palm she went back and sat down.

Millie rose.

Greta thought to offer her comfort but instead she went indoors. Yes, it was probably too much for her to digest as well. Charlene droned on with the names and details but Greta zoned out. The minutiae didn't matter.

Millie returned with a jug of iced tea. Poured Charlene a glass first, and then Greta. Greta focused on the ice cubes, heard them popping in the liquid and then watched as they slowly dissolved.

'While these matters are being investigated you are not permitted to move around without permission. Now I'm also aware of the incident at the supermarket. The police are obliged to provide these details to us. Unfortunate, but not your fault. I do worry though, you aren't a person that trouble simply follows are you?'

Greta was mute. It was a stupid question. How could she answer? So she didn't. That made it appear as if she was in shock and perhaps she was.

'Are you still cleaning?'

She nodded.

'As you haven't returned to the supermarket, are you intending to find other employment? I can't impress upon you the importance of keeping up repayments. But now, it also won't look good on these current cases if you cease contributing either.'

Greta tapped her foot, willing herself to remain in control. She focused on the tap-tap-tapping of shoe to deck. It helped and her breathing regulated.

Through gritted teeth she said, 'Since working I have contributed every week, even the smallest amount.'

'Excellent. But what will you do now?' Charlene flicked through her papers. 'Yes, I can see you are making payments and that might satisfy the court for the time being, but by golly, your progress is slow.'

'She's working for me, Charlene.' Millie had remained silent until now. 'As you are aware, I'm very successful and it has come to the point that I require a personal assistant on a full-time basis to manage my affairs.' Millie paused to cough, as if choking on her words, but the fit went on for a little too long. She had a sip of tea. 'It has become difficult at my advanced age to not only produce an extensive number of artworks for the ongoing exhibits I do, but to co-ordinate them is an enormous amount of work, to liaise with all of the interested parties and make arrangements. In addition to keeping my business affairs, you know taxes and the like, in order. It seemed like a perfect solution and with Greta's extensive management and organisational skills, she's the perfect fit. Plus, she's right here.'

Charlene listened, nodded, but her eyebrows crept to her forehead. She spewed forth a range of questions about terms, payment, the specifics. Millie answered without hesitation but Greta stopped listening.

'If that is all, please follow me to my studio.' The two women rose and entered the house. 'What is it you prefer, landscapes or French scenes? I have a small collection of both at the moment.'

The voices became muffled and Greta didn't hear the answer. Nor did she care. A baby kitten nudged her foot. It needed her. Greta leaned down and picked up the animal and cradled it. Right now, she wouldn't care if that poor, defenceless creature shredded her to bits with its sharp claws.

GRETA HID AROUND THE CORNER OF THE COTTAGE UNTIL Charlene left. Only when she could no longer hear the tyres crunching on gravel, did she emerge.

'Is that offer for real?' she asked Millie who stood on the bottom step watching the car disappear.

'I don't joke, Greta, dear. You should know that by now.'

'Don't you have a team of people to arrange your exhibits?'

'Usually, yes.'

'What's different this time?'

'This time I'm hiring you. I've never liked the pretentious young people they always assign me anyways. They dictate how thing should be, make outrageous suggestions and get cranky when I say no. Once they tried to convince me to open with a cabaret show with a scantily clad woman hanging from a trapeze. Oh, my Lord. This time I want someone I know and trust. I'll inform the gallery and assure them you'll work in unison. But you're in the lead, not only with this production but all aspects of my business. It's long overdue. I need some assistance.'

'Can you afford to hire me?'

Millie chuckled and the grip on Greta's stomach loosened.

'Have you had an assistant before?'

Millie didn't answer before she turned and headed back inside.

'How will I know what to do?' Greta shouted after her.

'Just get on with it and then perhaps you can stop worrying about everything all of the time.'

Not helpful. So in typical Greta style, she sat on the step and fretted.

THE VOLUME OF THE NIGHTLY NEWS BLARED AROUND THE ROOM. Greta and Millie sat in silence, neither in the mood for small talk.

In breaking news we can report that a group of self-funded retirees are not sleeping well tonight as they fear for their future after their investments were used for illegal purposes and the funds lost. A young couple, finance *brokers, already convicted of previous crimes, are being investigated on further embezzlement claims. They worked together in one of those flash and successful finance groups before becoming romantically involved. The company name cannot be revealed at the time of going to air. It is alleged that they swindled innocent victims of their money under the guise of offering them investment advice. It appears the duo got in over their head when drug debts piled up and they secreted away funds without anyone's knowledge. An attempt was made to repay the money, but it fell well short of the $800,000 that is still missing. No charges have yet been laid. The claims are being investigated and we will keep you appraised of developments.*

The voiceover segued into an interview with an elderly man, his head held in his hands while his wife stood beside him, gripping his shoulder, tears streaming down her cragged face.

These crimes were not hers, but she didn't have the strength to defend herself. And to whom? Millie? Crying poor at the unjustness of it was pointless. It didn't make any difference. She had no right to feel those same feelings as the couple on TV. She'd caused similar pain. She deserved to be ashamed. Could she repay this couple too? It would hardly make a difference to her debt.

Millie hadn't said a word as the interview dragged on. Greta rose, turned the television off and went to bed.

CHAPTER 18

'Maybe I'll take this one.'

'What? No, you can't. It's, it's… you're better than this.'

But in fact it was probably the best room they'd seen and it was still terrible.

It wasn't even lunch yet and the day had been exhausting. Poor Skye; Greta's heart sank taking in the young girl, hunched over and looking forlorn. Greta had been delighted when she'd asked her to tag along and help her find a room to rent. Finally she could do something useful. Not that serving up breakfast to women who wore faded bruises around their eyes and timid expressions, wasn't useful. But this young girl was different and Greta wanted to help, with her Greta could make a difference.

And selfishly, it was the distraction she needed. A world away from crimes and suffering elderly people, not that she would ever forget them, but for a few hours, the relief was tangible.

Initially, the attraction to Skye had been their similarities. But quickly, Greta learned they were not similar and thinking so was ridiculous. What she'd meant is that they had commonalities:

both were young, had a lot of life left to live and were both striving to make the best of it in difficult circumstances. Of course, their backgrounds could not have been more diverse and the more Greta had learned about Skye, the more her heart had broken.

When she'd relayed to Millie the girl's upbringing and expressed outrage at the neglect and abuse, Millie had tsked and said that for too long Greta hadn't lived in the real world. People struggled, she said, were unemployed, had addictions, not enough money to make ends meet, suffered with diseases and often violence. It was a shock, she'd confess, but as a result she felt intrinsically drawn to the young woman.

Where they stood, *this* was real life, not the world she'd been living in.

It had been a fierce slap in the face to Greta who had, up to this point, thought her life was a disaster. It was embarrassing now to reflect upon it. Around the corner from the comfortable home Millie allowed her to share with its warmth and clothing and food, there were homeless women fleeing the most abhorrent circumstances of violence. Those women had no money, no support. Whereas even if Millie had refused to take her in, Greta had any number of options, even if she didn't like them. She had a loving family that would support her. She didn't suffer trauma, those women did; they feared for their lives. By contrast, her experience was of a privileged lifestyle gone bad.

But Greta didn't want to dwell on her own circumstances or sit around and think anymore; she wanted to act; help and had become a regular fixture at *Beach Haven* and more particularly, in Skye's company.

However, today hadn't quite gone to plan and they were both disheartened.

The first place for rent was too damp with mildew climbing its walls. The second was beautiful but too expensive for Skye on her weekly benefits. The third little verandah room was cute but the sun shone too brightly through windows with no curtains and the male owner was a little too friendly. Greta couldn't wait to hightail it out of there. The fourth was a hovel that Greta wouldn't even let her cats explore. And now, well, the fifth wasn't shaping up much better.

'Greta, I don't have enough money to rent anything else,' and Skye went to slump onto the bed but after examining it more closely, thought better of it.

Greta moved closer and observed the stain the size of a large dinner plate in the corner of the bare mattress. She wanted to slump too. Was it really this hard to secure safe and comfortable accommodation?

Skye stood still and wrung her hands together, her brow furrowing in concentration. Greta looked around wondering if it could work. The room in the low-set fibro house was a reasonable size, dull with faded wall paint that would have once been white, now appearing a muted yellow and had a bed and a flimsy timber two-door wardrobe in the corner. There was a plastic outdoor chair randomly placed in the corner. The air smelled musty.

It was gross and her heart broke to think of Skye living in this dump. It was on the tip of her tongue to say she'd pay for her to live somewhere nice, but of course, that was a previous life where she had resources, now she was lucky she didn't have to pay Millie rent. If she did, she'd be on the other side of poor.

Skye stood up taller and brushed the wispy blonde hair from her eyes. 'You know what, it'll do for the interim, right? Until I get a job and have money to find something more suitable.'

Greta was not convinced. 'How long do you have at the shelter?'

'They would never shove me out without having somewhere

to stay. But, Greta, women arrive everyday needing help. I'm okay, comparatively, to them anyway, and they need the room.'

Grim, Greta nodded but then perked up. 'And you know there is heaps of stuff available at the op shops. We could make this place look amazing in no time.' The pair smiled at each other, buoying the other on. 'But you can't make a decision until you've seen the bathroom, that could be a deal breaker.'

They left the sanctuary of the room and headed down a narrow hall. Neither spoke as they arrived at the bathroom that was reminiscent of a retro seventies setup: laminate in oranges and browns with a plastic tub. Greta spied strands of hair in the basin and laying limp on the tiled floor.

They backed out silently. To get to the kitchen where the rental operator waited, they passed another bedroom with its door slightly ajar. Nosy Greta couldn't avoid a peek – if Skye was going to live here she was entitled to know her housemates, right?

The room appeared dishevelled but a glass jar of sorts caught her eye. Greta leaned in closer listening for an occupant and not hearing anything, pushed the door further open. No doubt about it, there was a bong and other smoking paraphernalia in the far corner, sitting on the dirty carpet. Greta had never seen a marijuana plant before, but from what she knew, she guessed the pots in the other corner conveniently located under a lamp might be suspect.

She backed away. 'No, you can't stay here.'

Skye took a gander and gasped.

After her experience with Charlie, drugs were not something Greta could entertain, but for Skye it was all too real with a mother who'd overdosed. There was no way the girl could live in a house where drugs were consumed, and perhaps sold and trafficked.

Greta grasped Skye's hand and tugged her along. Without stopping in the kitchen, she said to the man with the latest

Iphone to his ear and talking too loud, 'No, sorry. It's not suitable,' and rushed out the door.

'Let's take a break. Can I introduce you to my friend?' Skye agreed and Greta dragged her further along the boulevard until they reached the holiday park.

Luckily, Brodie was home eating his lunch at one of the outdoor picnic tables. Sneaking up behind him, she placed her hands over his eyes, and said, 'Guess who?' before giggling.

'One of my favourite people in the world?'

Greta dropped her hands as his words sank in and Brodie rose from the seat and turned. Her cheeks flushed at the rush of emotion tugging at her heart. This guy, he made the entire world disappear and was her safe place. His grin was broad and infectious and as he held out his arms, she sank into his warmth and softness and, immediately, the world was tilted back to rights.

Reluctantly pulling away, she gestured to the quiet young woman standing beside her. 'Remember me telling you about Skye? Skye meet Brodie.' Brodie held out his large man-hand and crushed the girl's small delicate one in his grip.

'So lovely to meet you, Skye. I understand you two have been house-hunting today. How did you go?'

Both of their grins dropped turning their expressions sombre. Brodie offered them a soft drink and they sat with him as he finished his lunch and told him the entire sorry story.

He wiped his mouth with his shirt sleeve and took a cool drink. 'I might have a solution.'

'What? No way. How is it possible you are able to solve every problem?' This man was incredible.

'I'll have to check with mum and dad but there's an old van, and it is old and hasn't been used for a while, out the back, near mine. If it was cleaned up and with a little repair, you could live there. I understand you need proper accommodation but you could use it until you get on your feet and find something nice.

My parents are kind people but they are running a business, so you'd need to contribute something for using the facilities and the site but it wouldn't be much.'

Skye's shoulders hunched up towards her ears before she dropped them with a squeal.

Brodie held up his hands. 'You haven't seen it yet. It might not be much better than what you've been looking at. But it's a full-sized van and comfortable, just needs a clean. My brother lived there and since he's shifted out, we haven't used it. Most people rent the cabins, families especially.'

Skye jumped on the spot.

'Brodie you are incredible!' And Greta jumped up too and squeezed him tight. 'Can we have a look now?' Excitement bubbled up and she placed her hand on Skye's arm. 'You'll be safe here, Skye. Brodie's family live on site and they are wonderful and kind and...' her words drifted away. 'This is a fantastic solution.' Then she turned back to Brodie, tears in her eyes and thanked him again.

'Don't thank me until you see the van. Let's go.'

It was a simple structure of panelled silver, in an old, vintage style. Inside was functional yet dirty and a bit out of sorts with unclean bedding that Dereck hadn't taken. They gagged at the sour milk left in the small bar fridge and the poo, possibly a possum, scattered across the linoleum floor.

Opening the windows, the van immediately felt larger and cooler and cleaner. 'I've got to run a few jobs for mum. Feel free to clean it out, pretty it up, whatever and I'll run it by my parents. I'm sure they won't mind and the extra quid will come in handy.' Brodie leaned into Greta and pressed his lips to hers and let them rest. Greta closed her eyes savouring his touch. Honestly, she thought herself the luckiest girl in the world.

Watching him walk away with the saunter in his step, Greta's heart was full to burst and with more alacrity, she realised, it was the small things that mattered the most. Helping someone in need, being loved and kind and caring. Brodie Quade was all those things. She dared to be as good as him. Yeah, he wasn't perfect, but he was pretty damn good.

After the misery of morning, Greta could not wipe the smile off her face that afternoon. With the park's cleaning products, together they scrubbed and cleaned until the van shone. She was confident it had never been so polished. Borrowing the car, they made a trip to the shelter to collect Skye's gear, another heart-breaking moment for Greta as she considered Skye's meagre worldly possessions. It reinforced her commitment to Skye as long-term, that is if she wanted her help. Brodie's parents insisted she didn't need to pay a bond even though *Beach Haven* would have funded it on her behalf.

'Don't be silly, love,' Henry had said at Skye's insistence, 'let the shelter spend that on someone else who needs it. They do such great work, I'm sure those funds can be well-spent elsewhere.'

Skye nodded and Greta teared up AGAIN. She was a blubbering mess. That van was simple and understated and colourless but when Skye with her white-hair stood inside and belted out the most beautiful heart-felt and dramatic opera tune, it was everything.

'It has fantastic acoustics,' she said and laughed and cried at the same time.

Greta watched Niamh and Henry clapping with broad smiles and Greta knew that being surrounded by good people, there was no chance she couldn't turn into one but she crossed her fingers just in case.

CHAPTER 19

'It's extraordinary,' Millie said as she moved closer, her fine artist's eye devouring each centimetre of the square canvas. 'This is unlike your usual work but the similarity is remarkable. I love it.'

Brodie didn't respond, only listened to the feedback. After a pause, he asked. 'Is it good enough?'

Millie slapped him on the arm. 'For whom? You? Me? The critics? I say this shows significant technique, particularly here and here,' she pointed to specific spots on the portrait. 'Plus, the colours are perfect, and the combination of the same colours instead of using multiple colours is striking. I'm not sure I would have thought of that myself. Why did you choose that palette range?'

'Because those are her colours, they represent her, her soul, her vitality.' He didn't hesitate in that answer. 'There wasn't any other suitable range. These colours are her.'

Millie nodded, 'I agree. You've not only captured the essence of her but the complexities she's currently experiencing and the anxiety. I can see it reflected in her eyes. Do you think it's finished?'

'It doesn't feel that way but I'm not sure what else I would add to it. What do you think?'

'I think it's completed, but perhaps your connection to it is so strong that you don't want it to be a finished product yet. Although …'

Brodie and Millie had a technical discussion about adding more depth of colour, stronger contours and the last finishing touches. Nothing other than tweaks and would not alter the dynamism of what he'd already created.

'What will you do with it? Have you shown her?'

His look of anguish answered the question and she chuckled. 'Brodie, boy, listen. You've done it. Done what I've always asked of you. You've created something special. Something to be admired. This is not a piece to be hidden away, it is one that deserves to be adored. You've heard me banter for years about the inherent beauty of paintings. I fully accept your other works and they are the soul of you and your style. They make a statement and are striking and important. However, this one is to be admired and considered deeply. I'm begging you, and I do not beg, please display your work at the exhibition. It can be all about me but let me introduce you to the world. Even if you don't wish to do it yourself. God forbid you don't even have to attend if you find it that affronting. And I accept it isn't pleasant having people critique your work, offering their lay opinions and saying they can do better or worse, that they don't like it. That unfortunately is part of the creative world. And that is the risk we must take. You need to decide whether you want to be part of that, or not. But if you wish to paint, you need to seriously consider why you do it. If it is never to show another human soul, then I ask you, boy, consider, what is the point?'

With that, she patted him on the shoulder and walked out.

He'd procrastinated over asking her opinion for days. Wanted her feedback on this one. It felt different. It was a stretch out of his comfort zone but still using his signature large brush strokes but not delicate and photo-like imagery. It was unmistakably his, but softer, more mellow and as Millie said, beautiful. Perhaps he could create beauty too.

But the thought of putting it on display, all those eyes over it. His legs trembled and his balance swayed. He couldn't do it. Another time. In the future. It was too soon.

Of course you can't do it. It's rubbish.

Everyone will hate what you've created, they'll criticise the most important things in the world to you.

They'll laugh and point their finger at you.

Take the easy option, you always do.

You'll never amount to anything.

But Millie said she loved it. Millie did not play with his emotions and she did not lie. If she didn't see value in the painting, she'd have spent the time telling him how to improve it.

Maybe he could do it.

No, you can't.

He'd think about it. For the moment he needed to get away, stop thinking so hard. He'd love nothing better than to head downstairs and wrap Greta in his arms and spend the afternoon with her. That girl was seriously under his skin. But she'd disappeared today; had been solemn since the revelations from Charlene. The world kept crashing in around Greta and she kept standing.

Incredible.

The hardships she faced, and she kept on. Brodie could learn a lot from her resilience and strength. She made him strong.

Stronger.

But he'd witnessed how Greta responded to adversity. She pressured herself to perform, whether it was the garden beds, or reading poetry to improve her reading and further train her brain or looking after the newest addition to the Osborne animal menagerie. After Millie offered her the job of PA, she dived straight in. Millie said she'd demonstrated that nervous flutter of excitement before grabbing a bag and heading for the bicycle. She said she needed to see the space; had set up a meeting with the manager of the gallery *tout suite*. Brodie knew as she cycled those pedals fast on the old bike, her brain would be formulating a list: advertising, marketing, brochures, decorations, food, invitations, it would be endless. He agreed it was beneficial to be busy… ah well, best he disappeared to spend some time with his neglected family.

Arriving home, panting and sweaty from the quick trip, Brodie entered the quiet living area and his senses went on high alert. Usually there'd be laughter, the babble of talking or the clatter of crockery. There was nothing, except for the shuffle of paper but it was the electrified atmosphere that made him pause.

His parents sat at the dining room table with papers scattered across its top. Both heads were bowed, scouring over details in front of them. His mother had a red pen poised in her hand that every few seconds she used to underline something on the page.

'Hi you two.'

They both looked up and offered him a perfunctory smile.

'What's up?'

His father responded with a heavy sigh and he wasn't a sighing sort of man. 'There might be some complication with our investment. We're checking the figures and the boring details.'

'We're sure it's nothing, but better to be sure. It'll all work out, these things always do,' his mother interjected.

They both went back to work. Like when he was a child, he had a sense his parents weren't telling him the whole story.

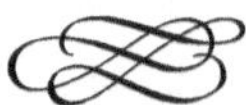

CHAPTER 20

'Brodie! Millie!' Greta's yell carried through the cottage.

The dining table was covered in paraphernalia: brochures, swatches, photographs, exquisite cream card, felt tip pens and magazines. What she focused on was the three different variety of embossed rectangular cards that sat face up. One, formal with traditional black block font and gilded edges; another elegant but less formal with cursive writing and flourishes and curlicues in each corner; then the third. It was her own creation using a print of one of Millie's landscapes forming a muted background over the card with gold lettering. Greta couldn't wait for Millie to choose one.

She poked her head around the studio door. 'Millie? I need you to pick an invitation for the exhibit.'

Millie didn't respond. Greta moved to the base of the stairwell. 'Brodie!' He obviously hadn't heard her the first time either. 'Come down here!'

Another squiz around the corner and Millie still held her paintbrush aloft and stared at the canvas in front of her. 'Have you painted all day? Have you eaten?'

Millie turned her head and gazed at Greta. She could have been an alien that had just landed on Earth such was her puzzled expression. A coughing fit erupted out of her and brought her out of her trance. Greta rushed over with a glass of water.

'Thank you, dear.' Millie immediately resumed her position.

'Millie.' Greta stretched out the word in a whiney tone. 'I need you to choose an invitation. Remember, we talked about this yesterday. I have to place the order at the printer today. Can you come and have a look? Tell me which you prefer?'

'Greta. I don't care. You choose the invitation, whatever you like best. It is of no consequence to me.'

The air whooshed out of Greta's lungs. She'd worked hard to make the invitations perfect but she needed feedback. Millie didn't seem like a formal sort, but who knew? Maybe she'd prefer the curly swirls.

'Are you still working on pieces for the show? It's only two weeks away. You sure are cutting it fine ...'

Millie turned towards her again as if remembering she was still talking. Her face was gaunt and her usually expressive eyes were sunken and surrounded by black pockets. 'Millie, you look exhausted. Surely you have enough paintings? You're working like a crazy woman.'

'I am not, silly girl. I'm doing what I do best and that is creating. Not fussing around with invitations and font and decorations and some such nonsense. I'll be there on the night with my paintings. Now be away with you because I want to finish.'

Righto. 'I'll ask Brodie.' Greta retrieved the cards from the table and took the stairs two at a time. Before knocking, she yelled again. 'Brodie, open the door.' Unlike the free thoroughfare in and out of Millie's studio, Brodie's studio door was always shut. He'd never said so, but she understood entry required permission. She wasn't sure if Millie was even allowed in.

Shuffling came from behind the door before it swung open.

'Which of these do you prefer?' She held three cards up in front of his face. Like Millie he wore a deer caught in the headlights expression and took a moment to register her question.

He moved further into the hall and shut the door behind him.

'What are these for again?'

'Urgh. You two are so frustrating. Invitations for the art exhibition. I've created them with the help of a graphic designer. Which one do you prefer? Millie won't say.'

He took a step back. His eyes darted between them in quick succession.

'That one,' he pointed.

Greta screwed up her face. 'Do you think?' She waited for him to say more.

'I don't know. Which do you like?'

'I need another opinion. That's why I'm asking you!' she screeched. 'I don't know why I bothered.'

His shoulders slumped and his jaw clenched making his lips draw in tight.

'What is it with you two? You are working crazy hours. Millie on who knows what given her stuff is ready for the exhibit. And you, you,' her words faltered, 'God knows what you're doing. But you're at it all day and night. Have you slept? Have you eaten?' She rambled not letting him answer.

'I'm okay.'

Greta shrugged. 'I have heaps to arrange and I need to get back to it. This exhibit is going to be the best. You wait and see.'

That bought the first smile to his lips. 'It will be. I'm sure.' Almost back to his usual self, he leaned down and kissed her. He aimed for her flushed cheek, but she moved her head at the last moment so their lips connected.

'I could be convinced to stop for more of that.' His full lips covered hers once more. The taste sensation of him exploded in her mouth with the unpleasant smell of his paints and turps and earthy tones.

'Me, too,' he whispered.

'Liar. If I tried to drag you out of there right now, would you come?'

'Y . . .e . . .s.' He drew out the syllables as if convincing himself.

'It's okay, I'm not asking you too. But thanks for not helping me at all. If either of you don't like the arrangements, it won't be because I didn't try to get your contribution.'

'Understood,' he said, one fist on the doorknob he rushed off a parting kiss.

'Urgh!' Greta said to no one in particular as she sped back down the stairs.

At the bottom she came face to face with Charlene who stood at the open front door. That was one sure way to dampen her mood. She'd become adept at pushing aside the troubling thoughts that always arrived with her parole officer. This woman with the crazy red hair and her sensible brown shoes and office wear made her shudder.

But perhaps today she could be of assistance?

'Charlene, what do you think of these?' Greta held up the cards and walked back towards the dining room table.

'Goodness, what are you up to?'

'Planning Millie's art exhibition, of course. She mentioned it at the last visit. I've been working on it flat out.' Duh, was Charlene not paying attention when they last spoke? Didn't she take notes?

Charlene came and stood behind her shoulder and glanced over in a covert manner, as if she shouldn't be looking. 'Oh,' she said, and moved out from behind her and picked each card up from the table and examined them closely.

Watching her, a dawning realisation occurred. Of course.

Charlene thought they had made up a fictitious job to please the parole officer; shuffle the books and make it appear as if the recently released crim had gainful employment. Well, in fairness, that's exactly what Greta had thought initially, too. And even worse, Greta wasn't convinced it wasn't a ruse, even now, but she was awfully good at pretending. Greta Johnson would be the best personal assistant Millicent Osborne had ever had. She'd prove herself to Charlene as well.

Greta puffed out her chest and stood taller and clamped her mouth shut. She wouldn't offer Charlene an explanation. She saw all she needed to know.

Charlene bent over considering everything laid out before her. Who would have thought that the person showing the most interest in preparations would be her? Thank goodness for her girl crush on Millie.

Charlene sat down. 'I haven't seen the space you're holding the event so I can't be sure on theme, I can only judge on what I think …' and she was off.

For the next hour Greta listened to her opinion. And it was good. She would never have picked her for being so aesthetically on point. The cards they agreed on were perfect. She made great suggestions about finger food to serve and when speeches should be held and other relevant timings.

As the meeting tied up, she finally turned to real business. 'Now, I can see that you are fully engaged and making some serious headway.'

Really? Headway, okay she'd take it.

'Of course, you're busy at the moment because there's an event. We'll have to determine afterwards how much work you are required to do in the downtime. I guess like everyone Ms Osborne has to pay her bills and do her BAS and she'll want help with that.'

Made sense, Greta nodded along but she couldn't think past the next couple of weeks.

'I have some news.'

More news? Greta wasn't quite sure she could bear it and avoided Charlene's eye. She was suddenly thirsty and couldn't get enough moisture in her mouth. The issue had been the metaphorical elephant in the room that had not been discussed. At least, for once, the darkness didn't threaten.

Millie's coughing drifted in, sounding worse and persistent. Did she need medical attention? Greta resisted the urge to jump up and attend to her. Instead she faced the conversation she dreaded.

'The pending embezzlement charges have been fully investigated and you've been exonerated. The circumstances have revealed that you were not involved ...'

The world was spinning; Greta clutched the sides of her chair.

'Why did you think I was involved?'

'The accused said you were.'

'And who was the accused?'

Charlene paused. 'It's public record because he's already been formally charged so I'm not telling you anything you'll not read about in the paper. Charlie Clarke.'

It was like she'd been punched in the gut. But she'd known. Of course.

'Bastard.'

'Hmm.'

'When did these offences allegedly take place? I have, I'm sure you recall, been incarcerated over the past months and so has he.'

'He may not be the person you thought he was, I shall say that. It appears he was involved in a much more elaborate ring than we could have imagined. Unfortunately for Charlie, he's in deep and the law has caught up with him--'

'Shit.'

Would he stop contacting her now? She'd had many missed calls…it was beginning to feel like a ticking time-bomb situation.

'Indeed. He was still stealing people's money, with assistance, when he was imprisoned. And that's enough. I've said too much. But the important part is that I'm sorry for the distress it's caused you, but I had a duty to inform you at that time. All you need to focus on is keeping yourself out of trouble and away from mischief.'

A wave of anger flared up. 'Isn't that what I've been doing, Charlene? I'm living in the middle of nowhere, staying away from people. I did nothing wrong at the grocery store, but everyone assumed I was guilty. Is this the future? People only have to comment about me and I'm investigated?'

'Of course not.' But Charlene's response was too slow.

Charlie Clarke was like a noose around her neck. In one way she was pleased. She was cured of him. His name didn't evoke any emotion, other than anger that the slimy sleaze-ball had incriminated her. How dare he keep contacting her? Was him implicating her payback for not speaking to him? If she got her hands on him, she'd, well, she'd not be very nice. To think that she once thought she loved him. She had loved him. What she knew of love anyway. How could she have been so stupid? That question AGAIN. The answer still made her stomach turn over.

'Anyway,' Greta shook her head of the demons, 'Thank you for your help with the show. I appreciate it.'

'I'll see you there.'

'You're coming?'

'Yes, of course, I wouldn't miss it.'

Greta paused, thoughts ricocheting around her mind. She had one last thing to do and she needed more help.

'Do you think you could assist me with one last thing?'

'Perhaps.' Charlene was always so even keeled. A stable plateau of emotion.

'Well, it could be useful for you, too. I have to do a run to the community centre where we'll be holding the event and drop off a precious delivery. Could you give me a lift? You can check out the venue at the same time. You know, to make sure we've captured the theme perfectly in the invitations and advertising?'

'Yes, certainly.' Charlene packed up her belongings, neatly stowing away her pencils, pens and stationery.

Greta had the packages ready for despatch. They'd been wrapped for days waiting for the opportunity to sneak them out of the shed. A ripple of excitement pulsed through her veins. It would either go well or very, very badly.

GRETA LEANED HER HEAD AGAINST THE BACK OF THE CHAIR. HER mind was a washing machine in spin cycle unable to grasp any coherent thought. Sometimes she didn't know when to stop, but the ache in her neck told her she'd done enough. As she stacked her belongings into a neat pile on the table, the cottage foundations creaked, the only sign the other two were home. Neither had made an appearance all day.

Retreating to the front room, she dreamed of a chilled Pinot Gris. She'd made her best efforts recently to restrict her drinking out of respect for Millie. It didn't feel right indulging when someone next to you, couldn't. Plus, she didn't want to tempt Millie. Greta wouldn't be able to forgive herself if she was responsible for a retreat into alcoholism.

Collapsing into the armchair, the cushion expelled its air at the same time she emitted a large sigh. Maybe she should read some more love poems. Wordsworth today?

She smiled.

Imagine if people knew she was reading the poetry of famous dead people. Her lips downturned slightly at the recollection she didn't have anyone to tell. Excepting Brodie and Millie. And Mum, she'd be delighted.

But her brain was mush. That counted out more of the delicious love letters from Reggie, too. Usually she could devour them all day. She had to pin down Millie about him and get some answers.

If the woman ever stopped painting.

A thick doorstop of a book sat on the coffee table. An art book, if the cover illustration was any indication. She recognised the famous Van Gough sunflower print with its vibrant yellow flowers and excitedly flicked through the pages searching for any reference to Reginald Smart. The pages were glossy and thick and reminded her of the books that filled her parents' home. Something fell out and floated to the floor. Mother cat gazed up as it landed beside her. It was a flat piece of faded green card with cursive handwriting across its lines.

A Girl
> *Born 24 May 1970 at St Elizabeth's Hospital*
> *Dr James Dr Simons*
> *12.37 pmGestational age: full term*
> *Weight: 7 pounds 5 ounces*
> *Length: 51 centimetres*
> *Parents -*

Who is this baby? And why is the card hidden in this book? It could have been inherited with the book if Millie had borrowed it or bought it second-hand, maybe. But it appeared brand new.

Greta turned over the remaining pages but there were no paintings by Smart. Towards the end, she discovered a photograph stuck to the back cover. She tugged but it remained steadfast so she leaned in close but couldn't see clearly. Getting up she walked over to the bay window and held the photograph up to the fading light.

In amongst a blurred green background sat a solid concrete tombstone. The gravestone was either terribly small or distorted in the image. Greta squinted her eyes to make out the words but none of them made sense.

Thunderclaps sounded down the stairwell. Brodie strode past the room and turned full flight and raced back when he spied her.

'Wanna go for pizza?'

CHAPTER 21

*B*rodie clenched his fist. 'How could this have happened?'

His mother and father looked at their family sitting around the dining room table in the modest chamferboard house in the middle of the campground. The property was the best on the block and reserved for the family only, always had been. His parents had paid off the debt on the park, too. Such a fantastic achievement but exactly what had landed them in this mess.

Today, Brodie noticed the faded paint on the bare walls with not a splash of colour, no art or prints. The scuffed, old sofa had stuffing escaping its edges. The rug covering the timber flooring, new last Christmas, did a poor job of providing warmth and vitality into the room. Sepia photographs lined the surface of the TV cabinet. Many were first day of school shots or pictures of gurgling babies. Two larger, more recent ones stood at the end, images of Thomas and Kristabelle, their smiles too broad. A few potted plants added greenery; he guessed it was the people in the room that created the colour and life.

'Look, we aren't sure. You're aware that being self-employed we don't have any superannuation. After we paid off the mort-gage we kept saving, for a rainy day like.' His father placed his hand on his mother's knee. Brodie couldn't see his hand under the table, but he knew he'd be squeezing it in a show of affection. 'We were clever weren't we, Niamh? We weren't going to get stuck in our old age, we were a couple who planned for the future. Anyway, long story short the money grew to our delight and we thought it was best to get it out of the bank and invest it. You know, get better return.'

'You got advice, right, on where to invest?' Leonie asked.

'Oh, yeah sure. We had no idea. There are loads of financial advisors around, we went and saw someone in Lismore. Beaut bloke, gave solid advice, or so we thought and made the invest-ment. That was a few years ago.'

Brodie almost couldn't listen. The pain of sitting through the story was excruciating when all he wanted to do was punch a hole in the wall. The same wall he'd then have to fix. Pointless.

His mother continued the story. 'This fellow left and new advisors came in. We didn't have a lot to do with them after the investment was made. We received notices of our return, and annual summaries. Honestly, we don't often think of it, do we, Henry?'

'No. Wouldn't have made any difference if we did.' He lowered his head.

'So, say it again, exactly how was the money lost?' Derek asked, slow to catch on.

No, please, not again, Brodie couldn't bear to hear the sorry tale repeated. He got up abruptly and went into the kitchen and filled a glass of water. All of a sudden he craved a beer and he'd chug a whole can down in one go and still be thirsty, no doubt.

'A new financial investor to our portfolio withdrew the funds and allegedly used it for his own purposes. He was only one person, but he was working with others, the police said that was about avoiding detection. Anyway, the fine detail is irrelevant. They withdrew the funds, gambling maybe,' his dad shrugged, and continued, 'the police didn't say, and then the idea was to return it before anyone noticed. But you can imagine with lots of money at your disposal, you borrow more, spend more and it catches up with you. The maths is easy- they withdrew the money, spent it and couldn't replace it. They forged authorities and everything. It's called embezzling.'

Brodie's head snapped up. Embezzling? The anger surging through his tummy turned to sick. The same embezzling that Greta had been involved in? He knew at some distant part of his brain that it wasn't the same case. She'd been caught and tried and sent to prison. But the same act. This is the effect it had on people? Were they all like his parents? Left stranded with just the miserable amount in their bank account, what they considered their life savings, gone? But then he remembered something else.

'But it has to be repaid right?' He said trying to quell his nausea.

'Ideally, upon conviction the police said –'

'Sent to the slammer, you mean!' Derek interjected but everyone around the table nodded.

'One order can be restitution where they are forced to repay the money but it depends on the number of victims. The police wouldn't say exactly how many, but we figure there's a few. So that means lots of money and realistically we may not see ours again.'

The words hung in the air and no one spoke.

Greta was paying the money she lost, back. It was important to her. She'd mentioned it heaps and more particularly, that if she didn't, she'd be back in jail. He knew she'd made small contributions each week. Now that he thought about it, unless she won the lotto, she'd be paying that debt back for years.

'This guy might have property that can be sold to recoup the losses?' he said, his mind grappling for solutions, options, a way ahead.

'Yep, if he does, it will be. I guess it just depends who's in line first.'

His parents sat there, their faces pale and drawn but calm.

He banged his fist on the table. The cups and saucers and plates jumped and rattled and everyone startled. 'How can you be so calm?' he yelled.

'We've had our moments son, trust me. Your mother has spent days in tears. And praying to that useless God of hers.' At that, his mother tried to hold back a sob but she couldn't and it came out like a strangled moan. That made Brodie calm the hell down. You couldn't make your mother cry. He stood behind his mother and massaged her shoulders.

'Don't cry, Mum. It'll be okay. You know we'll help out.' He looked to his brother and sister, heard his nephew and niece giggling in front of the television. How were they going to help? His brother's tradie income was good but sporadic between jobs and he lived elsewhere and had his own expenses. His sister had two small children and wasn't working while she cared for them. Mark had a good, permanent job but he wasn't earning a million dollars.

His father's words splintered his thoughts. 'We'll be fine,' he managed a tight-lipped smile. 'You're forgetting we have the park and it's fully booked over the summer. We still have an income and there's only the two of us. We don't have a safety net to fall back on at the moment and might need to keep working longer than expected. Who needs retirement anyway, right?'

They were the most unconvincing words he'd ever heard. But good on Dad for putting the positive spin on it. No retirement. Keep working his guts out into old age appeasing holiday-makers when they complained their cabin was too cold, or their campsite too small or the walk to the toilet block too far. When they didn't turn up for their booking and sites were left vacant. His parents had never been rolling in it, but sheesh, this was too much.

Before his parents had called them in to break the news, he'd been tackling his dad's repair list. The usual culprits: squeaky hinges, missing doorknobs, repotting plants and watering, sweeping and using the blowervac. Making the place presentable, as his dad would say. It was no skin off his nose to help them out; he often did. They worked too hard and he wanted to lighten the load but they always tried to pay him and he'd refuse. He'd never tell Greta but renumerating her the full freight for the cleaning was hurting and he was desperate to make up the difference. She needed the job, but what now?

Brodie couldn't bear seeing his family sitting at the table looking lost and devoid of hope. He needed to escape and order his scattered thoughts. He fingered the list of jobs in his pocket and extracted it. Without another glance, he stood up and left to get on with the chores. At least his Dad wouldn't have to work today.

He held the door as it threatened to swing back against the wall and breathed in, long and deep. His anger seeped away and he no longer had the urge to slam the door out of its frame. But the sick feeling lingered. As he stood outside on the narrow porch, realisation hit. What did people call it? An epiphany. That's what he had. It was up to him. He was the only one to help his parents and he knew what that meant. Goodbye dreams and hello reality. He'd have to get a real job.

'HEY, WATCH OUT!'

Brodie yanked the hose back in time to avoid drenching the passer-by with the high-pressure force. He'd been lost in his own thoughts. His mind still scrambled to find solutions and he failed to pay attention. Damn it, now he'd soaked himself.

'Sorry, mate!' he yelled at the man's departing back. The man held up his arm in a gesture, a sort of its-okay-I'm-wet motion but kept walking. At least it wasn't the finger; he deserved that.

He washed down the paths and pebbled drive until everything shone. Lowering the pressure, he watered the gardens that lined the communal areas and the few potted plants his mother nurtured near the picnic tables.

Brodie was torn between competing interests: helping his Dad do these jobs, sorting out his parents' mess and painting. The urge to express his feelings in liquid overwhelmed him. It would help sort his baffled mind that couldn't hold a decent thread of thought. It was his usual go-to coping solution and no doubt, in this mood, his fingers would fly across the canvas. The image formed in his head. His fingers twitched. There wouldn't be any pinks or blues, it would be ugly. Just how he felt. But that would have to wait.

First, he needed to check out the job possibilities, to discover there was hope. Of course, a few more minutes would make no difference to his parent's circumstances.

Then there was Greta. Now that he was on the receiving end of the act, he was trying to fathom how she could have been involved in something like embezzlement. He knew, of course, it wasn't quite that simple.

Urgh! He tossed the hose aside but then sighed and reached down and rolled it up and placed it back into its position. If he didn't, his mother would have to do it later.

Unable to stand it any longer, he grabbed a can of soft drink out of the garage fridge and hopped on his pushy. The majority of jobs were done, he'd ensure he completed the rest tomorrow.

First stop, the noticeboard in town. When he was a kid, they still had an employment centre. You'd go there, have a chat with a consultant and they'd try and hook you up with a suitable employer. In those days there was supreme confidence in a job being available for everybody. In a community like this, it was easy, everyone knew each other. Most often, it was a simple phone call and an agreement that the bloke or sheila would be on their way over to help. A slap on the back when you arrived and all was merry.

Now, it was much more complicated because everything was online. Maybe Skye could give him some tips; she'd actively been searching for a job. He didn't even own a computer and he couldn't sit in Mum and Dad's office and use theirs, particularly when job seeking. He'd know what they'd say.

Don't worry about us, we'll be fine

You don't need to find a job (that would be his mother)

Well, not for us, son, but a job would be good (that would be his father)

He didn't want to be distracted by their platitudes. Reality was he needed to help his parents because he'd sponged off them for years. He'd pulled his weight at the park but paid minimal rent (none). Like a crushing blow raining down upon him, he knew it hadn't been enough. What a lazy self-indulgent arse. His cheeks burned with shame.

The noticeboard advertised dog walkers, a holiday home for rent, a local paper run. He rode faster, the wind in his face. Only one place to go now.

'BREATHE, MILLIE. IN AND OUT, DO IT WITH ME.' GRETA crouched beside Millie on the floor. Having slipped from her artist chair, she was on her bottom, legs splayed in front. Her hat sat discarded a metre away.

At first Greta thought it funny; the silly old duck falling from her chair. But the fear in Millie's eyes made her pause. This wasn't a joke. Millie was not about to crack out a sarcastic comment. She coughed and her hands waved about her face, clutched at her throat.

A grip of fear seized Greta around the middle and she had to remind herself to stay calm.

'Is there something wrong with your throat?' Millie couldn't speak she was coughing so hard.

'Are you having trouble breathing?' Millie nodded. Greta made exaggerated noises of sucking in air.

Millie copied the same deep intake of oxygen and her chest rose and fell. The coughing stopped. A moment of hope flared within Greta. But then, Millie gripped her throat again, clutching like her airway was blocked. She panted, in and out in short bursts and her face turned a deathly pallor.

'Should I call an ambulance?'

Another nod.

She raced to find her phone, dialled as she sped back into the studio. The front door slammed shut and Brodie walked in.

'Brodie, oh thank goodness. Help me, Millie has fallen and is struggling to breathe.'

He rushed to Millie's side. By now, she made grotesque and loud gulps for air. That was a good thing, right? She was getting some air? Her concave chest rose like a plumped-up pillow and sank just as quickly before repeating the motion.

'Get the ambulance. I'm not sure what's wrong but this isn't good.' Brodie grasped Millie's hand, held tight and caressed his fingers upon its top. 'Millie,' he said with a smile, 'don't go doing anything stupid. You've got your show tomorrow. Don't you go drumming up more business by putting on a performance the day before. That would be cheeky.'

The frantic panic in Millie's countenance eased slightly, her eyes focused on him and his calming voice. He mimicked breaths in and out and Millie followed his example. It worked better than when she'd tried.

Within minutes Greta heard the wail of sirens and released the breath she didn't realise she'd been holding. Brodie talked softly into Millie's ear, her shoulders rising in a few short chuckles. Geez, he had the knack while she flustered around not remembering her left from her right.

Greta left them and waited on the deck for the paramedics. She bit her tongue to tell them to leave their bags of equipment outside let alone the trolley. It would never fit in the studio.

No need, they worked it out soon enough. Dumping a pile of gear, the male officer raced inside with the oxygen. They placed the mask over her aunt's mouth and within minutes colour returned to her face. Her eyelashes shuttered and she listened to their questions and answered.

To give them more room to work, Brodie moved outside with her. Greta wrapped her arms around his middle and clung on. 'Man, that was frightening. I don't know what's wrong with her. Maybe a virus?' She turned her head sideways as she spoke, the left side of her head leaning into the softness of his stomach. Brodie didn't envelop her in his broad and strong arms, nor respond. His gaze focused on the distance.

'Is everything okay?' She didn't let go.

'Um, yeah.' He shuffled free of her arms and moved into the kitchen to skull a drink of water. His back remained turned away, facing the window over the sink.

He must be worried; he and Millie are so close.

There was activity in the room and the two officers held Millie up under each arm and guided her out of the room. They placed her into a chair whilst one attended to setting up the trolley, ready for loading.

'We're transporting her to hospital. She requires breathing

support and to be thoroughly checked over. One person may accompany her in the ambulance.'

'If I go with Millie in the ambulance, will you follow?' Greta asked Brodie.

The hairs on the back of her neck stood up. Brodie stood, mute looking between her and the ambo. He rubbed his hands through his short beard and then raked them through the long strands of his hair.

Something was definitely up.

'No. I, um, have things I need to do this afternoon. You can look after her, she'll appreciate your company.' A bunch of newspapers were stashed under his arm.

What the fuck?

Greta didn't respond and followed Millie who lay on the stretcher.

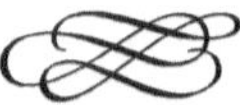

CHAPTER 22

The incessant beeping of a machine woke her. Opening her eyes, Greta stretched out her arms and legs that had been curled up on the hospital chair. Not one of those cheap plastic types, but a plush, sofa chair with a footrest. Not too shabby a place to sleep near your loved one.

The private hospital room had carpet and curtains and the room was so dark she had no sense of time. Rising slowly, she moved to the window and pulled the curtain aside.

Daylight.

The world was warming up, sun creeping higher, people leaving their homes and traffic building. It was still early but sound was muted through the insulated and thick walls. Instead, she heard indoor sounds: shuffle of feet in corridors, mumbled talking, carts on linoleum floors and that relentless bleeping.

Before rushing away in the ambulance yesterday, she'd collected the book of poems she'd been reading. Who was she? She didn't even know anymore – grabbing a book before leaving the house? Preposterous. Nonetheless, she flicked it open to a random page and scanned the contents.

'I love seeing you read. What is it?'

'You're awake.' Her insides relaxed; it had looked a bit dicey there for a while. Greta waved the book in the air. 'Tennyson poems. This one is *Crossing the Bar.* Do you want me to read it to you?'

In reply, Millie burst into coughing. Greta strode to her side and placed a cup to her lips. 'Jesus Christ,' Millie said after a sip, 'what, as my eulogy? That's an ode to death that poem and no, I do not want to hear it right now.'

'You're feeling better then?' Greta chuckled in relief at hearing the familiar caustic wit.

'Since when did you start reading poetry?'

'Well, since I realised they were beautiful and short. Much easier for me to digest because they're such little bursts of writing.'

'Yes, that's what poems usually are. You could move onto short stories next. They vary in length but some can be quite short. I think I have a few collections and they're lovely to read in brief sittings.'

'Good idea. I'll check it out. Now that my reading is sorted, how are you feeling?'

'Wretched.'

'Are you still having trouble breathing? I can call the nurse?'

Millie placed her hand over hers to pause her movement on the call button.

'No, it's just I'm worn out from all that palaver yesterday. What a circus.'

'Are you actually okay, though? They insisted on keeping you overnight for observation. A bit extreme, I thought. Check your vitals they said. But it's nothing more serious is it? Excepting of course for the fact that you should quit smoking before it kills you. They even lectured me to lecture you.'

'Just a silly chest infection. That's why I'm plugged up to this thing, helping keep me hydrated and all that. My chest certainly feels less tight than yesterday. When can I go home?' In her usual style Millie ignored the lecture.

'I assume the doctor will check you over this morning and you'll be discharged. You're very secretive, Millie. Why couldn't I stay when the doctor examined you?'

'My dear, I've been alone my entire life and managed fine. I don't need a minder. It was ridiculous you sleeping in that chair last night.'

'I wanted to.'

'Well, find a poem to read to me that's a bit more cheerful so we can pass the time. I hope the doctor doesn't take too long.'

'Why? Do you need to rush home and finish a painting before the show tonight?'

'Ha, ha. You are so funny. But actually, yes.'

'What? No, you can't they've all been delivered and are probably in place by now.'

'Okay, well, it's one I'm working on but doesn't have to be for tonight. Next show.'

Greta sat on the edge of the bed and her aunt shifted over to allow her to fit. She flicked through the book looking for a poem.

'Millie?'

'Mm?'

'Why do you love Paris so much?'

Greta didn't look at her aunt as she composed her answer.

'Paris is the most exquisite city in the world. And for artists, it's a living gallery. There is beauty everywhere. The streetlamps with their ornate steel work, to the classic architecture and oh, the street painters. What other city is crowded with so many people behind their easels creating either landscape scenes inspired by what's in front of them or portraits of those that pass. And the bookshops and the food. Their food is art, too.'

'Did you meet anyone special during your summer?'

Greta watched her aunt over her eyelashes and saw Millie pause. She opened her mouth and shut it again. Then unclasped her hands and gripped them together once more.

'I met many special people. Some of whom remain my closest friends.'

'Surely there were gorgeous men throwing themselves at the beautiful young Australian girl?'

She smiled then, her eyes diverted to the window and her gaze distant. It seemed as if memories were clouding in on her and she was losing herself to another time.

'Of course,' she laughed. 'I had a great time let me tell you. I'm only human. But they always wanted more. Demanded more of my time and that I see them regularly. When I refused, they became resentful. I was there to paint, Greta. I wanted to paint and draw every day. Not accompany someone to the gallery for their purposes, but for my own. I guess I've been quite selfish.'

'But if you were never prepared to sacrifice for someone special, surely you didn't love them?'

'I'm not sure it's that simple. I loved their company, some more than others. But that didn't mean I wanted to spend all my time with them. I craved my time, for my art. It's all I've ever wanted. And I couldn't have both.'

Her aunt's eyes were shrouded, not teary, her voice faraway, with a twist of wistful. Millie was rarely reminiscent. Perhaps she was back on a Parisienne street, the agony of choice before her?

Greta held up the book. 'As I said with Brodie's help I'm trying to read more and get better, not be frightened of reading. I've been going through your library and I found–'

The door opened and in walked a young man resplendent in a white coat and a stethoscope hanging loose around his neck. He wore turtle-skin print glasses and held a clipboard in his hand.

'Wait outside, dear,' she said to Greta, her hand pushing her gently off the bed.

Damn it! She was about to get Millie to open up; ask her about the letters, the photograph.

Talk about timing.

'I want to stay.' She stood.

'And I want you to leave. I'll give you a shout when we're finished and it's time to take me home.' Millie offered the doctor a saccharine smile. Greta hoped the doctor realised it was a warning. If he wasn't here to advise Millie she could return home, he'd best get on to seeing his next patient.

'FOR THE LOVE OF GOD, CAN YOU PUT THAT CIGARETTE OUT? Not only should you not be smoking because of your health, you'll stink!'

Greta faced off Millie who was sandwiched between her and Brodie. They stood outside the community hall building on the narrow deck leading to the entry. Millie's bright floral dress contrasted with the white verandah and picket paling fence. The fairy lights strung up by the committee placed the historic building in a beautiful glow.

Greta stared with dagger eyes at Brodie. Normally he'd back her up, tonight he remained tight-lipped.

'There's pretty much only one thing I won't tolerate and it's being treated like a child. You know too well by now, Greta that I will do as I please and when I bloody well want. I want this smoke and I will have it and finish it. Be damned with anyone else.'

Greta pinched her nose with her thumb and forefinger. 'Sorry, Millie. I know. I'm more nervous than I anticipated. It's important everything goes well.'

'You worry too much, child. What can possibly go wrong?'

Greta heard Millie's words but her mind was tuned into Brodie. He'd been strange the last few days and tonight wasn't any different. Each time she tried to broach the subject of something being wrong, he fobbed her off. Right now, she wanted his tight arms around her and whispering in her ear that everything would be all right. She wanted to feel the prickle of his facial hair along her check as he leaned in close. His warm breath as it tickled her eardrum. What was wrong with him? But he stood stock-still and didn't say a word. She didn't know what to think, so she tried not to worry about it at all. Plus, she had other things on her mind. Greta flicked into work mode.

There was one main room, and it was filled with people talking, drinking and having a lovely time if the mood of the room was any gauge. Each wall displayed Millie's paintings. Even for Greta, it felt overwhelming. All those pieces she was intimately familiar with, staring back at you. Millie had mentioned how surreal it felt to have your work on display. And worse, have everyone staring at it and voicing their opinion. Greta guessed you had to remain confident that the people present liked your paintings or the artist, at least, and would be kind. Of course, it wasn't quite so simple.

She looked at each wall with their multiple works grouped into similar style. It was an explosion of colour. Greta could not believe that those boring old plain vases with flowers could be so amazing. Or the way Millie made the simple rooms of Banyan Creek with their VJ walls, the sofas and the trinkets all come to life so vividly. What a feat. A burst of pride washed through her. These were her aunt's work and she was talented. She guessed she took it for granted being surrounded by their beauty each day. But, here, today, their effect was stunning. How could everyone not love what she produced?

Unable to control herself, she scanned the room for Brodie. Of course, this room was allocated to Millie's exhibition, but there were other rooms with ongoing exhibits, other local artists, schoolchildren's work and function rooms. He could be in one of those.

Greta thought she knew no one in this small coastal town that had become home. However, she recognised Brodie's parents, Henry and Niamh. Henry held a beer and sipped while Niamh fiddled with the rosary beads at her neck. Henry balanced from foot to foot and took another sip in quick succession. Niamh didn't hold a drink. Smiles spread across their face as a young woman approached and they exchanged kisses and cuddles. Two little people appeared and hugged their legs. That seemed to brighten their mood. Such a happy family.

In the far corner she spotted Constable Reynolds. Out of uniform tonight, he stood next to a woman gripped in animated conversation. They stood close, their bodies touching; his eyes did not leave her face. Not far from them Greta saw Kathleen. Despite the circumstances of Greta's departure from the supermarket, she liked Kathleen and made a vow to talk to her later.

Standing near the bar was Robyn from *Beach Haven*. They'd worked together most mornings on the breakfast shift. Next to her stood a beaming Skye. When they caught glances, the girl waved. They'd gone shopping and found the feminine but modern dress she wore. It made her look older, but it wasn't the dress that Greta noticed. Burden had shifted from Skye's shoulders and she looked lighter. Her troubles were far from over, but it was a start.

Her parents had arrived with great fanfare stating they wouldn't miss the event for the world and she was grateful. And despite her mother's protestations about Millie and her unconventional lifestyle, she adored her sister. Oh, no, they were with Charlene Harris. Good to her word, she'd arrived, too. That was a no-brainer, that woman loved Millie. But still the trip on a Friday evening after work, was a commitment. Hopefully she wasn't here to check on her. Greta wondered if she was married but she couldn't detect a wedding band and she was unaccompanied.

No Brodie. Where was he? Why was he acting so weird? She'd come to accept his brutal honestly and tell-it-how-it-is-policy, but, for whatever reason, he'd shut down. Gone silent. Perhaps being a creative sort he was nervous for Millie. Goodness knows why anyone would be anxious for her, though. At one glance, Greta saw that she held court, a group of five or six adults surrounding her. She held an empty champagne flute in her hand.

Greta went through a mental checklist. She might do a quick walk around and confirm everything was in order. She'd pass Millie and confiscate her glass but before she moved a cacophony of noises behind made her turn. Other people too. Raised voices came from the entry and Greta raced outside to investigate.

Charlie Clarke stood on the verandah. Like a wild animal, his hair was mussed and while wearing another deep-blue navy suit, his tie sat askew, and one jacket sleeve had ridden up to his right elbow. Fumes of alcohol radiated off him.

'Gretie!' he shouted and moved towards her.

Within reach, she shoved him backwards with a palm to his chest, almost toppling him. He grabbed for the railing to steady himself.

'What are you doing here?' she said through gritted teeth.

'Came to see you, babe. Aren't you glad I'm here?'

His pupils were dilated and his eyes open extra wide. He wasn't only drunk.

'You need to leave.'

'But I've just arrived. We need to sort things out, get back on track. Whadda you say?'

The sight of him disgusted her. How dare he? 'This is Millie's special evening and you're not invited.'

His voice rose an octave. 'I can do what I damn well want. Now, where's a drink?'

He tried to push past her but she stood firm. He gripped her forearm and attempted to move around her, but she wasn't budging. Without any assistance from her, Charlie toppled sideways and crashed into a large potted pine tree with Christmas decorations adorning it. One sat at each side of the door. He righted himself on wobbly feet but then swiped at the tree with uncoordinated hands. It fell and the ceramic pot smashed into shards across the timber deck. Grains of dirt mixed in with tinsel.

'Greta!' Charlene's shrill voice came from behind her. 'A condition of your parole is that you cannot associate with known felons. You cannot associate with him,' she repeated.

'Okay, I understand Charlene. But it's not quite that easy, is it?'

'Young man. You have thirty seconds to decamp. You're awaiting trial for serious offences and are taking a big risk demonstrating this behaviour.' She moved in closer and took a big sniff. 'Are you high?'

Greta was in one way amused at the tone of Charlene's words to Charlie and on the other hand, enormously proud. The woman had balls.

Go, Charlene.

Charlie moved in close to Charlene and laughed in her face. Spittle bubbles flew out of his mouth and Greta recoiled. Constable Reynolds joined them, making the people standing on the narrow verandah four abreast. Poor man, he wasn't even working tonight. Guess you were never off duty in a small town.

The policeman bent his knees as he was a head taller than

Charlie and leaned in close to his ear and said words she couldn't decipher. His arms went out to his side, as if offering options. One or two.

Charlie's head bowed; his body slack.

Her parents appeared beside her. 'What on earth?' her mother muttered.

'How did he know about tonight?' Greta asked.

'Um, I might have told him,' her mother said, her voice a whisper.

'What? Mum! Why?'

'He keeps ringing the house and asking about you. He's distraught, dear. I've been quite worried about him. So I've kept him informed of a few bits and pieces about what you've been up to. This event came up, only because we're so proud and love that you've achieved something so wonderful.'

'You know, don't you Mum, that's he currently charged with further offences. More money that he's stolen from people and he's still taking a cocktail of drugs and of course, I can't go near him because I'm on parole.' She raised her voice on the last phrase. Her mother wasn't stupid, but sheesh, she could be dumb.

Charlie hadn't moved so Constable Reynolds grasped his elbow and escorted him away. Charlie shook off the hold but kept walking. Her father raced to Charlie's other side and accompanied them. Greta watched until they disappeared into the darkness. Her mother offered her a lopsided smile of sorts.

Greta re-entered the hall and at the first drinks waiter she saw, she swiped a cold, tall flute of champagne. She drank it down in two gulps and reached for another.

CHAPTER 23

A fork dinged against a glass and the chairperson of the gallery rose to commence his opening address. Millie stood to his left and coughed, more like an annoying tickle. Someone passed her a glass of water and she drank greedily. A few minutes passed while everyone listened. Then the cough started again. Greta heard the rattle of Millie's chest as the hack fought its way up her windpipe and exploded outwards. Then the phlegmy snort as it pounded on. Millie found a chair and sat, bent double.

Greta gave her two minutes, but it didn't stop. She lifted her up by the hand and guided her outside.

'I need a cigarette and it will pass.'

'Are you seriously kidding?' Greta responded.

'No, I am not. And as I'm the one about to give the speech, I think you'll indulge me.'

Millie's hands shook so Greta did the unsavoury and lit the stick for her.

'Hurry up, at least, before someone sees you smoking out here.' The woman was like an impossible child.

Millie inhaled and sure enough the convulsions stopped. 'Greta, a tipple now to calm me, just a wee little dram to drown out the nerves. I'm an old lady now, it hardly matters.'

Greta passed her a fizzy glass of sparkling wine. Geez, what was she doing? Serving alcohol to the alcoholic. A new low. Just get through tonight, Greta, tomorrow they'll all be on a diet and sober.

As Millie downed the drink, her name was announced.

'Millie, your hat. Give it to me,' Greta insisted.

Millie resolutely shook her head and linked arms with her and they walked back inside the venue to the waiting crowd.

Bloody stubborn, that's how she'd remember her aunt. That grubby old hat sat on her head, never to be removed, it seemed.

'After so many exhibits and shows, I still can't believe that people show up to see me and my art.'

Greta couldn't believe that Millie was nervous. The woman owned the room with a captivated and adoring audience.

'I'm incredibly grateful for your ongoing support. I look around and am amazed at all the red dots, that people want to purchase my paintings. That is what spurs me on to keep going. Well, that's not true actually,' she tittered, her voice wavered. 'I would paint regardless. It's what I was born to do and it's a compulsion. If no one bought a single one of my creations, I'd be poor, but I'd still paint. I gain so much out of capturing the everyday beauty around me. That is why, with this show in particular, I wanted to showcase our very special part of the world. There's my usual interiors and still lifes, but landscapes, too of our area, for everyone to enjoy.'

Millie paused, glanced around the room and the crowd seemed to hold their breath. Greta waited for the eruption of a cough but it didn't come. Had the nerves finally overcome her?

But Millie continued. 'It's fair to say that I'm getting on in age, but age does not stop me. In anything I do. In fact, rather than being here hobnobbing with you lot tonight, as lovely as you are, I'd rather be at home painting. There's always work to be done.' She smiled, seemingly back on track, her tone less serious. 'People ask for the message in my paintings. I say there isn't any. Enjoy the beauty. If it doesn't make you feel something, go on to the next, even if it isn't one of mine.' People laughed. Millie did too. 'Don't waste your time on things you consider ugly. It's all about beauty. Life is about the beautiful moments. And my tips for keeping things beautiful–don't do the housework. If your house gets messy, buy some fresh flowers.' The room erupted in laughter. Her acerbic wit on show, Millie was at her best.

'But tonight is about the young people. The young *artistes* coming through, the next generation. Let's foster them everyone, but don't forget about me,' she giggled, 'and nurture the next generation of work. I am not a judge of the young art competition. I have left that to the committee to make an independent choice. But I cannot wait to walk through those doors,' she pointed to her left, 'and not only view the winner, who will get to work with me for the next twelve months on a paid bursary, in addition to a prize of $25,000, but all of those who entered and were shortlisted. I know I will revel in their talent.'

Rapturous applause sounded around the room and Greta clapped along with them. She experienced another swell of pride, her chest might even have puffed out. God, she loved that woman.

Another committee member took the microphone. Greta glanced around, nervous this time for a different reason. Where was Brodie? She spotted him in the far corner, standing alone, his arms folded across his chest. She dare not move closer to him. The announcer talked about the breadth of talent not only in the room, but in their local community. How lucky they were; how fortunate to have such support from Millie, their patron and greatest contributor.

Another couple of people made speeches; the words blended for Greta and she lost focus and collected another drink, crisp white wine this time. Like her aunt, she needed to calm her nerves.

Greta swayed on the balls of her feet. 'Now to the important and one of the most exciting moments of the evening. Tonight we have the great pleasure of announcing the twenty-third winner of the young emerging artist competition. After the announcement all entries will be on display in the Rembrandt room.' The gentleman pointed to his left. 'I'm pleased to advise that the judges were unanimous in their decision. A clear winner stood out this year for their vision, outstanding technique and the transparent passion in their work. Congratulations to Brodie Quade.'

Cheers filled the rooms and heads turned to spot the fresh new talent. Greta tried to resist but couldn't, she turned too. Brodie's arms had dropped by his sides but his mouth gaped open, his head shaking in confusion. His mother was by his side in an instant, expressing her glee, patting him on the arm. Then presumably the rest of his family embraced him, the children jumped up and down and squealed.

'This year the winner receives a cash sum of $25,000 plus a year of working with Millie Osborne. What a prize! Don't be shy, Brodie, come and collect your prize from Millie.'

Brodie was ushered forward but he was clearly reticent. Millie moved into position, a static smile on her face. Their eyes caught. The smile stretched for Greta's sake and she relaxed.

Brodie rushed forwards, as if he was in a hurry to get it over with. He briefly shook the announcer's hand but immediately bowed his head to Millie and exchanged private words. The announcer interrupted, handing a cheque to Millie to present to Brodie. As if they were strangers, she handed it to him, he bent and kissed her cheek and as he rose, his eyes sought out Greta. He found her and he shot her a look that she couldn't read.

A mixture of sick and elation somersaulted in her stomach. He'd done it. Brodie deserved this award and she was ecstatic for him. The sick part was the realisation that he hadn't entered his refugee pieces. She had.

THE DOORS TO THE ANTEROOM SWUNG OPEN AND FROM HIS vantage Brodie saw his refugee on display. All three of him. He wanted to barf. Could he go and rip them from the wall? That would cause a scene, but did he care?

Before he could move, Millie was in his face. She clasped his two hands in hers. 'Look at me, Brodie. You deserve this award. It was independently judged. They adored your piece.'

His face screwed up in disgust. 'It's not a piece to be adored.'

'Don't be facetious. I won't stand for it anymore. You know what I mean. They understood your message. Agreed it was important. But more than that, they thought it was well-executed. Technique proficient and the way it was presented was powerful. If you don't believe me, go and talk to them. I didn't judge it. People who don't know you, don't care who you are, declared your pieces the winner. Can you please accept this accolade? Your work is worthy of attention. You must learn this. Accept it. It is becoming quite wearisome trying to convince you. I'm an old woman, you know.'

He tried to speak and she silenced him.

'I don't care what happened in your past. This is the now and this is your future. You are a talented artist. Listen to the people if you won't listen to me.'

She dropped his hands. Others took hold of them. Strangers slapping him on the back and congratulating him.

'I saw that article. Shocking. Now you've given that fellow a voice. We can all remember him and what he went through.'

Shivers raced up Brodie's spine.

'I don't know a lot about that man, but the three versions of him that you've painted, it's incredible. So clearly depicts his stages of life and his loss and the tragedy of his passing. Thank you.'

The comments came thick and fast. He couldn't move without receiving another compliment. Eventually he made it into the room. There they were, but he couldn't look at the man he created. His gaze diverted to the other pieces.

Landscape. Nice. A self-portrait. He liked the style. A vase on a table. Nowhere near as proficient as Millie. A Picasso style contorted face. He liked the colours. A street scene. Pretty good. And there was his. He had to admit. It was striking. Sent an immediate arrow to the heart. Struck a chord. Made you uncomfortable.

'I knew you could do it,' his mother whispered to him. Her breath tickled and warmth spread through him.

'Mum, I didn't enter. It was entered for me.' He glanced in Greta's direction.

'Well, you have a lot to thank that girl for. She's done you a favour.'

He pulled up short. 'Done me a favour? Entering my work without permission. That's a bit rich.'

'Stop it. Listen to yourself. You were never going to enter this competition, or any other for that matter. I don't know what it is, Brodie, but you can't accept your talent. Listen to these people, enjoy it. Accept that you create special pieces that make people feel something, even if it's discomfort. That is special. You are special.'

'You can't enter someone's stuff without their permission.'

His mother groaned. 'If you weren't my son, I'd slap you

right now.' Then she became more serious and leaned her forehead against his large bulk of a shoulder. 'Please enjoy this. You are being recognised for your hard work. You're a talented artist. Take a moment, let it sink in, be grateful and most of all, be kind.'

Gosh, only Mum could make him cry. Tears pooled in his eyes. Why didn't he listen more to the real voices instead of the ones in his head? Why did he let those voices dictate his life and his beliefs? It was hard to overcome, that's why. When you're told you're useless, it sticks because you believe what people tell you, particularly knowledgeable adults who must be right. But maybe they're not always right. He was worthy. He was talented in his own quirky, unusual way with his outlandish paintings and his view of the world.

Why then couldn't he approach Greta? Because she betrayed him. He thought she knew him better than anyone but if that was true, how could she expose him like this?

'IT'S A LOAD OF CRAP. I MEAN LOOK AT IT. THEY'RE SUPPOSED TO be faces but they look grotesque, can't even tell who it is. He could have prettied it up a little. Is that blood?'

Greta had drunk too many wines. A result of trying to cope with the aftermath of her decision. And Brodie still avoided her and that hurt most of all. Surely, he understood she did it for his own good? Didn't others act when you alone could not?

'Excuse me, do you paint?' she asked the two young men standing in front of Brodie's pieces.

They looked up in surprise. 'Yes, actually,' one answered. 'We both do. That is my piece over there and my friends on the other wall.'

Greta glanced at both. She'd learned a little about art living with Millie and Brodie. The first was a rather banal ordinary portrait of someone she didn't recognise. Rather realist, like a photograph. The other, a car, perhaps a Holden Escort?

'How are your paintings any better? I mean, these won, right. Yours didn't. Tell me about what you've tried to achieve with your works? Are you sending a message, trying to change the world?'

'It's not about that. Millicent Osborne said so. She appreciates beauty.'

Greta turned back to both canvases, in case she'd missed something. 'Is that what you've created?' The sarcasm in her voice obvious.

The two men spluttered.

'I'll tell you one thing I do know. It's a small world so best not to dish fellow artists but learn how you can do better and be humble and congratulatory towards your colleagues. Otherwise, you'll never get ahead.'

Dickheads, she said as she walked away. Brodie might be pissed with her right now, but she wouldn't tolerate them denigrating his work. Not within her earshot anyway. Greta savoured the mouthful of another cold drink; the dry oaked wine tasted perfect.

CHAPTER 24

Greta pulled the door shut to close out the world. Her throat was as dry as a desert. And yet, she still craved the zing of another white wine. One more sip and the world might go back to rights. It had to. But, she was sober enough to know that only water would quench this thirst.

Brodie and Millie stood huddled with Henry and Niamh. Greta found a bottle of water and guzzled it. Then she surreptitiously collected dirty glasses and strewn serviettes along with scraps of food from every available surface while glancing sideways at the intimate group huddled together.

Brodie held the cheque in his hand and handed it to his father. Henry shook his head, refusing to take it, but faced with his son's insistence, he folded it in half and placed into his back trouser pocket. Niamh held a tissue to her nose before they embraced, and Brodie showed his family out.

Was her fuzzy brain playing tricks on her? What was going on?

Brodie had ignored her all night; not said one single word. But he'd spoken to everyone else in the room.

She was striding towards him before she had time to think.

'Why did you give your dad the prize money? You need it. That money can tide you over without the need for another job —' Her tone was all wrong, brusque and abrupt but the words flew out of her mouth and she couldn't stop them. Blame the alcohol but she was also hurt about how he'd treated her.

He held a flat palm in front of her face. 'Why? Because my parents have lost their life savings. And guess how?'

Her shoulders drooped but that was nothing compared to the rollercoaster ride her stomach was on.

'Their financial advisor decided to borrow their funds. Now their money is gone. They have nothing left except the park. Nothing to fall back on. No safety net. That's pretty low isn't it?'

Her knees went weak and she shrank in front of him. *No. No. No.* This couldn't be happening. It wasn't her fault! Not this time. 'It wasn't me. You know that, right?"

'Yes, but Charlie is facing more charges, isn't he?' Brodie stared hard.

'Yes,' she squeaked. And added as an afterthought, 'they'll get it back.'

'How much has Charlie repaid?'

She shrugged and avoided eye contact.

'Exactly. So that is why Greta, I gave my parents the prize money because they can start saving again and rebuild their retirement fund. They deserve that.'

'Yeah, they do. I'm really sorry.'

'Sorry is not enough, is it, Greta? Sorry doesn't replace the money. Doesn't take away the pain and suffering my parents are feeling right now. And the other victims too.'

A hacking cough erupted from Millie and Greta rushed to her side. She silently thanked the Lord for the distraction. How the hell was she supposed to respond to Brodie? She had no words. Instead, she focused on Millie and offered her water.

Saliva filled her own mouth as she watched the cool water slide into Millie's. Her tongue felt heavy and furry.

'Millie, are you okay? You've been ill. Should we get you home to bed?' Brodie stood beside her, holding one arm, before leaving briefly to retrieve a chair.

Millie stalled. 'Is there any hot water left in the urn?'

'I'm sure there is. Brodie?' Greta asked.

'Yes, please.'

She watched him comfort her aunt while she made three cups of tea. A couple of sips in and Millie had regained her composure.

'Stop bickering, you two. Greta, this was a fantastic event that you've pulled off beautifully. Not that I think it's important but you've redeemed yourself in everyone's eyes and made it a raging success, thank you.'

Warmth spread through her at the compliment. The evening had been better than she could ever have expected, everything had gone off without a hitch. Millie's collection of paintings had sold, the community had finally accepted Greta, Brodie had won the art prize and everyone had a good time. Perhaps she had a future as an events co-ordinator?

The only downer of the night was Brodie. And now that dreadful news about his parent's savings. Could she recover the situation?

'Brodie. I know you're pissed at me but I wanted you to see that people would love your work. And they did. I was right.' The look he gave her chilled the blood in her veins. She looked at Millie for reassurance then. 'Isn't that right, Millie?'

'I've been telling him exactly that for years, Greta. I think he's seen it tonight. Or at least understands that whilst not everyone might love what he does, they can appreciate it and in Brodie's case the message and importance of what he's trying to say. Do you get it now, you silly boy?'

The first smile of the night. It was all teeth and spread up to his eyes making them sparkle.

'You should not have entered my work without my permission. That wasn't a decision for you to make. I would never have exposed you like that.' He turned away from Greta and faced Millie. 'But I admit, yes, most people liked it. Or thought about the person behind the face, his experiences and trauma.'

'Exactly!' Greta exclaimed.

Brodie shot her a barbed look. 'Most of them know me, they are being kind.'

Millie and Greta emitted a low groan at the same time.

'Ah, despite what you say, I think you understand. Being creative is a hard pursuit. Not everyone will agree with your decision not to have a real job, or like what you create. We cannot make everyone happy. But when you have this gift, Brodie, it becomes a duty to share it. You can no longer keep it to yourself.'

He hung his head and Greta prepared for a further rebuke.

'The problem is Millie I want to spend every minute on my art. But, now, Mum and Dad are in strife. I can't sponge off them any longer, shouldn't have for this long. I need to help them get back on their feet financially and that means getting a job.'

'You gave them money,' Greta interjected.

Brodie acted as if he didn't hear.

'You have twelve months with me, Brodie. You lucky man.' Millie tried to smile but coughed instead. Recovering, she continued, 'That's an income, so you'll have money. I'll double it so you can focus on your art. Now is the time, no more excuses. No more looking after other people. If you have too, give that money to your parents. I don't care what you do with it. I'll feed you so you don't starve. But by golly, you are not going back onto any construction site if I have a say.'

Brodie's shoulders appeared to tremble and for a moment Greta thought he might break down.

'Make the most of this, boy. Use it. This is an opportunity, a chance, don't forsake it.'

Brodie pounded one hand against his chest, over his heart, and looked at Millie and then rose up like the giant he was and engulfed the tiny old lady.

'Only problem is…' Millie paused.

Brodie pulled back. 'I knew it. What, tell me, are there conditions?'

'Always the cynic,' she said to him but turned her gaze between the two of them and licked her pale pink tongue across her lips.

A shiver ran up Greta's spine as she waited. Millie wasn't usually one for theatrics but she kept them in suspense. As Greta waited she noticed how particularly tired she appeared. Her skin was translucent and darkened in spots like it was bruised. It was hard to treat Millie like an old lady when she never acted like one.

'I'm sick.'

'I knew it.' Greta jumped out of her chair. 'I've been thinking for weeks that something wasn't right. 'Is it bronchitis, pneumonia? What's the treatment?'

'Oh, you silly girl.'

Ouch, harsh, chastened she sat back down.

'I'm not telling you to make a fuss. Life will continue on as normal but it's only fair to tell both of you because you are the closest to me'. To one cheek, she placed a bone-thin hand with the skin blotched pink. 'Greta. It's been such a delight having you here with me. I'm sorry for all the bother that made you come but I'm glad it happened because otherwise, you might have continued to live the life you were. This will be the making of you, my girl. You're a wonderfully kind and open-hearted young woman. You need to find your feet and once you do, I'm confident you'll fly. I have no doubt that you'll achieve great things.'

She removed her hand and placed it onto Brodie's broad knee. 'And you, my stubborn young man. From the day we met I knew you were special. And I don't say that often or willy-nilly. And I don't tell people they have a gift unless they do. Unless they are talented. I do not waste time mincing my words. I've fostered you and nurtured you because I can't bear to see it go to waste. You cannot waste this life you have. You're loyal and loving and can both chase your dream and look after your parents. I confess art is all-consuming to those who are committed. Perhaps I should have given a broader life a try, but nonetheless I didn't. You can do it, Brodie. And please, try to create beautiful things sometimes. There is beauty within you.' Millie's lips curved into a delicate smile.

Greta's heart shifted in her chest. She felt truly loved by Millie and she was sure Brodie did, too.

'But the thing is,' Millie continued. 'I have emphysema. I'm dying.'

Greta replayed the words in her head. She must have heard incorrectly, but it sure sounded like Millie said she was dying. Glancing at her aunt, the realisation it might be true caused nausea to swirl in her stomach.

The door burst open and the sound of shoes on the hardwood floor clacked in their direction. Greta looked over her shoulder to see Charlene approaching at a brisk pace. Could Charlene tell she'd had too much to drink? All of a sudden everything felt topsy-turvey. Millie was dying and what did Charlene want right now?

'Greta, Charlie has committed suicide.'

For seconds, the silence stretched; the world around her blanched. Then every emotion hit her at once. Bile churned in her stomach and rose up scorching her throat and before she could quell it, she vomited all over Charlene's Doc Martens.

~

Brodie used the white roller to criss-cross up and down the canvas. His strokes were rough and heavy as the blurred colour became white. The movement was invigorating, he loved a fresh start.

Millie had loved this painting but he knew it could be better. He'd improve it and show her; she'd be proud. He'd work hard on making it pretty. No, not pretty, that was superficial; a thing of beauty. Nothing else would do.

That supernatural force that overtook him when he worked, compelled him once more. Colours mixed and ready, his brushes primed, his blank canvas ready.

He had another purpose too: to release his anger. It simmered inside of him ready to explode like fireworks popping on New Year's Eve. The same sensation when he was witness to an injustice that needed to be righted. A feeling of overwhelming fury that could only be overcome by expression.

Millie was sick; Greta had deceived him.

He wasn't angry at Millie. He was distraught that his closest confident and mentor was ill. In typical fashion, she'd refused to be drawn on diagnosis or treatments and all that bother as she'd called it. That information was her private business and she'd keep it that way regardless of her condition. Good on her. But that didn't make him feel any better.

He couldn't describe his feelings about Greta at the moment. Thinking of her caused his chest to tighten and his balance to sway. He didn't know how or what to think.

He'd thought he was falling in love with her. But the thought of her entering his pieces made him stab the canvas hard. The thought of what she did to those innocent people made him want to punch a hole in the canvas. She'd exposed him and committed unforgiveable acts.

Now, loving her felt wrong. How could he love someone like that? Who was she? Greta had arrived a damaged person, but because of the hurt she'd inflicted on others. Yes, there were reasons, but everyone had an excuse for their behaviour. How could she even be associated with that slimy character, Charlie? But he immediately stopped those thoughts. His mother would say you cannot denigrate the dead.

Poor bastard. Killing himself was not the solution. Easy option? Probably. Jail might be that bad. And if you can't get your addictions under control, it would control you. He was wise, wasn't he?

He wasn't. All Brodie knew is he had to paint. And it had to be her. The image would change this time. The pinks and purples and bruised melee was her before. Now, she was after. She'd appear older, more complex. But the colour palette still suited. She was bright and frothy shades of magenta and maroon and strawberry.

His brush paused before the first stroke. Was he able to forgive her? Or did the events of her past determine the core of who she was? Could they be overcome? He didn't know. Perhaps the answer would be revealed to him through the paint. The only thing he did know, was that he wasn't going to stop until the painting was finished.

CHAPTER 25

*D*eath. It was everywhere: Millie, Charlie. Greta couldn't help wondering what Charlie had looked like after he'd gassed himself in his ridiculously expensive car. Had his mouth hung open with spittle in the corners of his lips? Had his skin turned green from lack of oxygen? Or had it been peaceful and he'd drifted into a dreamless sleep, perhaps one of the best he'd had in sometime, his heavy head resting against the back of the leather seat?

The day of the funeral was a clear, humid summer day. Not fair really. Like in the movies, it should be cloudy and overcast and as you stood at the gravesite, rain should pummel the earth. Did the weather mock Charlie and his decision to end his life? Or was it a greater meaning of celebration and happiness as he moved onto another world?

As if Greta knew.

She'd never erase the memory of Charlie's mother reaching for the coffin and preventing its descent into the deep, open hole. His mother's guttural wail sent shivers up her spine and immediately formed a migraine at her temples. But ever since, the sound had reverberated around her empty head. It dinged to one side and then the other. Often the image was interrupted by Charlie's father trying to reef his wife away only to cause loud protestations when she swatted at his arms violently.

Through the service, she'd stood alone. Of course, Charlie's friends were there. Some she'd known well. Others only in passing. His sister and brother. Everyone present seemed to gaze at each other with disbelief, it being incomprehensible that they were standing at Charlie's funeral.

Millie would have accompanied her, but as if her confession had given her body permission to wilt, she'd spent the week in decline. Her health not up to the car trip to Sydney. And Brodie, well, once he might have come, too. But now he avoided her. Ironic, given they traipsed around the same house and if they happened to pass in the hall, it was all sorts of awkward. Skye volunteered to join her but with so much grief in the young woman's life, Greta couldn't add to it.

So acting like a big girl, she went alone.

Now, back at home after her morning breakfast shift at *Beach Haven*, Greta cuddled mother cat. Her chest tightened and she felt like crying, but she didn't. Her emotions zoomed between Charlie killing himself, Millie's illness and cold-hearted Brodie. At any given moment, she couldn't make up her mind which was worse. All three situations made her sad.

But there was also anger. Charlie chose the easy option. He'd done some bad and unforgivable things and wasn't here to pay the price. He could have done his time, gotten clean and sorted his shit out. Just like she'd been trying to do these past months. It felt like two steps forward and one back. But as long as she was always one step ahead, things would be okay. Obviously, his demons were too large, too difficult. She'd never been addicted, so couldn't understand the lack of discipline associated with a fix. He could have sorted out the other stuff; the legalities, paid the money back, rehabilitated himself but if the drugs remained like a noose around his head, well, that was a tough road.

Deep down inside, she was also wracked with guilt. Should she have done more? Helped him when he cried out? He cried out for drug money though, so if she had, would she now be crying that her money had killed him? A no win situation. Greta knew what Millie would say. It wasn't her fault and she agreed it wasn't, but nonetheless, he was dead. Someone she'd cared about had killed themself and that one and the same person had contributed to her own demise. But she was on the rise back up, wasn't she?

Too many questions, too many thoughts. That's why she was keeping busy, it had become her mantra, particularly now as her role of PA had slowed.

At the cemetery, a beautiful young woman had approached and introduced herself as Charlie's girlfriend. She was rake-thin, platinum blonde with gel-tipped nails and the latest designer clothes, and early twenties at best. She'd actually smiled at the time picturing Charlie perfectly with this woman. In that moment, she knew he hadn't changed.

'My name's Poppy.'

Of course, it is. 'Lovely to meet you.'

'We hadn't been dating long. It's fair to say he was a bit of a train wreck.'

He hadn't been when we first met.

'He told me about you. I used to be jealous because he got this twinkle in his eye when he spoke of you. A fondness. But now, I can see why.'

Really? Greta did a double take at her plain blue-wash jeans and white blouse. No name, no brand. Nothing special. She ran her fingers through her loose hair. She couldn't even remember if she'd brushed it. She'd lost her habit of the strong, bold straight bob and a face full of make-up.

'Anyway, he raved about how good you were at your job. So good with people and money, wise investments. I'm in real estate. I know that you can't, well, your restricted in your work options. But we have a great team at *Red Rock Realty* and if you want, we are hiring. It pays well.' The girl swung her arms wide indicating herself and her image. It was on the tip of Greta's tongue to ask what car she drove.

Poppy went on to detail her latest bonus and how they only sell high-end prestige property. Sales talk she'd heard before. Different industry, but the same.

She'd shot her down quickly, refused her kindness. In true bulldog fashion Poppy shoved her business card into Greta's hands, refusing to accept no. What Greta thought was a no-brainer had her ruminating the what-ifs. She pulled the card out of her pocket; pushed her thumb into its sharp-card edge.

Had she been too swift to dismiss it? For a fleeting moment, she imagined the income she could apply to her debt.

Something moved to her right. She returned the card and saw Henry and Niamh meandering down Millie's drive. Greta placed the cat down and smoothed her palms down her skirt.

'Hi, Henry, hi Niamh.'

They greeted her with a kiss to her cheek.

'We were so sorry to hear about your friend. It's tragic when someone young dies, no matter the circumstances.'

She nodded. The tears only just kept at bay.

'Brodie is here, upstairs. Do you want me to run up and fetch him?'

They shook their heads in unison. 'No, we've come to see you actually.'

'Me?' She couldn't imagine why.

'Yes, we've come to ask some advice.'

'Um, okay. I'll put the kettle on and we'll talk inside. Millie is painting, too. Those two are like peas in a pod.'

Brodie's parents laughed and followed her into the cottage.

After the first sip of tea and cake that she'd found in the kitchen, Henry said, 'We understand you're very experienced in the finance industry and wondered if you wouldn't mind steering us in right direction.' He pulled out a pad with some loose papers on top.

The Madeira cake she'd just taken a bite of stuck to the roof of her mouth. She swallowed it as a hard lump. 'I'm so sorry for what happened to you. I simply feel sick about it. Not only because I know you, but because, well, it makes me understand the impact of what I was involved in. I'm ashamed and embarrassed. I can't understand how you can even sit across from me knowing that my ex-boyfriend did this to you.'

Henry held up his hand. 'We aren't here to make you feel bad and it goes without saying that we don't blame you and none of what happened is your fault.'

Her smile was weak. 'I'm happy to help.'

'Well, the money that Brodie gifted, we intend to pay it back, but we want to invest it and make it grow. We aren't shy of further investing. We completely understand this was a random act and we were unlucky. I've done a bit of research and what do you think of these?'

He pushed the papers across to her and mentioned what he'd found and his views. Without ruminating about the past or dreading the future, Greta got lost in the moment. She knew the funds they referred to and could help them.

'Avoid this one …' After half an hour, she sat back. Her throat was dry, but her mind swam. She'd helped, been productive. And they were grateful. Niamh helped clear the table as stomping came down the stairs and the house shook.

'Dad, what are you doing here?' she heard Brodie ask as she emptied the remnants of tea into the sink. His mother went out to join them. Her stomach turned into a tightly strung coil of knots.

Brodie's voice raised in response. Okay, she'd stay where she was. She found the dishcloth and wiped an already clean bench.

Voices echoed through the doorway but she didn't budge. Niamh came to extract her to say goodbye. Damn it!

She entered the dining room but avoided Brodie. His parents proffered their thanks but Brodie remained silent before turning and following his parents out.

Greta thought she'd grown: she loved helping at the shelter and had made a difference, she was working hard and there was a shift; she viewed life differently. She wasn't the same person anymore. But since Charlie, Brodie refused to talk to her and Millie didn't need her, despite her illness. Except for Skye who was perfectly capable of looking after herself, there was nothing tethering her to *Banyan Creek*. Maybe she should take that job and return to Sydney.

BRODIE'S CHEST BUBBLED WITH EXCITEMENT. HIS MOOD BUOYANT. His feet wanted to move. Is this how it felt to believe? To feel content? This might be the first piece of work that he truly liked. He soaked up that feeling; it was unusual. He wanted to feel it a million times over.

Perhaps he was good enough.

Everyone might be right.

Before he could change his mind he packaged the canvas with the most delicate of care. The bubble wrap went round twice. He obtained the address and labelled it and double checked. He was not going to prevaricate, overthink it or allow the doubts to creep in. This painting he would enter into *The Olley Portrait Prize* himself.

No deception, no surprises. If he didn't win or short list even, it was on him and he could live with it. Whatever. At least he tried. And with a piece he loved and was happy for others to admire.

Millie would be proud; Greta too.

He knew deep down Greta didn't act in malice. Naivety yes, but not out of nastiness. But he couldn't forgive her yet.

He needed to forgive himself first. It had never been his fault. Could he truly live those words and let it go?

It was time to be honest.

CHAPTER 26

But of course, she was needed. After all that had happened, she was still a foolish stupid girl. Greta had to learn, once and for all, that not everything was about her. It became quickly apparent that her aunt needed her.

'Millie! What's wrong? What are you doing?' Greta tried to keep her voice steady but her stomach did flips.

Millie sat on the floor of the front room, detritus in the lap of her dress and across the rug and cried. Large, ugly tears that Greta had never seen her shed. Heaves rose from deep down inside her lungs, escaped her open mouth and turned her face blotchy red.

In an ironic twist of fate, the afternoon sun streamed into the room through the front bay window and cast the room in a golden glow. And Millie, too. Dust mites floated in the rays, dancing to an unknown rhythm. The fierce scrutiny of light made the parlour appear both delightful and old simultaneously.

Greta sat next to her aunt and pulled her into an embrace, like she might cradle a baby. Millie's body leaned in, resting. In one hand she clasped a solitary bootie, knitted and once pink. In her lap was a jumpsuit, aged and ever-so tiny. Next to it a rattle and a cubed toy of multiple colours. Greta picked it up and at the pressure it released a squeak. On the floor, was a hospital tag cut in half with a clip missing. The spare bootie to the pair sat further away.

Mother cat sensed the mood and curled into Greta's side.

'Shush, Millie. It's okay. It will be all right.'

Will it?

'What's all this stuff that has made you so upset?'

Her aunt held the bootie to her cheek, closed her eyes and kept crying. But then she whispered, 'Eleanor'.

'Eleanor?' Greta repeated. 'Who's that, Millie?'

No answer. The weeping quietened into a sniffle. Her aunt fingered the items one by one. There was a faded photograph, the old sort with the traditional white border. A chubby rosy-cheeked newborn in a pink muslin wrap was asleep.

'She's beautiful,' Greta murmured.

'Yes, she is,' Millie agreed. She lifted her head and gazed red-eyed at Greta.

Like a switch had been flicked, Millie's clouded eyes cleared, she wiped the moisture away from her cheeks and sat up taller, her weight no longer resting on Greta. Then she frantically gathered the things around her. She dragged the box close and returned everything, working silently. When each item was back in place, Greta motioned to take the box, meaning to place it safely away.

Millie held tight. 'I love you, Greta.'

'I love you, too, Millie.'

'Sometimes we think we're living the good life and we lose focus. I've never lost focus but it's possible my focus was not always in the right place. I thought it was. So regardless of anything else, I want you to know that you've been a darling niece to me. I've treasured these last few weeks. I don't know how you are Grace's daughter.' The first sliver of a smile.

'Thanks, Millie. I promise to always do my best. But why are you so upset? What is this baby stuff?'

Millie tugged the box closer under her arm. 'Some things are best kept a secret. It's my pain to own, not yours. You should not concern yourself with my past sorrows.'

'I'm happy to listen. I want to know.'

I really want to know!

Why was Millie so bloody private!

Millie didn't hide the box though. She pushed it under the armchair and Greta memorised the spot.

'I will however, need you to help me get up. This old body is not like it used to be and my legs have cramped from being crossed for too long.'

Greta gently pulled her upwards. Her body, once such a frightful force, was light under her grip; her limbs brittle. She held her arm while Millie gathered her balance before she wandered slowly away on wobbly feet. Afterwards, Millie slept for two days straight and didn't get up again.

MILLICENT MARGARET OSBORNE WAS MANY THINGS TO MANY people. She was a much-loved Australian artist, sister, friend, mentor, confidante, but to me she was my Aunt. She was a war baby, born in the spring of 1944. Her parents were Toby and Louise and they had three children. Millie was the eldest and a sibling for Joseph, and Grace who both survive her and are here today. She reports that her young childhood was free and filled with joy. She used to run through the fields of sugar cane in their North Queensland home. The family moved around a few times before settling in Sydney for a while where Millie went to art school. However, once she found the northern New South Wales hinterland, she never left. She loved living here and adored her isolated and run-down cottage, Banyan Creek.

Despite her isolation, she had many friends and was quite known in her early years for her outrageous parties that lasted all night. And often with the glitterati of the art world and famous actors in attendance. It's rumoured if you turned up the following morning after one of her dos, sleeping bodies were strewn across available floor space, lounges and even on the deck. Of course, with a party lifestyle comes consequences. It took her a long while to realise and accept that whilst she lived a wonderful life with her art and family and friends, she had a demon. Alcohol was not her friend. In her usual style and discipline she gave up the drink, admitting it controlled her. To be fair, if it hadn't affected her art, I don't think she'd have ever given up. But when the grog affected her painting, it had to go.

Unlike those disgusting cigarettes. A habit she refused to give up no matter how many lectures she received. And of course, that habit had consequences too. Ultimately it killed her. Diagnosed with emphysema she still refused to stop smoking. She was a stubborn old bugger.

A tinkle of laughter rose up amongst the gathered crowd, dressed in green, Millie's favourite colour.

Her worn-out lungs made her prone to chest infections in her last days and it was a dose of pneumonia that caught her in the end.

*Some might have called Millie a recluse or perhaps an eccentric and maybe she was. But for sure, one thing I know, is that she was funny and kind and compassionate but she was most passionate for and lived for her craft. She dedicated her life to it. She never longed for anything except time at her easel. If she could, Millie would have spent every day in that painting chair, wearing her painting hat—*Greta held up the worn old red hat*—surrounded by all that stuff. Her painting studio made me shudder with its clutter but to Millie it was all inspiration. From the vases, flowers alive and dead, driftwood, trinkets, cups, photographs, postcards and then of course, add to that her equipment – varieties of paints in more colours than I thought imaginable, tubes empty and full, clean and dirty clothes, brushes of varying lengths and styles, and the God-awful smell. The turps and methylated spirits, it permeated everything. She was immune to it of course.*

Millie is most famous for her still life paintings. She loved the simplicity of an indoors scene or capturing the smallest of detail in a domestic panorama. However, her talent didn't end there, she was prolific in creating landscapes, particularly of her beloved France where she spent a glorious summer when she was twenty-six years old. She never did stop talking about the beauty of the country. She fell in love with it. Those scenes are some of my favourites.

When she had established herself as one of our great painters, she used her skill and knowledge to help other aspiring artists. Over her later years she mentored many young students, encouraged them and provided endless advice. The most recent recipient is one of our own and local resident, Brodie. She saw enormous talent in him and never let him forget it. I'm sure Brodie won't mind me saying but there could not be two more diverse artists. Millie created beauty and objects to be admired and swooned over, Brodie creates important scenes that convey messages and can be quite dark, but in amongst all that they adored each other despite their differences.

Not even those she loved avoided her honesty and acerbic wit. Anyone who knows her well will have been at the receiving end of one of her barbed comments. You always knew where you stood with Millie. And that was one of her many wonderful traits. Another is that you could be certain of a delicious home-cooked meal or a pudding or dessert. Only of course, after she'd finished her painting for the day.

I guess unlike the rest of us, she leaves a legacy. Her artwork will live on forever. It won't surprise anyone here today, that almost, right up until she was confined to bed, she was painting. There is a piece still sitting at her easel and I think, perhaps two or three more behind her, waiting for her final flourish.

I can't express how much she meant to me over these last few months and how grateful I am that I got to spend this time with her. Because of her, I survived. She is famous, a renowned artist, a wonderful woman but she was my aunt and I loved her.

THIS WAS A PRIVATE CELEBRATION FOR HER FAMILY, FRIENDS AND local townspeople. The government of New South Wales announced they would hold a State funeral to honour her and her commitment to the Australian art industry. Greta wasn't sure she would attend; this was her intimate farewell.

All members of the community were present. Brodie's family had offered to hold the wake, but Greta wanted to be surrounded by her aunt. Of course, holding it at *Banyan Creek* was out of the question, unless it was demolished first. So, they held it at the community hall where her art still hung, not yet having been sent to their new homes. It felt right.

Brodie remained silent, caught up in his own grief, she guessed. But he stood by her side and she felt his presence. A few times she looked away from the person talking to her and caught his eye. He stared at her. Looked as if he wanted to talk.

As soon as her family left, she whisked out the back door. That was enough, she was exhausted and hadn't had a moment to digest that Millie was no longer here.

She got on the trusty old bicycle—it had served her well— and rode home. Without parking the bike properly but leaning it against the front stairs, she rushed inside. Straight to the box and extracted it from under the chair. Then she got the coffee table book and found the card and photograph. She wanted answers. Greta carried the objects upstairs to Millie's bedroom. It was hardly prying now that someone was dead, was it? The roll of her stomach acknowledged that it felt wrong, like she was invading her aunt's privacy, the privacy that Millie guarded so fiercely.

The room was ordered and clean and everything in its spot. Millie's floral fragrance hung in the air. She guessed it wouldn't be long before that disappeared. Greta flopped down onto the bed pulling her legs up under her. She opened the lid and emptied the contents and placed the card and photo in amongst it.

Who was this baby? She'd asked her mother after the funeral

but she'd had no idea. It was 1970, Millie would have been twenty-six and only recently returned from France the end of the year before. That brought Reggie to mind. Did he have anything to do with this? Was it a friend who had a baby? But why then was she so sentimental to Millie? She shifted the items around on the bed, turned them upside down and looked into each bootie. What did it all mean?

Running her hand along the edges of the box, she felt nothing until her hand jagged on the corner. A piece of paper. She lifted the box up to look inside and sure enough, there was a tiny scrap of paper stuck to one side. Tugging at it, a yellow and aged newspaper cutting came away. The print was small and Greta held it up close to her face to read the words. A death announcement. Such an old-fashioned tradition. Did anyone do that anymore? No one had suggested an advertisement for Millie. She was pretty sure Charlie hadn't had one, but perhaps some people still wished to formalise the death of a loved one. Who knew?

Her shoulders slumped as her eyes swept along the words and realising it was the death announcement for Eleanor. The dates indicated she lived less than a week. Greta scanned the small print for more information. Child of Millicent Osborne.

She read the words again. Eleanor had been Millie's child. Greta picked up the photograph again and to her, it was a pudgy baby, could belong to anyone.

A shooting ache spread across her chest; the pain so fierce she wanted to double over. It felt like someone was stabbing her with a pointy knife. Greta had not expected that. Not once had she considered the child was Millie's. Her aunt had never expressed any interest in children, or a family, never had a steady boyfriend to father a child, and had not uttered a word of this to anyone.

Greta fondled each item. Poor Millie—what sorrow she must have kept locked up inside. She'd had a child and lost her within days. Picking up the article again she noticed there was no mention of a father. Greta kept the belongings close and lay back on Millie's bed. The painting on the far wall caught her attention. It was brightly coloured similar to Millie's work but this wasn't one of her own. It was a French scene of boats on a harbour and old buildings along the edge. Greta smiled, not surprised that Millie liked it and hung the piece in her private space. It had a calmness about it, a serenity but the detail was captured in the late afternoon light. A single seagull appeared in the foreground eating a fish; a gold name was written in cursive print in the right-hand corner. Was that a 'g'? Greta bolted up right and the items scattered. She rose and raced over.

The name said Reginald Smart.

CHAPTER 27

'We are gathered here today to read the will of the late Millicent Osborne.'

The words sounded more like the opening to a wedding.

Brodie and Greta sat together at the dining table. It was cleared of debris and for once, nothing was scattered across its tabletop. Mr Trevor Porter, solicitor, sat at the head. He'd been Millie's advisor almost her entire life, since she'd moved to the hinterland at least.

Funny, Millie had never mentioned a lawyer but it seemed there was a lot that she failed to talk about.

'This is a straightforward division of her estate. I am the executor and so will attend to the distributions on her behalf. You are both here because you are beneficiaries, or in plain speak, receiving something out of the estate. There are a number of other beneficiaries also but there's no need for them to be present, I will make the necessary arrangements.'

Greta glanced at Brodie who returned her gaze, looking as solemn as she felt. Mr Porter was taking his job very seriously and it felt as if they were sitting in an important meeting, which she guessed it was.

'Okay, to get on with it. Greta, you are left this property which she owned in her sole name and was unencumbered, or to explain otherwise it had no mortgage or debt owing on it. You will take a straight title.'

Holy shit! She reached for Brodie's hand under the table. He let her grasp it.

'Everything in the house is also yours.' He looked around him then. His gaze took in the spaces beyond the living room and he comprehended exactly what that meant. 'Of course, because you own the furniture, belongings etc, you are entitled to do what you wish with it.'

Both Greta and Brodie listened. When they didn't respond, he continued. 'What I mean is you can dispose of it, keep it, give it away, anything you like.'

Greta nodded. Suddenly any joy she might have had about diving in and cleaning up the joint, held no appeal.

'It's important to note of course, any artworks that remain in the house belong to you also. Millie had pieces she was working on and there may be some other completed ones. They become your property. Have a think about that, Greta, and when the time is right, come and seek some legal advice from me. And of course, in the interim, I'll ensure that the insurances are main-tained on the house and contents.'

Greta couldn't keep up; the house was hers and everything in it including Millie's paintings. The insurance part was confusing. Her expression must have given her away.

'Greta, the paintings are valuable and we need to keep them safe.' Brodie intertwined his fingers with hers, gripping tighter. It provided immediate comfort as his warmth flooded through her. It was so nice to touch him again.

She nodded, understanding but her chest tightened at the responsibility. She'd better keep the doors locked.

'Brodie,' Mr Porter addressed him then. 'Millie has provided you with a bursary. There's an important difference, let me explain. Other beneficiaries are to receive cash lump sum of a stipulated amount. You are to receive an annual yearly income with terms and conditions.'

They both smiled at each other then.

'Usual Millie style,' Greta commented.

'It's to be your income so that you are not otherwise employed. What that means is that for the life of the bursary you are not to have another job but to show commitment and dedication to your art.'

'How long for?' Greta asked the question she was sure Brodie was thinking.

'Five years.'

'Wow' she whispered.

'Yes, wow,' Brodie reiterated. Then Mr Porter read out the yearly income and neither were capable of speaking anymore.

'I haven't invited your parents here today, Brodie, but they are also to receive something. This was a late change. Millie was gravely concerned that their current plight distracted you from focusing on your art. Therefore she has provided them with an amount to invest for their retirement.' He advised of the figure. 'I will of course, be speaking directly to them about it.'

'They can retire now on that sorta money,' Brodie uttered. 'This is going to change their life.'

The lawyer ran down a list of other recipients, most of them not-for-profit associations, galleries or charities. The very last was *Beach Haven*. Greta couldn't help but express delight for the organisation that so badly needed the resources.

'I'll be in touch further in relation to the paperwork and finalising the details.' And with that he shoved the pile of papers into his tan leather briefcase and stood. The meeting was over.

Brodie rose too and let her hand drop. Greta hid her disappointment.

'I need to go and see Mum and Dad. Tell them the news, make plans.'

'I understand, of course, go.'

'We need to talk, Greta. Let's do that soon.' He paused and she thought he was going to kiss her, forgive her and their relationship could return to normal.

Ha. Wishful thinking.

Brodie dashed away.

Such fabulous news for his parents, she was stoked for them.

Greta washed and put away the cups they'd used for tea. The house was silent, and she was alone— it continued to feel strange. She'd never experienced loneliness when Millie and Brodie were at home and busy painting. Now, solitude blanketed her like a shroud.

The essence of Millie was everywhere, but particularly in the studio. Of course, that awful stench remained but it too personified her aunt. Where once she'd longed to pick each item up and dust and tidy, now Greta couldn't bear to touch anything. It felt sacred, like a memorial. This was Millie's space where she created her work. Greta whipped out her phone and took snapshots of the room from each angle. Just in case. Then she did the same in each other room of the cottage and from the outside as well.

The garden. A swell of pride overtook her as she considered the beds she'd created. As someone who didn't paint or create anything, she could admire the garden like Brodie or Millie might their work. The thought flicked into her head before she could stop it—she could finish the yard now. But would she? Or would she only do that to ready the property for sale?

The lawyer was right about the art works. At least three pieces stood against the wall in the studio, facing out and one sat on the easel. To her naked eye, it appeared finished. Another still-life, this one a collection of teapots with a matching cup and saucer and a bowl of bright green Granny Smith apples. Did her breath catch because Millie was gone or because the painting was stunning? Probably both.

Her arms ached to be embraced in a roly poly cuddle, where Millie's arms were soft yet strong, where she was pulled in too close and the scent of Millie's hair was all she could smell.

Instead of a hug, she collapsed into the vacant painting chair, her legs no longer capable of supporting her.

Millie was dead. This was her stuff. Greta's shirt became damp from the splatter of tears. On the small table near the easel sat her aunt's straw hat. It belonged here, in this room with her favourite things. There was no doubt, Greta felt her aunt's spirit swirling around the room and it delivered her a strange level of comfort.

Looking around, Greta remembered the small adjoining room and her heart rate sped up. There was one room she could tidy. Caked with dust, it wasn't going to be easy. First thing, she wiped her palms across her wet cheeks, swiping those tears away. Then she strode across the space to get access to the tiny room.

The boxes and paint tins were where she'd last seen them and the canvases remained against the far wall and turned away from the viewer. Why? Millie loved art. Why would she hide away anyone's work? Unless it was modernist pieces. She'd made clear her view on unusual modern and abstract work. But why wouldn't she donate them to someone else to appreciate?

There was a tower of boxes in her way and she dragged them to the side. She sneezed three times in quick succession as dust clouds drifted up her nose. There were three frames. Greta leaned the first away from the wall to reveal an early work of

Millie's. She ignored her disappointment. Perhaps a painting Millie didn't like? It didn't make sense for her to hide-away any of her work, it seemed very out of character. Even if not her best, Millie Osborne didn't hide her work and if she hated it that much she'd paint over and start afresh.

It was a French scene of Paris, Greta assumed. A narrow cobblestone lane ran the middle length of the painting and drew the admirer's eye. Hedging the path were terraced houses with planter boxes of a variety of brightly coloured flowers. The old-fashioned black streetlamps illuminated the scene in a soft, yellow glow. The pavers glistened like it had been raining. It was beautiful and deserving of admiration and Greta drank in its magnificence.

Greta couldn't fathom why Millie would hide such a scene, no doubt one she loved. A mystery, so she moved on to the next one.

It was another of Millie's because she recognised the style, but this one was not like anything Greta had seen before.

A pale pink muted background housed a round angelic face in rest; a baby with its eyes closed. A small tuff of blonde hair was evident on the scalp. The child appeared so small in the vastness of the picture.

Greta stepped back, one hand covering her open mouth and emitted a soft 'oh' sound. But certainty seized her, she knew who this baby was - this was Eleanor. Greta moved the painting so it faced outwards but still leaning against the wall and sat down on the dusty and cramped floor, pulled her knees into her chest and gazed at the portrait.

She was transfixed and didn't want to pull her gaze away, but she extracted the third frame and leaned it against the opposite wall.

It was not a familiar piece. As she lifted it away from the wall, a line remained as a marker of the time that had passed. She sucked in her breath. This one was similar to the painting hanging in Millie's bedroom. Her eyes darted straight to the right-hand corner and a flurry of fireworks exploded in her tummy.

Reginald Smart.

She was surrounded by precious art. Pulling out her phone, she Googled Reggie again. This time refining her search to the value of his paintings.

Again, her screen went crazy with results. Most of his works remained in France. Some had travelled to special exhibitions around the world but were borrowed for a short time only. The articles said his works were difficult to price because one hadn't been sold in many years. Frustration crept in until the bottom article, dated fifteen years ago, commented on the purchase of a rare find, a piece that hadn't been heard of since its initial unveiling. It was six digits.

Greta dropped her phone and crept backwards, away from the painting as if being near them was criminal. Her eyes diverted between the pieces and her thoughts flowed like a gushing stream. There were two Reginald Smart paintings in Millie's possession. Six paintings by Millie remained in the house. There was some valuable property located in this isolated, country cottage. Greta jumped up, conscious all of a sudden that she sat in a secluded back room while the front door remained open.

Rushing out, she closed the door and latched it twice. Then did the same at the back. But Millie had known, of course, and hadn't taken any precautions. Did she have it wrong and the paintings were worthless? No, Porter had said they were valuable, too.

These works needed to be on display in a gallery. A spark of an idea formed, and her lips curled up into a smile. She couldn't do it alone. In a speedy whirlwind, she moved the paintings into her bedroom upstairs. Placing them at the back of her wardrobe, she ensured nothing encroached on their space or any random old item accidentally brushed against them. She shut the wardrobe doors and then opened them again. Could they over-heat? Didn't galleries have their temperature set to freezing? But they'd lasted here for so long. Who knew? Best to be careful. Comfortable in the knowledge the house was locked up like Fort Knox, she collapsed back onto her bed and punched out a text to Brodie. He'd know what to do.

*A*s he approached *Banyan Creek*, he heard Lola yapping. Unusually, the dog stood guard at the top of the stairs. Brodie lowered his hand to her muzzle and she instantly quietened at the familiar smell. No sign of the cats.

He expected the door to swing open because Greta must have felt the foundations shaking. He turned the knob and it held fast and the first tremor of discomfort passed through him. The front door of the cottage was never locked. Made sense that Lola was edgy.

He knocked and waited but there was no response. He knocked again.

Eventually it swung open and Greta stood in the doorframe, her hair not curly or straight, more like a bird's nest, matted and knotted. Round and large eyes peered at him through long lashes that were moist. Her pale face made her appear like an apparition.

He wanted to reach for her and sink into an embrace. Not yet. 'What's wrong?'

'I don't know,' she hiccupped through tears. 'I was fine yesterday. Found things, sorted a bit. But the house is deathly quiet without Millie, and you,' she added. 'I couldn't sleep. I heard noises I'd never heard before. Shadows danced on the walls. It was awful.'

She hiccupped again.

Man, she was hard to resist.

'Now, all I do is cry.'

'That's normal. You've lost someone you love, life has changed. You have to allow yourself to adjust.'

'I know. That's what's unfair. I'd adjusted to life with Millie and now she's gone.'

Brodie patted her back to offer perfunctory comfort but touching Greta sent a bolt of pleasure through his body. God, he'd missed her; her closeness, her touch, her warmth, her everything. His heartbeat quickened in his chest. Was he being stubborn? Why did he always have to take the moral high ground?

'I'm sorry. I should have been here.'

'No, it's okay. Your family needed you. Were they happy?'

'In shock, still are. Can't believe it and are uncertain about making plans in case it's a dream.'

'They deserve it.'

He nodded, avoiding her gaze, trying to let his body cool down.

'Everything will be all right, Greta. It will be. I know it.'

'Yeah, but you're always Mr Positive, even when everything has gone to shit.'

'That's a good trait, right?'

He smiled down at her. The timing was wrong. They hadn't talked, cleared the air but he couldn't resist. Her swollen lips were so close, her moist cheeks pink from crying, it tugged at his heart, made the blood run faster through his veins. A damsel in distress. She gazed at him like one of those poor defenceless cats left abandoned.

Was his decision made? Did he forgive her? Or was his lust uncontrollable?

Brodie held the nape of her neck and kissed one eyelid closed, then the other. He kissed the tip of her nose and formed a trail of feathery light touches down each side of her face, starting at her temples until his lips brushed her jaw.

Greta stumbled as if her legs turned to jelly. He caught her and was transported as she responded with her open lips on his. They tasted of the sea from her tears and were warm and soft to touch. His body responded; he wanted more of her, but he forced himself to gain control and gently pushed her back, providing them with space.

'What did you want to show me?' he asked.

She tugged on his arm, pulling him forwards until he was upstairs, in her room. 'Close your eyes.'

His body tingled, nerves alert wondering about the surprise. He ached to touch her again. Did she know? Had she forgiven him for ignoring her and being rude? The kiss indicated she had. He'd be honest with her, he'd decided and now all he wanted to do was wrap his arms around her, hold her close and breathe in the citrusy scent of her hair and feel her body against his. His body stirred at the prospect.

'Open your eyes,' she said. Two paintings leaned against the bed. He recognised the style but not the artist.

'They're beautiful. Millie would like them.' Greta nodded in agreement.

'Do you know Reginald Smart?' she asked dancing up and down on her toes.

He shook his head.

'Reginald Smart is a famous French impressionist painter,' Greta's hair whipped around her face in excitement as she spoke.

'Where were they?' he asked the question as he moved closer

to examine the name and the back to see if it revealed any information.

'One was hanging in Millie's bedroom, the other in that funny little nook off the studio.'

Now, he took a step back and examined them at arm's length. Greta continued, 'he was famous for his French scenes, landscapes and streets, but all of his adopted country. He wasn't French but lived there his entire life.'

'How do you know that?'

'I've done some basic Googling. His works are worth a fortune and the latest article I read said they can't be valued. They are only owned by galleries, and all of them in France. Excepting for the piece Millie purchased all those years ago for Australia, there isn't another Reginald Smart painting in a private collection around the world. That's unusual right?'

'I'm no expert on art history but yes, I guess so. You hear all those stories of finding long-lost paintings of dead famous artists. Picassos and Van Goughs have been found I think. But let me understand this. These two paintings were here, in the cottage?'

Greta agreed.

'Millie never mentioned that she had two Smart paintings that potentially could be worth millions?'

'Millions,' Greta whispered.

'Holy shit, Greta. This could be the greatest find this century.' He stared at them, his heart hammering in his chest. His mind ricocheted with thoughts.

Greta stood closer. She was silent as they both took in the moment.

'We need to get an expert to verify they're real. What if they're prints? Or replicas? It happens all the time, people copy famous works. That's why there are so many vases with bright yellow sunflowers. It happens.'

'Do you know anyone?'

'Nah, not really. But I can find someone. Someone we can trust. We don't want this to get out, particularly if we're wrong.'

'Okay, can you do that? I've hidden them, along with some of Millie's pieces, too, at the back of the wardrobe.'

'Wait. Is that why the door was locked? You found these yesterday?'

'Yes.'

'You understand, don't you, Greta, that you own these. They belong with the house. If they're real, you are … you are rich?'

'Let's get them back in the cupboard real quick!'

Back downstairs and over a cuppa, Brodie had spent the last twenty minutes on the telephone.

Finally, he found someone that would take them seriously. And only because of Millie. If they hadn't been found in her home, he wasn't sure anyone would have come.

'This guy has cleared his schedule. He's coming tomorrow.'

'Is he qualified, and does he think they are real?'

'More qualified than you and me.'

'I'll stay tonight.'

The nerves in her tummy dissolved and became fluttering butterflies instead. 'Thank you, I'd love that.' Suddenly, awkward, her words were stilted. Things between them had been weird. Now he was here. And staying. 'Um, I'm starving. Let's find something eat.'

Greta streamed music on her phone and skipped the slow and romantic songs. Only a short while ago, she was comfortable in Brodie's presence. Now, she thought about every word, each movement.

'Okay, there's some frozen chicken breasts.' Brodie's head was deep in the freezer. 'Chicken and salad sound okay?'

'Sounds great. I bought fresh bread this morning so we can have that as well. I'll do the salad.'

They worked companionably. Brodie hummed the words of the latest song and Greta tried not to chop her finger off with the sharp knife as she sliced the cucumber. 'Wine! We need to have a drink,' she said and extracted the bottle of Pinot Grigio she'd also purchased. She poured them both a generous glass and offered him one. Brodie tossed the chicken but paused to clink his glass with hers. She was acting like a young girl on her first date—silly and nervous.

After serving up, they retreated to the front room. It remained the most inviting spot in the cottage. The last of the dusk light entered the room creating a muted glow. The heat of the day lingered, heavy and oppressive. Brodie sat on the floor at her feet.

'Uh, let me show you something. It relates to Reginald Smart. *Reggie*,' she said in exaggeration. She leapt up and located the bundle of letters from the top shelf.

Greta tugged at the red ribbon to loosen them and a lump formed in her throat. She paused for a second, blew her fringe out of her eyes and sucked in a big breath of air.

Brodie's large hand held hers. He didn't say anything but stared deeply into her eyes. His pupils moved taking in her entire face. She appreciated that he let the silence continue rather than fill it with words of reassurance.

She'd get used to this tightening of her chest; at the thoughts of Millie that flooded her mind at the least expected and convenient of times. Would it get easier though? She didn't know.

Opening the bundle, she went to the bottom this time, wanting to ensure she read a different letter. She ate a couple of mouthfuls of chicken before commencing.

'I found this bundle of letters ages ago. Accidentally, of course, when I was looking for a book. There's other stuff in here too, important belongings to Millie that we have to protect.' She pushed her foot further under the chair and felt for the hard edges of the box. It was still there.

'Brodie, these are letters from Reggie to Millie.'

He coughed, covering his mouth from exploding chicken and salad. 'Do you mean to say that they were, what? Lovers, friends, art colleagues?'

Greta grinned, chuffed at his excitement. 'Well, they were definitely more than friends from the few letters I've read.'

'Greta. Was there a relationship between Reginald Smart and Millie?'

'To be fair, I don't know. But it appears that at least at one time, while she was in France for that summer, that they were close. Reggie's letters are definitely love letters. He adored her.'

'Okay, the two paintings are making more sense, I guess. If they were friends, it's possible he gifted them to her. She might have done likewise. But if they were lovers, it's even more likely. A love token.' Brodie was smirking now.

She placed the letter she'd opened in her lap and had some more dinner. 'Why do you think she kept it a secret?'

'She never did talk much, was pretty good at eschewing the big topics. And very good at avoiding the painful ones.' Greta considered this. So much to tell Brodie. She hadn't yet mentioned the baby, but she would. 'Yeah, I think you're right. Maybe it's the darker memories that she doesn't wish to remember. But if you read these letters, wow! These two had something going on.' Greta swooned and looked at Brodie. 'Imagine being loved like that.' They kept eye connect. 'Tell me what you think,' she whispered.

JANUARY 1971

My dearest Millie,

A deep melancholy has come over me. It's been a year now since you left France. I still don't understand why you left. I know I was becoming attached to you and it affected your art, even though you never said so. You said my art was being affected too, you scolded me for producing too many portraits of you. But I've produced other work, look at the accolades I've received since last summer. Everyone loves my latest pieces. I hear you have also done incredibly well and I am enormously proud of you. Your last exhibition was a smashing event! I keep track of your success in the papers, as much news as we receive.

However, since my last show, it's been a bumpy road for my own art. Strangely, the only thing I wanted was to focus on was my work after you left; to forge ahead. To keep producing. The events of the last year have hindered me and it has not been as expected. My muse has seemingly deserted me in my hour of need.

Perhaps it is the weather turning me sour. We are enduring a deeply cold winter. Wind that whips over the hills and chills you to the bone. Even indoors, the hearth is never dry, and I find I cannot get warm. At those times I dream of those dry and warm days you described to me in Australia. You would complain it was stifling and the paint would melt from your brush. I adore that weather. The heat provides fond memories for me of our summer together, too. And of being with you, of course.

At least the days for me will grow warmer soon. Your days will cool. Your painting productivity will increase in the cooler climes, I'm sure. Please, inspire me, dear Millie, what are you working on at the moment? Is it a new series of works? For an exhibit?

Please write. You haven't written in so long, I do hope you are well. I long to hear your news. Perhaps you can have an exhibit here in Paris and can visit me?

Reggie xx

. . .

'Urgh! I'd love to read Millie's responses to these letters. She wouldn't be all gushy, would she? I think she maybe had commitment issues.'

That didn't raise a smile in Brodie. 'She was quite emotionally compact, I guess.'

'Compact? Distant? She was always so warm to me, and to you. To others. So she wasn't frigid.'

'I also think she dealt with her emotions through painting.'

'Mmmn, like you?' Greta questioned.

'Yeah, I guess. I deal with my anger and resentment and the wrongs in the world through my art.'

'What are you angry about?'

CHAPTER 29

Greta felt the heaviness of his pause. She drew in a big intake of breath.

'In year seven my mother insisted I go to a Catholic high school. She wanted me schooled and raised in the bosom of her devout church, under its guidance and direction. I didn't care. Dad didn't either, he agreed with Mum. My sister went to the local girls' school and I went off to the local boys'. I should have cared a whole lot more. Because that commenced a year of hell for me.'

Her stomach swooped. 'No, no, no, Brodie, please don't tell me—'

He held his palm up flat and cut her off. 'No I wasn't sexually abused by the parish priest. So you can put that out of your mind.'

'You'd tell me if that was the case.'

He nodded. 'Yes, but it isn't. Does sound lame in comparison, I guess. I mean that would have been the worst thing to happen, right?' He paused, seemingly collecting his thoughts. 'There was one teacher. He was a Father and a cruel man. I entered school as this quiet rascal sort of kid who liked running amok outdoors and getting into innocent mischief. I wasn't a bad kid. Except, he, for whatever reason, didn't like me. Or the more I've thought about it over the years, maybe he liked me too much. Anyway, he subjected me to endless punishment and taunts and abuse.'

Greta reached over and clasped his hand, held it tight. 'What do you mean exactly?' Greta tasted bitterness at the back of her throat.

'Even when I was young, art was my thing. Outside of being a silly bugger. I'd draw all the time. Doodle in my book when I was supposed to be doing maths, but to me, they were never mindless sketches. They were always more; they were important. Very quickly he cottoned on that I was often lost in this other world. It started as punishment for not listening but then it became personal. He'd ridicule my drawings, destroy them and throw them away. He'd belt me and do things like hit me over the back of the head as he walked down the hallway, like a school kid. I can still feel the whack of the leather against my bare legs, bum, upper arms, everywhere and the words he'd utter while doing it: saying names to belittle me, tell me I was useless, would amount to no good.' He looked away into the distance at the darkening sky outside the windows and flinched. 'That would happen at least once a day, often more.' He turned back towards her. 'As I said, it does sound lame. Kids have suffered much worse. But when it happens on a daily basis and those messages are shoved down your throat, you believe them. As a twelve-year-old, I thought I was the most useless kid in the world. He'd say it was evil to be so frivolous and spend time drawing pictures, particularly pictures that were so bad. I should be spending my time on God's work and doing good.'

'Have you ever told anyone?'

'No.'

'Oh, Brodie, I'm so sorry. That is an unforgiveable thing to happen to a child. Children are innocent. It wasn't your fault. You know that right?'

'Of course. As an adult you learn it isn't your fault. I didn't do anything to deserve that treatment. But those voices in my head speak up at each opportunity that I'm unsure of myself. And when you do think that is? Each time I finish a painting, sometimes before I'm even finished. The words echo in my head and I find it so hard to make them stop. To turn it off, not to listen.'

'Yeah, I get it.' She dropped to the floor and sat next to him. 'Thank you for trusting me. Telling me. I know that can't have been easy. I need to say, again: it isn't your fault. That man was wrong, mean, evil. He did bad things but that doesn't mean you're bad. You are talented and clever and wonderful and kind and sexy...'

Water pooled in Brodie's eyes before tears rolled down his cheeks. Greta wiped away the moisture with her thumb and then stroked his cheek.

'The things that happened don't define me but help to explain my actions. I find it hard to believe in myself. It's when I'm most vulnerable. So when you entered those pieces without telling me, I was piping mad. More than that, I felt betrayed. That you could deliberately do something that I was so fundamentally against.'

Greta touched her fingers to the corners of his lips.

'But you were right. I would never have entered that contest. Would not have taken the risk. There's a darkness that lives within me. It isn't explosive, I would never hurt anyone ...'

'Brodie, you are the gentlest man I know. I'm more likely to hit out than you.'

'Well, yes that's true.' The beginnings of a smile tipped the corners of his mouth. Greta moved forward so she sat closer, almost touching his crossed legs.

'It's dark, but it's not evil. But that part of me drives that vehicle for change, the issues in the world that people need to know about. It craves justice. Fairness for all.'

'Is that why you like me? Am I a pet project, someone to save?'

He shook his head.

'Okay, I get it. I really do. Yours is not a beast that controls you, but there's something deep inside that drives you.'

'It feels like a beast sometimes. But it would only ever affect my feelings and emotions and thoughts. Not my actions, other than expressing myself through my work.'

She leaned in, wanting to kiss him.

'I want to kiss you now, too. But—' He held up his hand again. 'I can forgive you for entering my work without my permission. I kind of deserved that. But I understand now the true ramifications of what you did. Greta, families are suffering. Innocent victims. They have nothing left. Well, I assume they're like my parents. It was their savings. You allowed that money to be stolen. My parents are in their sixties, Greta, had planned their retirement and were looking forward to slowing down. Now, they can't. The future looks different...'

Still the urge to defend herself, but she didn't. That was the old Greta. 'Brodie. Stop. I understand. I agree. Those people haunt me every day. I am desperate to pay back every cent.'

He bowed his head. 'Yes, you've been desperate to pay it back. To stay out of jail.'

The words hung in the air.

'That was the impetuous. Not the reason. I've always vowed to repay the money. And please, don't forgive me if you can't, but it wasn't intentional or malicious.' Her voice cracked for the first time. 'My worst crime was stupidity. And I've paid dearly for it. I vow to you that those people will get their money back.'

They were standing on a precipice. She felt it. It was now or never. She'd be okay if Brodie walked away. But she'd prefer he didn't. And she'd do all she could to stop him.

Greta kissed him, her soft lips meeting his, only their mouths touching. The flush of heat that came with wanting flooded her body. Brodie responded, and she came alive with hope. The kiss became deeper and they moved closer, Greta inching forward until she was almost in his lap. In one swift movement, he cradled her bottom and lifted her until she sat on him. His muscular legs supported her, and she wrapped herself around him, felt his desire.

But she pulled back. There were still so many unsaid words. 'Brodie, I'm sorry for everything. For stealing people's money and loving Charlie. For making a monumental mistake. For your parent's situation. For Millie dying and me being such an idiot.' She leaned her forehead against his. He didn't push her away and her hope blossomed.

'You aren't an idiot. Okay, you did a dumb thing. Like choosing Charlie. But since I've known you, you haven't made poor choices. I've been frightened, angry. But you're a good person.' He arched back then so he could see her face and stare into her eyes. 'You are a good person,' he repeated, 'and bloody hot. Right now I want to be a bad person and rip all your clothes off and ravage you right here and now on the rug.'

She gave him a deep, hard closed kiss on his mouth. 'The door is locked, please be a very naughty person to me right now, Brodie Quade.'

AN ARM SNAKED AROUND HER MIDDLE, RESTING BELOW HER breasts. Her nipples went hard. She smiled, keeping her eyes shut against the brightness that permeated her bedroom. Brodie's bronzed nakedness lay next to her and she caressed her fingers up and down his back. Goose pimples formed and she spooned her body around his, relishing the feel of skin against skin.

Lazily opening one eye then the other, she said, 'You should talk to your mum. About what happened. She'd understand. Be distraught, most likely, but you should tell her. And your dad. It would help them understand you. Do you think you should see a counsellor too? Just to talk it through?'

'Good morning to you too,' he rolled over and kissed her with his sweet morning breath.

She nuzzled into his neck, feeling the tickle of his short beard. It wasn't the only thing she wanted to feel right now.

'Why haven't you told them?'

His hand rested dangerously close to her groin. 'I thought she would blame herself because she insisted on sending me to that school. And she will, won't she?'

'Probably but she still has a right to know.'

'Yeah, you're right. It needs to be out in the open. It will make sense to them. They knew something was up at the time. Coincidentally, I went off the rails. Went from being an innocent muck around, to naughty. Drinking under-age, joyriding in cars that weren't mine, petty theft, a few fights. Mum was desperate at the time to work it out. It was too fresh and real back then. But now, there's distance and maturity ...'

Greta picked up the pillow and slapped him. 'You're so mature, Brodie!'

He grabbed the pillow and pinned her in place. 'You're trapped. My prisoner.'

'Oh, I can't wait,' she giggled as his head lowered. Lola commenced barking, so loud it was like she sat next to the bed.

The walls shook indicating someone was climbing the outside stairs.

They looked at each other.

'The valuer!' Brodie leapt out of bed and raced around

finding his clothes that were strewn in each corner of the bedroom. He hopped on one foot as he placed the other into his shorts. Greta laughed and covered herself with the sheet.

'C'mon. Get up! I'll have to bring him up here.'

'Oh, yes.' At his command, she jumped up and bounced around making the bed. Brodie paused; his gaze was like red-hot pokers against her back.

The knocking on the door downstairs echoed up through the cracks in the old house.

'Argh,' he groaned and left. She laughed at his departing back.

Mr Archibald was short of stature, wore dark-rimmed glasses and a white shirt and tie. Every so often he reached up and tried, unsuccessfully to loosen the grip around his neck. Within the first fifteen minutes, Greta wanted to rip that tie from his throat.

He didn't talk much. But made lots of sounds from the depths of his throat. He asked a few questions; examined the paintings with a magnifying glass to the front and with a feather light touch at the back.

'It is my conclusion that these are original Reginal Smart works.'

He said it deadpan like they hadn't struck gold. Did he realise the implications? But of course he did.

'I will have to research the value and confer with my colleagues at the gallery, but it is likely to be excessive. My greatest concern right now is their safety. Paintings of this value should be secured in a gallery. Plus the conditions. The heat is disastrous to them. I suggest we take them for safekeeping and then we can negotiate the purchase.'

Whoa! What?

'The purchase?' she queried.

His head titled in question. 'Well, yes. These are priceless pieces of art. They simply cannot be holed up here, for a range of reasons.'

'They belong to me.' Greta folded her arms across her chest.

'Yes, they do. But as I said we can negotiate the terms of sale.'

'They aren't for sale.'

Are they? She hadn't thought this part through.

'And I see there are a number of original Millicent Osborne works as well. We would be very interested in purchasing those also. They are highly sought after now, after her ... passing.'

'They aren't for sale either.' Greta stomped her foot.

Brodie stepped between them. 'Mr Archibald, thank you for confirming what we thought to be the case. We appreciate your visit, but Greta will have to think about what she's going to do now.'

Mr Archibald looked incredulous. 'Yes, all right. I will return to the gallery and formulate an offer. You'll have it this afternoon. It will be one I'm sure you can't refuse and then we can ensure their safe passage.' He closed his briefcase and saw himself out.

As the door slammed shut, Greta released a scream, grasped Brodie's hands and together they danced in a circle.

In between rounds, Greta said, 'I thought all artists were quirky creative people. Mr Archibald doesn't fit the bill with his leather brogues and grey slacks.'

'Ah, but he's the expert, the historian, not the artiste himself. He doesn't have to have personality, just the knowledge and the power to wield the big offers, one that you won't be able to refuse.' They collapsed into more giggles. For the first time since Millie died, Greta felt lighter, freer, a semblance of hope burning within.

That didn't last. Her feet stilled and the world crashed around her. She dropped Brodie's hands. She wasn't free of burden was she? She sat down, hunched over, all the air released from her lungs.

'I need to sell them, don't I, Brodie? The money from these paintings, even just the Smart pieces will repay my entire debt.'

Suddenly, she didn't feel so excited anymore.

'Greta, you can't. These meant something to Millie. That's why she kept them. She didn't sell them and she knew their value.'

She considered his words. 'But I have an obligation. A duty. I have to do the right thing.'

'But you will, you have. You aren't reneging your responsibilities.'

'Do you understand how long it will take me to refund the money? Years. And that's with a job. A job that I currently don't have. Those people have to wait. If I did this, they wouldn't have to.' She held her head in her hands, covered her eyes.

Brodie's mobile rang. He moved aside and spoke to his mother. 'Sure, Mum, I'll come right away.'

He cradled her head with his large hands. 'Mum needs me to fix a leaky tap and Dad's away in town. I'll come back later, okay?' He tilted her head up to gaze at him. 'Don't make any rash decisions. Let's talk more when I get back. And, lock the door.' He kissed her.

God, she loved those lips.

CHAPTER 30

Greta ruminated; thoughts slammed into each other.

Choices. Decisions. Life. Death. She could do this; she could do that.

Lola whined at the foot of the bed and she leaned over and picked up the little dog and they snuggled in together. Mother cat joined in but the now-grown kittens were too rambunctious to stay still. Greta gave Lola a big cuddle. Since Millie's death, she'd wandered the cottage, into each room, rubbing herself against the corners of walls and mewling, searching for her beloved master. Sort of how Greta felt, too.

Now, Greta had an urge to be in Millie's studio, surrounded by her and her belongings. She pushed the animals aside and rose, collected Millie's paintings from the back of the wardrobe and went downstairs. She placed one delicately on Millie's easel, in front of her painting chair, the other on the ground. Zooming into the front room she retrieved the box of baby things and the bundle of love letters. They joined in amongst the other stuff in the ramshackle room where everything remained untouched.

Looking around her, damn, she wanted the Smart paintings too. Needed everything in front of her.

Since realising their value, she'd been reluctant to touch them. One scratch or a sweaty finger smudge could slice off a million dollars.

Ouch.

Nonetheless she made two more trips up and down the stairs.

Lola followed her into the studio.

One thing became alarmingly clear to Greta, if she stayed at *Banyan Creek*, this room had too as well. It couldn't be dismantled, that would be like burying Millie all over again. This room was her aunt. It represented who she was and everything that was important to her. But how could she live in this house with the studio right smack in the middle? The mess, the smell…

Did she want to? Was she entertaining thoughts of staying?

Yes. Yes, she was.

She stood in the studio and listened. Crystal clear clarity hit her. Yes, she would stay, live in this house. Brodie would continue to use the rooms for his own painting workshop and she would, she would, she didn't know. It was as if Millie was channelling her and soon enough the answer would become clear.

Her heart raced erratically as the adrenalin kicked in. That will teach her for not stopping for a coffee on her return from *Beach Haven*. An image of a shiny new coffee machine installed in the kitchen came to mind. She bounced Lola up and down in her arms. She needed a drink. Not coffee. Greta checked her watch. Yes, it was a respectable time to enjoy an icy cold white wine. Unlike before, the fridge was now regularly stocked with the staples, of alcohol that is. Back on the floor, Lola went to a secluded spot in the corner and curled up on a dirty old painting cloth that probably smelled of her aunt, and hopefully not, of nasty chemicals.

Returning with her wine in one hand, Greta sat on the floor next to Lola.

Greta was now the owner of a home and significant assets. But of course, none of them realised, so no cash and no income. The sounds of talkback radio blared into the room from the kitchen. Oh, sheesh, she'd have to change the channel. But it captured her attention for a moment as the dominating and deep male voice droned on. The announcer interviewed the widow of a recently deceased singer. A famous name she recognised.

Obviously, she'd been living in her own bubble and hadn't realised he'd died. Suspected drug overdose, another talented person gone too soon was the gist of the interview. The widower said she would do everything in her power to have him remembered.

That would be easy, Greta assumed. His songs would continue to play on the radio and his admirers would download or depending on their age, play their CDs at home. But it did raise an interesting question – how do we remember someone? Comparisons were made to Elvis Presley and his legacy. His home open to tourists, his image reproduced, events held in his honour. Those terrible movies played over and over.

Millie's artwork hung in galleries around the world and she hoped they'd continue to display them. Was there a time limitation on such things? Like when a new, mega talented artist was discovered, would Millie lose her wall space? Be relegated to the back storeroom? Surely not, but Greta didn't know about such things. The likes of Sidney Nolan, Arthur Streeton and Russel Drysdale, they were not forgotten, and people still flocked to see their works. Van Gough had his own museum in Amsterdam. The *Musee D'Orsay* was devoted to Impressionists. Relatives of famous people came out with snippets of hidden history and interest was maintained in the secret aspects of their lives. Long-lost relatives were often discovered.

Museum.
Gallery.
Café.
Shop.
Oh Lord! She had it. Could she pull it off? She downed the remainder of the Chardonnay as she thought about it.

BRODIE COUNTED THE MINUTES UNTIL HE COULD RETURN TO Greta. It was a strange sensation, the feeling he'd had since he'd left her side. A flutter in his chest that kept it tight. It was like a wild bird thrashed about in there. It was also a propulsion to keep moving forward. A sense of jitteriness. Was this love? Is this what it felt like to be connected to someone? He hadn't yet made the commitment to Greta, but he would. He couldn't bear being separated from her. He listened to his mother, fixed her leaky tap but the whole time this crazy city girl filled his head. But she wasn't a crazy city girl anymore. Like a young pup, he was an excited bundle of energy. Finished, he headed to his mobile home and passed Skye as she tendered to a flower-box garden she'd created. The colours were brilliant; she'd made a home in that caravan.

Brodie grabbed some clean clothes because he didn't anticipate returning anytime soon. Mail sat on the small Formica table and he snatched it up and ripped open the envelope—an official one with the windowpane in the front. Acknowledgement for his entry into the art prize. Geez, his heart had sped up there for a moment. God, how stupid, did he really imagine he could win or even shortlist? Anyway, one step at a time.

The cottage was lit up by the time he arrived. A pine scent hit his nose as he entered. He followed the Christmas carol tunes playing.

'Hi there,' he said before kissing the nape of her neck.

'Hi,' she said back before they kissed again.

'You've been busy,' he commented as he stepped around streams of tinsel and Christmas decorations.

'I found these in the spare room and I had a tree delivered. Come and see.' She wove her fingers through his and lead him back to the deck. An enormous pine tree sat at the far end.

'I've never had my own tree before. In the apartment these last few years, we didn't bother. I bought one of those pretentious small plastic white ones and decorated it with a few sparse blue glittery baubles.' Greta eyes held a faraway gaze, remembering other times and places, then she grounded herself back to where she was. 'The man took pity on me. Who knew Christmas trees were so pricey? When he saw the look on my face at the amount and then realised I'm Millie's niece, he let me have this one.'

Brodie looked at the tree in the better light. It leaned to the left and had a bare patch bereft of pine needles on a section near the bottom. A reject. It seemed like they both liked saving things.

But,' Greta squealed, 'it's only a few weeks to Christmas. And I want to decorate and get in the spirit.'

He paused. 'So, you're staying then?'

'Yes, I'm staying. And I have a plan. I hope you don't think it's stupid.'

His heart did an unexpected leap and he stopped listening after the words *staying*. Greta was staying. Brodie drew her in close, held her too tight. But then he realised he didn't have to, she was here and always would be. His Christmas had already arrived.

'But, let's talk about that later. Let's decorate. Will you help me haul the tree in? It's rather tall.'

She stared at him with those large chocolate eyes. Those eyes he easily got lost in. 'I'm glad you're staying.' His voice was low, husky. 'I want you to stay and for us to be together.'

'Yes, me too, more than anything,' she said before his lips were on hers once more.

As he drew back, he took in the size of the tree and laughed. 'Yeah, it's bulky. You know what, this is going to be fun. I can't recall decorating a tree since I was small. We'd all gather around on the first of December and fight over where the baubles went and of course, who placed the star on top.'

'And, who did?' she asked.

'My mother was diplomatic, dad always did it.'

'We had an angel that was way too heavy and made the top of the tree droop, but my mother refused to buy a new one.'

As they positioned the tree in the front room—that was the only spot for it—Greta said, 'Given your mother is quite religious, I'm surprised she had a good old commercial plastic tree.'

'Yeah, that part was for us, the kids. For her it was all about worshipping. The Catholics have Christmas Eve mass, so for years we'd go to bed early and be woken at eleven p.m. for a snack and then dress for church.'

'She still goes?'

'Yes.'

'When was the last time you went?'

'The year before I started high school. It caused a hell of a scene when I steadfastly refused to go the following year. They cajoled, and then tried to punish me, but there was no chance in hell I was going to church to show devotion to God, the same deity the Father worshipped. I decided then and there, there was no God because if there was, he would not have allowed that man to treat me like that. The Father would have been there too, at the church, it was the same parish.'

Greta nodded, solemn.

'Over the years we've all dropped off, so Mum's had no choice but to accept it.'

'Even your dad?'

'Yep, she is the only remaining believer.' He chuckled but didn't find it remotely amusing.

'Did you talk to her?'

'No. I thought about it, but it didn't feel right.' He reached over and clasped her lower forearm. 'But I will, I promise. Promise myself,' he said.

'Well let's get into the spirit of a non-religious, very commercial Christmas. But we do have a real tree, so that counts for something,' she said.

'It does,' he agreed. 'It adds authenticity.'

'Will we fight over the Christmas star?' Greta giggled.

'Nah, let's do it together.' And as cheesy as it sounded, Brodie thought that that was how they would do things into the future. A joint team effort.

'Oh, I forgot to tell you. I received an email from Mr Archibald.' Greta placed the sleigh on a tree bough and reached for her phone. 'Read this.' She handed him the phone.

'Is this for real?' Brodie pulled the screen closer to his face.

'Uh huh, can you believe it?'

'No, I can't.'

Greta turned the carols louder and the animals hid in the corner under the couch while they finished decorating the tree.

CHAPTER 31

'What do you think?'

Greta's stomach crunched into a tightly strung coil of knots. A sea of eyes stared back at her. Brodie's hand rested on her knee.

She hadn't been this nervous since she waited in the dock for her prison sentence to be handed down.

Her mother spoke first. 'After all you've been through, are you sure you're up to this?'

Her father's head remained bowed, scribbling in his notebook.

Niamh jumped in. 'It's a fabulous idea! What a legacy! You two are going to make a great team.'

'Guess it's as close as Brodie is ever going to get to a real job.' Henry said it with a smile and slapped Brodie on the back.

Grace, Niamh and Henry all talked over one another as her father spoke. Greta strained to hear him.

'This is a fantastic business opportunity. Of course, there are many things to think about: zoning permissions, renovations, business licences, food and beverage grants, logistics, marketing, advertising and most importantly, security.' Her father paused, looked up and caught her gaze. 'Greta, this could be amazing.' He cracked his first smile and she relaxed.

'Well, we know it's a big task but that's why we gathered you here. To help guide us and make sure it isn't a hare-brained idea.'

'I had no concept her artwork was that valuable,' her mother added.

Greta pounced on her. 'Yes, you did. You just never wanted to believe it.'

Grace shrunk back into the chair.

'Will you handle the legalities, Dad?'

'Of course, I'd love to be involved. And at no cost. I will make it a donation. Depending on the status of the venture, might be a charity, not-for-profit or simply a business. That's something I'll think about.'

Greta jumped out of her seat and hugged her father from behind. 'Dad! That's awesome. Thank you. I'm worried about the cost of setup. It's ironic isn't it, given the value of the work I've hidden in the bedroom,' she whispered those last few words as if people might hear. 'You'll liaise with Mr Porter, the solicitor who administered the estate? If you need to, that is.'

'Yes, darling. He can be the man on the ground.'

'How did you two come up with this idea?' Henry asked.

Brodie jumped in then. 'It was Greta's idea and I can't take credit. And it's important moving forward, Mr Johnson, that you understand, this is Greta's business. I'll be involved in any way possible, but she is the owner-operator so to speak.'

Her dad gave a curt nod but didn't disagree. Her dad would always have her back.

'But Brodie remains working out of the building, has his studio and produces his works that will go into the private gallery.

They'll be available for purchase and we'll have an online shop as well. But however we choose to set it up, there'll be another space, for the Smart paintings and the last few of Millie. They are only on display and not for sale. So Brodie will keep his earnings from selling his work.'

Her father frowned, 'But he'll rent the space?'

'I'm not sure, Dad, not officially. I don't want to charge him rent!'

'Okay, no, I understand, but for business and tax purposes it might be best to have an agreement in place. There are many ways to work it out. Lots of thinking to do.' Matthew loved a challenge, particularly a legal one.

Henry was caught up in the excitement too. 'Let me get my old head around this before we discuss too many fine details. You own this land, Greta, and house. In the house are two incredibly valuable paintings by a French artist, if I forget later, can you please tell me how that is even possible, and then there are some paintings left behind by Millie. You are going to develop a gallery with those works including our Brodie here, plus there will be a café, gift shop, Brodie's workspace and a museum. Is that right?'

It sounded like an impossible venture when summarised like that. 'Yes. The gallery part is straightforward. The café is for me so I can buy an espresso coffee machine as a tax deduction.' The room erupted in laughter. 'But more seriously, I'm imagining that if people travel here, it is a place to go. A journey. So when they arrive they might want a coffee before they look around, or alternatively, will be hungry once they've finished. It's pretty hot here in summer, so even to enjoy a cool drink after working their way through the exhibits.'

Everyone nodded. She assumed they thought it was a good idea.

'And the museum, what's that, Greta?' Grace's tone had softened.

'Well, that's a grand idea, I guess. Millie is one of our country's finest artists but no one knows much about her. She was incredibly private and only told people what she wanted them to know. So the idea started with her studio because I can't destroy that room. It feels like a betrayal, or more, like we would be removing something sacred. So, my thoughts were, it would be like a shrine to her and her work. But then, there are many objects in this house that represent Millie and secrets, too.' She paused, wanting those words to sink in.

'It creates a dilemma. She kept her private life private. Do I have a right after her death to advertise her personal life to the world?'

'What sort of secrets are we talking?' her father asked.

'I'm not one hundred percent sure, but there was definitely a relationship between Reginald Smart and Millie during the summer she spent in France in 1969. It could have been a friendship, but I don't believe that. I think they were deeply in love. To explain Henry, I'm assuming Millie was gifted these painting as tokens of love. The scenes are images that Millie talked about loving and also, there's a stack of letters from Reginald Smart to Millie that I've discovered. Love letters. And there is reference to Millie adoring his Paris paintings, especially those of the cobble-laneways. Plus she spent time in a seaside village, and I think the second painting is a homage to that.'

'Love letters! But Millie loved nothing but her art!' her mother's voice had taken on a tone of hysteria.

'But Mum, there is more. Remember the baby I asked you about? It was hers. Millie had a baby in 1970. A baby who died shortly after she was born.'

'Oh!' her mother covered her open mouth with her hand. No one spoke.

Greta waited a heartbeat.

'So the long answer to the original question is I want to create a little bit of history about Millie. Even if we reveal her child-hood, Mum you can help with that, her passion for her art and what she did throughout her life. I don't want to shock with long-held secrets, but public is interested in her.'

'They are,' her father agreed. 'And now is the time to strike from a business perspective.'

'But Dad, there is one problem I can't think of a solution to.' Her father put down his pen. 'I need to significantly renovate. We've tinkered with some plans and it's a bit of reno and new development. How do I fund that? Can I borrow money against the value of the paintings?'

Even as she said the words, Greta knew she could never obtain a loan. Who in their right mind would take the risk?

'That is a problem—'

Brodie interrupted. 'I can borrow under my name.'

'Son, you don't have any collateral. You need property against which to secure a loan,' Henry said.

Greta saw her father's brain ticking over.

Henry coughed. 'Greta, Brodie, we'd like to invest our funds from Millie into this venture. It's significant sum and will allow you to undertake the renovations.'

Simultaneously Brodie and Greta said no. Unacceptable. No way. Not going to happen. It's for your retirement.

'Would you prefer we made alternative financial investments where other people benefit instead of you?

Greta looked at Brodie, he stared at her and then back to his father.

'Dad.' Brodie said in his serious adult voice.

'We can enter into a formal arrangement, either by way of contract for loan or they take a percentage of the ownership and operation of the business and therefore get a return. It's like investing in a company. No different,' Matthew commented

Greta squealed. 'Are you serious? You'll let us borrow those funds to develop the site?'

Niamh and Henry nodded. Jumping out of her chair so quickly it fell backwards against the floor, she hugged them both so hard they gasped for air. 'That's so kind. I can't thank you enough.'

Brodie nodded his head towards his parents, his eyes misty.

'Mum, Niamh, will you help me work out the café and gift shop. I want postcards. Niamh, you may not be aware but Millie was obsessed with postcards. She bought them from every place she visited. Said they had to be prints or replicas of painting scenes most of the time. I'll keep her collection as part of the museum, but I want to sell them in the shop.' Her mother's eyes clouded. It must be sad, Greta realised, to know nothing much about her only sister. 'Mum, you can help with this aspect. It's important to develop her paintings into postcards and prints. They sell like hotcakes at galleries, everyone wants to take home a piece of their favourite art but I don't know how to go about that, can you help?'

Grace offered a weak smile. 'I'd love to.' She stood. 'I'll put the kettle on.'

Henry and Brodie chatted detail. Niamh jumped up to assist Grace.

'Dad, I need to make enough to pay off my debt and as quickly as possible.'

'I know, sweetie. You have to be realistic, it'll be hard at first. No one makes a squillion on their first day in business. It's usually a slow burn.'

'Turn on the news,' her mother shrieked from the kitchen.

No one reacted but Grace raced out and turned on the television. Breaking news flash crossed the screen.

Reginald Smart paintings found in desolate old cottage in the hinterland.
'Hey,' Greta voiced, 'that's not fair!'

The voice over continued with images of the beach at Bronte Bay and derelict houses God-knows-where being flashed onto the TV. Not Millie's house, thank goodness.

It is a story that gives us all hope. That one day we might find a valuable gem hidden away in our own attic, only to be discovered as a famous old artefact and worth millions.

For one lucky resident of the NSW hinterland, this is exactly the story they've got to tell. Two paintings have been found after the owner, reportedly an artist of some repute, died. One hung in her bedroom and the other, tucked away in an unused room. It was not until the owner's death that the relative who inherited the home uncovered the finds. Experts from the Gallery of NSW have examined the work and confirm that they are authentic, Reginald Smart, circa 1970s.

'I think they've got the timing a bit wrong,' Greta commented.

The first, a scene of a famous Parisienne street, is thought to form part of a limited edition collection produced around this time and made famous by Smart. All other pieces in this particular series remain owned by the galleries of France. It was thought there were only ten paintings in total; it seems everyone was wrong.

The second is a lesser-known scene of a harbour on the coast of France. Experts are still trying to determine the exact location. Whilst it is in signature Smart style, it hasn't yet been attributed to any one collection. Standalone or not, both are rumoured to be valued in the millions. And the spokesperson at the gallery said they were in talks with the current owners to acquire them for their collection as soon as possible.

One thing is certain—the art world is abuzz tonight with the revelation of more famous art works being discovered. It seems that everyone can hold out hope that perhaps, the forgotten acrylic in the kitchen might just be a long-lost relic.

'That bastard. Archibald must have leaked the story. He is the only person outside of this room who knows of the paintings,' Brodie said.

'Bastard,' she agreed. 'Isn't he subject to some cone of silence or something?' she muttered.

'That might well be the case, Greta, but you have bigger problems now,' her mother addressed her father. 'Doesn't she, Matthew? The world knows. They didn't provide the address, but astute people can join the dots, surely?'

'Yes, I agree, Grace. Security, Greta. That's the issue. You have millions of dollars' worth of paintings, currently stored in the house. I suggest two things, a news release confirming the facts and circumstances and a statement advising that they are being kept in safety under lock and key at the gallery — '

'Are you suggesting I put them in the gallery, like on a loan. How do I get them back?' she interrupted her father.

He put up his hand, signalling that he hadn't finished. 'No, I'm not suggesting that. I'm saying you tell the public that is what you've done to ensure people don't start sniffing around here. As a matter of urgency we have to get a safe, large enough to store them, the best we can find and build it, have it delivered, whatever. We can make it a bunker, it doesn't matter as long as the paintings are unable to be found.'

'Today?'

'Today,' he confirmed.

'Right, let's get onto it. Henry, we'll need to call on that investment *tout suite* to get things moving.' Chairs lifted, cups rattled in their saucers, last bites of food taken.

'Greta, if you're smart and you are, this is the perfect time to advise that the paintings will feature in a new gallery providing never-before seen Osborne pieces alongside a history of her life. A picture-perfect gallery with museum and shop nestled in the original home of Osborne in the hinterland and open for operation sometime next year.'

'Brilliant,' offered Henry.

'So clever, Matthew,' said her mother.

Niamh nodded.

'You're incredible, Dad. So we're marketing already?'

'People will want to know more. Why not give it to them, in teaspoon doses and attract interest now while the topic is hot.'

Far out. This was really happening. Her body was all a tingle and her mind raced. So much to do. One step at a time.

CHAPTER 32

'You know what?' she asked Brodie as she leaned over and kissed him, wearing only her underwear. It was stifling in the van with its tin roof and cooler not to wear too many clothes. Brodie lay on the bed in the caravan they'd shifted onto the site at Millie's while work commenced.

'What?' he asked in between feeling her near-naked bottom and returning her kiss.

'I quite enjoy living in this miniature van with you. It's cosy, isn't it?'

'Would have been even cosier if you'd insisted on keeping the tree,' he chuckled and pulled her on top of him.

'Well, lucky we have the tinsel,' and she held up a green piece that spanned the van before she laid back, her hand landing on something. 'What's this?' She held up the cream envelope.

'Oh, the mail came earlier and is addressed to you.'

Greta flicked it over, prepared to open it later but she spied an airmail stamp on front so turned it back to check the return address. 'It's from France!' She moved off Brodie and sat next to him, propping herself against the wall of the van.

She ripped it open and scanned the contents.

'Oh my God. You are not going to believe this. This is a letter from,' her eyes roamed to the bottom of the page for the name, 'Angelique and she says she is a descendant of Reginald Smart.'

'Does she want the paintings?' Brodie asked.

Greta sat up taller. 'No, she can't, ownership isn't disputed is it? They're mine. She might be asking for them to be donated or something like that. Deliver them back to France, maybe?' She swatted him with the letter. 'Let me read on and find out.'

It was with such excitement that we heard on the news that two of my great-uncle's paintings had been found in Australia. So far away from home! To explain, my great-grandmother was his sister and her name was Amelie and she managed the Estate after his death. She was some years younger than him. Quite an unusual state of affairs back then, usually a man's job, I'm told! Amelie was my grandfather's mother. Over the years we've all taken a great interest in the history of our uncle's work and his lasting legacy. My mother is currently responsible for the business of the Estate and his work. Quite a job for someone so famous. As an art history buff and amateur painter myself, I, too, take great interest.

So, I hope you can understand why we are fascinated to hear of this discovery. We would love to know more. The news told us such very little. But we are daring to be excited!

There was a tiny mystery that we never uncovered when my uncle was alive and the plot has thickened over the years after his death and since. A puzzle we have been unable to solve. And perhaps now we can.

'How funny! What is she on about?' Greta tucked her legs up under herself.

Our uncle spoke of unrequited love. Of a love found and lost.

Greta couldn't help but shake her legs up and down in excitement, anticipating what she hoped was coming.

Uncle Reggie never married. My great-grandmother revealed a time in the early seventies where he grew quite melancholy and grumpy. But more seriously, he isolated himself and became more eccentric, if that is possible for a painter. However, it is known as one of his most productive times as an artist. He told his sister very little but enough that it was over a woman who had left him. He never spoke of it again, and everyone assumed he would find another love. He didn't. Reggie remained enamoured with Australia and none of us could ever work out why. Not long before his death, he again spoke of Australia and of his lost love. He talked of her and called her Millicent. After his death we tried to find her, but failed as we had no information. It was impossible.

We wonder – is there a link? Were the paintings owned by Millicent? Is this lady our uncle's long-lost love?

Greta jumped up squealing and danced on the spot. 'Oh my gosh, can you believe this! It's incredible. They knew of Millie, we learned of Reggie. What happened between those two? I have to write back, we need to piece it together and solve this puzzle. I'm going to write now, give her my details, maybe we can skype or email. It'll be so much easier and faster.'

'That's brilliant news,' Brodie agreed. 'Who'd have thought Millie would have left us with such intrigue, secretive old thing she was. That's awesome,' he said and kissed her on the cheek. 'I'll leave you to write your letter and I'll go check out the site and see what's happened today. The concrete was meant to be poured.'

Greta settled herself at the table and wrote back to Angelique.

THE CACOPHONY OF NOISE IN THE QUADE FAMILY LIVING ROOM WAS deafening. Greta could not help but compare it to her civilised family Christmas gatherings. Her parents and siblings never spoke over the top of each other and during present giving, everyone waited until the present was unwrapped and admired before the next was gifted. Her mother collected the discarded wrappings before the rubbish had time to hit the floor, their antique oak table gleamed with silver you could see your reflection in with cotton napkins and the special festive-themed crockery that only came out once a year.

And they never invited anyone who wasn't family. Greta smiled at Skye who looked as overwhelmed as she felt.

Funny, she'd never questioned her family Christmas before. Here, the youngest grandchildren tore through the living area screaming; everyone spoke at once so that Greta could not keep up with any conversations; the barbeque smoked unattended outside and the pile of opened gifts was so big another two families were surely joining them. She wondered how Millie used to spend her Christmas. Except in her earliest memories Greta couldn't recall her aunt at their get-togethers. They would have seemed so demure to someone so full of life.

'This is for you,' Brodie sat next to her and handed her a rectangular wrapped present with a white bow. With him so close to her, the room suddenly became starved of air and the noise, so penetrating only moments ago, faded away.

'Hey, that's not fair. We said no gifts and I stuck to it.' She'd had no choice. Her bank account was dwindling in fast proportions.

"I know. And I didn't buy you something, so it's sorta fair.'

'No, it's not!' she insisted. 'I don't have any skills to make you a present.'

'I'm sure you can make it up to me in other ways,' his smouldering eyes bore down deep inside of her.

'Okay, I guess I can.'

As she ripped the wrapping, the room quietened. She hadn't received any gifts this morning and was surprised at how excited she felt. Her mother had telephoned and said a package was on its way, but it hadn't arrived in the last mail delivery yesterday. She slowed her fingers savouring the anticipation.

'C'mon, Greta, hurry up. Tear the paper,' Brodie's nephew yelled, standing right in front of her, blocking everyone else's view. Leonie placed gentle hands on his little shoulders and steered him away to be distracted by the plethora of new toys spread around the lounge.

The present was heavy, solid and yet small. Inside the last of the wrapping was a layer of tissue paper. Undoing that layer, the object was upside down and she turned it over.

'Oh my gosh.' Tears sprang into her eyes. Joyful pinks and maroons jumped off the postcard size portrait of Millie. It captured her perfectly in his signature style. Sweeping broad strokes even on the five by seven-inch card so that colour carried into each corner. Excepting the centre of her face, white spaces were left between her features – the nose, eyes and mouth. Brodie had painted this for her. She would forever have this image and she would treasure it. And, add it to Millie's collection of postcards that she now treasured as her own.

Her eyes watered and she avoided looking at him out of fear they'd become sobs. He hugged her tight and before she knew it, a human pyramid of hands and arms surrounded her. They held tight for too long and she fought to breathe; at least that distracted her from the crying.

'Oh, Brodie, that is beautiful,' his sister cried when they released her. 'He must really like you, Greta, he never paints for anyone else.'

'I've given Mum a painting before. Fourth grade, self-portrait. It still hangs in her bedroom.'

'Seriously, bro, that is good,' Derek piped up. 'I can't remember seeing something you've done before.'

'That's because you never pay attention.' His mother swiped Derek across the head, mussing his hair. Niamh took it from Greta's hands and held it with great care. Greta watched her consider it, properly, not brush over it like the others. It was like she examined each shape, line, dot. Her eyes misted over.

'It is beautiful. A striking resemblance to Millie and such a special thing to do for Greta.' The smile she offered him lit up the room. Brodie's chest puffed out and he sat taller. Greta had met his number one fan. It reminded her she must check with him to see if he'd spoken to his mum. His mother adored him; she would understand and want to help.

Skye smiled. Niamh had ensured she had a gift too, an old record player with some LPs of opera. It was perfect.

As quickly as the gift had created a quieter scene, everyone resumed their rambunctious behaviour.

'Lunch is ready!' Niamh announced. Little legs sprinted for the best spot at the table, adults cleared away dishes with leftover nibbles and glasses, poured more drinks.

Brodie helped Greta to her feet and she hugged him again, as if he provided her a lifeline. She was beginning to think he did. 'Thank you,' she whispered.

He kissed her in response.

'Brodie, son, this came for you in the mail a couple of days ago. I left it here to remind myself to give it to you. Looks official,' Henry said.

The two of them wandered into the dining room and claimed the only space left sitting on the piano stool at the corner of the table. Greta noticed Skye snagged one of the best seats.

Brodie picked up the envelope and turned it over. His face drained of colour. Greta stood a little closer. Bad news on Christmas Day? With speed, he ripped it open, pulled out the letter so that its corners got stuck. Once out, he held it in his forefingers and read.

'Holy shit.' It was faint but audible

'Holy shit,' little Thomas copied.

'Brodie! Thomas! That's enough,' Niamh admonished.

Greta waited for him to speak.

'I'm shortlisted in *The Olley Art Prize.*'

The chorus of 'what's that' sang out.

He looked at Greta, held her gaze before he spoke. It felt like her eyes were in her forehead they were opened so wide.

'It's a portrait competition and one of the most prestigious annual art prizes in the country. I spontaneously decided to enter. Millie saw the painting before she died and said it was the best work I'd ever done. She said it was pretty.' Brodie paused, smiled at the memory.

Greta's lips turned upwards, slowly at first, but then realisation dawned.

'Brodie! Is this for real?' and she stole the letter and read for herself. 'Millie has never won that prize. It's, it's so, well, one of the top contests. Sought after.' She jumped up and down. The family realised it was big news and got out of their chairs and made double the noise of before.

'Okay, okay. I haven't won. I'm shortlisted.'

'Yes, but you're the guy who won't even let his own family see his work. Who won't enter anything for fear of others hating it. This is incredible!' Greta said.

It was Skye who asked. 'But who's the portrait of?'

The room went silent.

Brodie gazed at his feet, shuffled one shoe back and forth; glanced up and looked around until his focus turned back onto her.

'It's a portrait of Greta.'

TWELVE MONTHS LATER

Brodie avoided Greta's eye as he slid the cloth off the framed painting. It was no longer a canvas; no longer a piece in progress; no longer a painting he hoped someone might admire. It was a prize winner. *The Olley Portrait Prize* winner to be exact. It had been framed specially since its win. The gilded frame made it even more important; made it real and special.

Keeping his back to her, he carefully curled the fabric over the corners, making sure it didn't catch. He'd spent ages this morning hanging it just right. The most appropriate wall, the perfect spot on the space; the right height. With the new *Millicent Osborne Gallery and Museum* ready to open, it was a test run for the special and expensive lighting and temperature control they'd had installed. Like any gallery, it was set to freezing and even he rubbed his hands over his arms to gather warmth anytime he was inside.

'Will you hurry up!'

He knew her patience would run out.

With a dramatic flourish, he let it fall. Brodie had not let Greta come to the special ceremony when he was awarded the prize. He'd tried desperately in the few short months since to keep her away from media articles and news. It had been hard work, but worth it. This moment had to be special.

Greta's hands flew to her mouth, covering its round 'O' shape.

'I'm speechless,' she said.

He stood at her shoulder, letting her absorb it. 'Wow, that'd be a first. I hope it's in a good way. Not in the way you want to shout expletives at me because you hate it so much.'

Greta dropped her hands and took two steps closer. 'It's in a similar style to the portrait of Millie you did for me.'

'Yep,' he nodded. 'Still my style, though, but it looks different with those colours. Bright colours might do that instead of severe black and grey. Much easier to have those broad, sweeping strokes with a larger picture, too.'

Unlike the postcard of Millie, this was large. The canvas inside the frame was over two metres in width and height and adding the frame, it was luminous.

'You've stuck with the pink shades as well.'

'Yes, well, I did this one first and those same colours seemed to suit Millie. They are definitely your colours. No red hat for you though.'

'But of course, you've kept my hair black and that fringe. Boy, it makes a statement,' Greta laughed.

'Your midnight hair and that blunt fringe define your features. A lot less face to detail as well when your hair covers your forehead.'

'It's striking,' she said.

'You're striking.' He reached across and took her hand in his, caressing the top of it with his thumb.

'I'm not sure I'll ever get used to seeing myself up there gazing back, looking all intelligent-like. People will think I'm smart.'

'You are smart. I've painted you as I see you.'

He watched her stare hard into her own face.

'You've captured that vulnerability, the uncertainty I try so hard to hide in my eyes. I can see it.'

He cuddled her from the side, his arms around her waist. 'It's part of you, it needs to be there. And it's part of what makes the painting great. It's meant to be an accurate reflection, but also my reflection. When others look at you, I'm sure they see the confident young woman that you are. All brash and bold.'

'Hardly,' she said. 'I'm so grateful, though, you showed me first without it being unveiled at the official ceremony.'

'Yeah, me too. This painting is for you, Greta. For making me get off my arse, for seeing what I couldn't see, or I guess, making me realise what I could see but didn't want to admit. Of course, this painting was an easy option to start with, as Millie would say, this isn't confrontational or ugly or uncomfortable. It's beautiful, so people shouldn't shun it. But despite that, I have learned to have faith, to trust myself. I can create beautiful pieces as well as making statements.'

'You sure can.' Greta waved her arm around the space. 'My portrait is what, only one or two of the beautiful pieces,' she said. 'The rest are ...' She didn't finish.

'I guess I still have a lot to say.'

The small gallery room off the main floor space where the other colourful paintings hung on white walls was in stark contrast to Brodie's dark blacks and slate-grey with some splotches of army green.

'Man, you sure do. But why would it be any other way? It's incredible, Brodie. You've created all of these in the last twelve months. You've come from being afraid to show your work, to having an entire gallery filled with it. How do you feel standing in here?'

'I thought for real, I would hate it. But I don't. It feels strange, surreal that these are mine. More so, that this room is for me and my stuff.' He laughed, a funny sort of uncomfortable chuckle. 'I am slightly worried that they'll all still be hanging here in another twelve months because no one will buy them, but hey.' He shrugged.

'I get it. But don't worry. The critics love you and are scrambling for your work. Remember, it's not going to be the locals purchasing your art at these prices.'

He nodded. 'I know. It'd be great for Millie to see it, right?'

'Yes. At least I can talk about her without crying now. But that might not go so well when we open tomorrow. Talking of which, we still have heaps to do. We'd better get back to it. But thank you. It's special having someone paint you in such a flattering light and then to win a prize with it. I know it was never part of the plan, but honestly, winning that prize has garnered huge interest in this place. You know that, don't you? Our success could all be down to you.'

'Nope, doubt that. I'm sure it's helped, but it's also the hard work you've put in. Plus the fact that we have two original Reginald Smart paintings and a few of Millie's that no one else has ever seen.'

'Plus, the museum. What time did Angelique say she was arriving?'

''bout 4 I think.'

Greta rattled off the list of chores she had to complete before she arrived. They'd down tools then and give her a private tour and talk, most-likely nonstop about Millie and Reggie and the past. Greta raced away.

He knew it was her dream, this place. Her idea. Of course, he'd been on board and had loved the concept. But he stood now, for a few more moments relishing the fact that he was in the middle of a room of work he'd created. All him. And it was for sale. People might actually buy some and he could eventually, one day, hope to live off his own income as an artist and not the bursary Millie left him. Thank God, she had though. It had kept both of them afloat these past twelve months.

It had been blood, sweat and tears to use the colloquial saying, and he could still feel the cool, wet surface of his skin and the smell of acrylic and turps still hung in the air, it was that recent, but it was a pinch-me moment that he didn't think he'd ever forget.

Could he have done it without Greta? He didn't think so.

THE FRENCH ACCENT MADE EVERY WORD OF ANGELIQUE'S SOUND exotic and Greta found herself staring stupidly at the woman when she spoke.

Together with her unfailing elegance in clothes and grooming especially in the blazing heat, Greta determined that France was a place she had to visit. Mixed in with Millie's love for the country, a trip had to be in her future. Once her debt was paid.

It was official. All three of them agreed that there must have been a stormy—that was Greta's word—relationship between Reggie and Millie during the European summer of 1969. Angelique preferred the words *love affair*, as she'd poured over the letters, clutching at her chest and covering her heart as she did so. Greta had jabbed Brodie with her elbow because she had clutched at her heart when she'd read them, too, therefore she commenced calling herself half-French.

She wished.

That elegance would forever escape her. But not long ago she recalled wearing trousers with frilled blouses and stiletto heels. A past life. She reminded herself to straighten her hair tomorrow for the opening.

'You know much more that we do. My grandmother says that

as he aged, Reggie talked more of Millicent. He called her by her full name, even though I notice he calls her Millie in these letters. My grandmother reports that he spoke with great pain, as if he was reliving the agony of their parting. It was quite distressing for her. And then, of course, after his tragic death, and sorting out his belongings we found a collection of sketches, all of one woman. We guessed, we hoped it was his beloved Millicent.'

'I'm sorry to bombard you with news, but I also found these.' Greta had kept the baby things in their original box, deciding at the very last minute they wouldn't form part of the museum, particularly when it was speculation, and so deeply personal. She explained the items and her conclusions to Angelique.

She did the heart clutching thing again. 'Reginald and Amelie's grandmother was named Eleanor!' Her voice rose in volume. 'It is not a coincidence, no?'

Angelique rose in one streamlined movement, whereas Greta would have flounced off the chaise like a dog chasing a butterfly and retrieved a package from her belongings. It was a box inside a box and carefully wrapped.

'This is a gift for you,' she said, but continued to unwrap it. There was a layer of bubble wrap and tissue paper and plastic. When it was free of its coverings, she revealed an object about A4 in size and held it up.

'Is this your beautiful Millie?'

Larger than Brodie's postcard and in a distinctly different style, was a portrait of her aunt. It was like a mirror image, a photograph. Greta stifled a sob. Brodie moved closer. It was Millie as neither of them knew her. Her face less creased by the years, a different hat on her head, a smile, something that was rare and there was something else.

Brodie noticed first. 'Do you see her eyes, Greta? They're sparkling. Those eyes are turquoise with a glint.' He grew quite animated. 'I never saw her with that look in her eye. It's a mischievous streak, like she's up to naughty business. And her shoulders are bare. Huh!'

'Do you think, is she naked? Is that how he painted her?' Greta giggled.

'She's so much younger, our age, I'd guess. That smooth skin. So, Millie did have a youth,' he concluded.

Angelique handed it over. 'This is yours to add to your collection. It belongs here. Particularly if what you say is true. There are larger, more complex images of her at home, but this one, I agree, is special. It shows, I think, that she is directing her joy at Reggie and displaying her love for him. It makes me happy to think at some point in their lives they enjoyed this.'

'Oh, Angelique, this is too much! This must be worth a fortune, we can't accept it. The two we have in the collection have exceeded our expectations and now you deliver more.' Angelique continued to hold the painting as Greta refused it, shaking it away with her hands.

'I understand. But it means a lot to me and my mother. We want you to have it. To reunite them now after all these years.'

'Well, when you say it like that. What a beautiful idea. I absolutely adore it.' She hugged Angelique in a very non-French way. When she pulled back the woman kissed her on both cheeks instead.

'I only wish we knew the answer to why they parted. Why did Millie return to Australia? Why didn't she stay or he come here? That is the one answer we don't have.'

'Yes, it remains a mystery. But we are satisfied because we have found his heart. His love. Yes, they were parted and he was devastated but they did love each other. There is no other ending.'

Were all the French so romantic? Greta loved Angelique more each minute she spent in her company.

'Are you happy for us to allude to this relationship in her past, in the history of the museum?'

'Yes, of course.' She threw up her hands. 'We celebrate it!'

'Well, that's what we're gonna do. Celebrate. It's so wonderful that you're here for the grand opening. Do you want to take a tour now and we'll decide where to position this painting?' Brodie gestured onwards. Greta hooked her arm through Angelique and they followed him.

They stopped first at the scrap book of photographs. Brodie had diligently taken before and after photographs for austerity sake of the original house now that the whole site had changed dramatically.

'This is the original house but with extensive changes. We've maintained her studio exactly, but my art room is downstairs on this floor when it used to be upstairs. The centre is on this level with the museum that leads into the gallery and then further on is the gift shop and café.'

'Where do you live?' Angelique asked.

'Our living quarters are upstairs. Maybe one day, we'll build another home on the site. There's plenty of room and then we can convert the upstairs to office space and the hum of operations. At the moment the spare room is our office. But you must be dying to see the paintings, let's go.'

Angelique allowed herself to be pulled along by Greta. The main gallery was a compact room and only had the two Reginald Smart, soon to be three, paintings and the five works of Millie. The adjacent room had Brodie's works and it was larger because he was likely to produce more and be a living, extending exhibit.

Angelique stopped abruptly as soon as the paintings came into view.

'I know what they look like from your photos, but seeing them in real life, my goodness, they are breathtaking. I would know they are his without even checking. Those sail boats, those streets. He loved the Parisian street scenes. He had such a talent.'

Greta, usually inclined to jump in with her own platitudes, let their new friend enjoy the work in silence as a homage to her dear relative.

'And these, your Millie painted these?'

Brodie and Greta nodded. 'These are the ones she left behind in the house. Most of her works are in private collections or galleries. That is what makes these so special. They are unseen and the ones she was working on at the time of her death. Right up to the day before.'

Greta had not included the painting of the baby. Like the other mementos, it was too private, too raw. The woman was entitled to some secrets. For the time being, it remained hidden away in their private quarters.

'Incredible. These are beautiful. The detail so fine, the colour and image, so delicate.'

Brodie walked past his room, intending to walk on to the museum. Greta redirected Angelique. It took a moment for him to notice.

'And these are Brodie's paintings and other works. A couple of sculptures in there too.'

'Wow!' she said.

Greta noticed Brodie brace himself. Would he ever not?

'These are amazing! I know exactly what you are saying here. This one relates to your Aboriginals, no?' she quizzed him.

He cleared his throat. 'Yes, exactly. It demonstrates their displacement from their own land.'

'The colours are magnifique! Those oranges and reds. The colours of your dessert, yes?'

Angelique considered each of the fifteen pieces and stopped at the portrait of Greta. 'Aha, you. So fabulous and so different.'

Brodie had moved on by this stage and they showed her the

studio which she exclaimed was a pigsty and how could anyone possibly work in such mess.

'We agree!' they chanted.

She considered each of Millie's artefacts and knick-knacks that had been preserved and strategically placed. Including the impressive postcard collection. 'So many of France,' she commented.

As the tour came to an end, Greta suggested a drink in the new café. 'Wait till you see it. We worked hard to make sure it was in exactly the right position. It overlooks the bushland with a view out to the hinterland and further, a glimpse of the ocean on the horizon.'

Greta opened the glass doors to the indoor section of the café where everything gleamed shiny and new. She continued through to the outdoor deck.

'The trees!' Angelique exclaimed.

'Yes, gum trees. They provide the most glorious shade and canopy over the deck.' Brodie returned with an Aperol spritz for each of them and a stubby of beer for him.

'To Millie and Reggie,' Greta offered and held up her cocktail. 'I don't know exactly what Millie would make of this but I think secretly she'd be pleased at the fuss and the recognition of her work, I'm not so sure about the expose of her personal life.'

'She has achieved great things and I think she would be enormously proud of you both for what you have accomplished here.'

Greta's face ached from all the smiling but she thought it was true, too.

CHAPTER 34

Greta listened to the operatic words and her body seemed to float. The elongated sounds resonated beautifully around the snug space; the range of high notes leaving the crowd mesmerised and held in silent awe before erupting into applause after the climax. Chills raced up her spine at the spectacle that was Skye.

She'd been unsure what reception the young opera singer would receive. But now, in this moment it had been another perfect occasion in an already perfect day. But the performance wasn't about her or her new business; it was all about Skye. She watched the girl's confidence grow with each deep breath until she beamed with delight at its conclusion.

The day had been an overload of emotion and wasn't over yet. Once again, like many times throughout the day, certainty crashed down upon her like a real, living thing. For Skye, like her, Greta Johnson, this was just the beginning. Greta felt it, knew it and was filled with pride for the young woman who had overcome such adversity that she could stand up in front of a strange crowd and sing.

It hadn't been easy of course. But six months into her stint at the conservatorium of music where she'd received a scholarship to study, and she had the confidence to perform. The school had changed Skye's singing from something she was good at and enjoyed, to her passion, her purpose. Greta had watched the development with delight. Skye was now living the life she was meant to.

Greta also knew they would both be okay, along as they continued to push themselves to achieve great things.

After Skye had finished, Robyn and other ladies from the centre bombarded her with kisses and hugs and jubilation. Greta vowed that she would continue to help girls like Skye. As the juke box commenced playing its next tune, she snuck outside.

'You understand you're still on parole?'

Greta had successfully avoided Charlene the entire afternoon. Now the sun touched the treetops and was sinking to meet the ocean and the breeze had picked up. It was beautiful on the deck away from the frantic crowd of indoors, and for watching the dusky sky turn pink. The gathering was thinning now, the official part of the day over. Finally, it was about celebration. Without her noticing, Charlene had slunk over to stand with her. Greta looked toward the horizon.

'Yes, I know.'

And that was exactly why she'd avoided Charlene. Her presence was a reminder of her past, the past she continued to run from, desperate to forget. Impossible, when it seemed to follow her everywhere.

'You've done well here. Congratulations. I think you're going to be all right. I underestimated you, but you've excelled. Greta, your crime doesn't define you. Some people need a life-changing event to put them on the right path and that was the case with you. You didn't know you were lost, until you were. You would never voluntarily have ended up with Millie here in the hills and yet here you are and the happiest I've seen you.' Charlene turned to face her then. 'I will reduce my visits to quarterly.'

The punchline.

'Quarterly? Uh, that's wonderful, thank you. But you know what, Charlene, you're right. Even now I'm still trying to run away. I can't, my past is not going to go away no matter how much I will it. I need to accept what I did and that it was a dreadful mistake that I have learned from. If it hadn't of happened, I would not have rekindled my relationship with Millie and have this place. And of course, found Brodie. That cheesy old saying is right, isn't it? It was all meant to be.'

'I don't do cheesy, but in this instance it's true. You've done it, Greta, stay true to yourself and stay focused. This place is going to be a massive success. You've created it. Enjoy the spoils.' Her parole officer gave a tight smile and started to move away.

'Charlene, thanks for coming. You haven't had to come to any of these events, but you've attended all of them.'

'I did have a rather large crush on Millie and her work. It's fabulous.'

'True. That helped. But she's not here now. And you helped when I asked for it. Thanks for believing in me.'

Charlene gave a curt nod. It wasn't going to get any more sentimental than that. But that was enough.

Greta's heart was full. It was true, pride made your chest swell and made you inches taller. It also gave you confidence. She felt like she could be soaring above the clouds right now. She'd never realised the depth of love that surrounded her, that she'd willingly abandoned. For what? For nothing.

Someone inside turned the music up and it seeped through the cracks in the glass screen doors. People talked louder and glasses clinked. The after party was in full swing. The day had been exhausting but exhilarating. And a success. That ridiculous concrete carpark that filled part of the long drive to the centre had filled to capacity. Locals, tourists, supporters, the media; they'd all turned up. Feedback had been encouraging. Some people loved the original works, others preferred the secret inside to Millie and her creative process. The printed postcards were a hit and they'd have to restock before opening again tomorrow.

As Charlene disappeared, her father appeared and handed her a Kir Royale, its raspberries bobbing to the surface.

'Thanks, Dad.'

He kissed her cheek, his lips lingered and he made one of those ridiculous smooching noises that only a dad can. 'I'm so proud of you. You could have knocked me over when you came to me with this suggestion. What an idea! It was grand. I was a little worried at first—'

'You never said!' she interrupted.

'You were so keen, so enthusiastic. I've never seen you like that. Never in any of the projects or ideas you've had before. And you know why?'

She shook her head.

'This one matters. This is important. Preserving Millie's legacy, keeping it in the family and promoting new talent. I can also see that Brodie needed that push. You gave him that confidence. It's something you might like to think about for the future, continuing Millie's support of new talent. She had a lot of money to funnel into it of course; it's a thought for down the track. But you could offer an art competition or prize or a bursary like Brodie had.'

Brodie came and joined them; his face was flushed.

Greta gave him a quizzical look. 'Lots of people in there,' he said by way of explanation. He needed to escape too.

'Dad just had this brilliant idea.' She repeated it to him.

'Matthew, I love that idea. Millie was so passionate about nurturing future generations. If she hadn't found me, honestly, I'd still be swiping that paintbrush around with futility.'

'It's great, Dad, but my first priority for the first few years is paying my debt.'

'I know, I know. I could never forget. Let's talk about that, not today, but perhaps you can consolidate the balance somehow with your collateral, we'll arrange something. I'll give it some thought. I didn't realise how much the guilt has been eating you alive—'

'As it should be.'

'Granted. It's an important step for the future and to provide you with some comfort that the money has been repaid and those people don't have to wait any longer.'

Greta stood taller, hopeful. 'Yes, please. Let's talk more about it tomorrow.'

Matthew agreed.

'I feel so good about the future.'

'And so you should.' Brodie linked his fingers through hers. His touch still caused a shiver to race up her spine.

Mr Porter rushed over. The whole town of Lucas Heads had turned out today in support. Kathleen had come along dragging Jasmine in tow. She'd had the decency to appear sheepish and only muttered a brief hello. Other customers, many of whom had shunned her at the supermarket all those months ago, approached and congratulated her. Greta had no hard feelings against Jasmine or anyone else; Greta trusted these people and now they returned that trust. She had become part of their community.

'First review is out,' Mr Porter said holding up the local rag.

'What already?' Greta's stomach dipped dangerously.

'Yep, hot off the presses.'

Others had heard the call as they'd drifted outdoors. The fairy lights turned on and the deck became illuminated like a magical wonderland. Her mother and Niamh and Henry came close so they could hear, and Brodie's entire clan. She'd become quite used to the rambunctious group.

The Millicent Osborne Gallery and Museum opened its doors today. Located on the original site of the home of our late and dear local painter, Millie, it features original artworks mysteriously located after the artist's death by Reginald Smart and the last few pieces she'd been working on at the time. If you'd paid the reasonable entry fee just for those exhibits, you wouldn't be disappointed. But there's more. An exact replica of Millie's painting studio is the main feature of the museum which provides a lovely insight into the life of the artist herself. Infamously private during her life, she revealed little. Now we get to know her better and what a joy it is to learn that she collected postcards and travelled overseas which was the influence for many of her early works. And her painting hat is on display, in all its ratty original and well-used form. But the greatest joy is learning of her relationship with Reginald Smart, who knew! Endorsed by Smart's family, they've generously donated a portrait Smart completed of Millie when they met in France.

After spending a delightful hour or more in the company of Smart and Osborne, we are transported through time to the present and the impressive and courageous work of Brodie Quade. What a sensation! This man makes us think, reconsider our values and the world we live in. His pieces are of the modern age and demonstrative of the issues we should all be thinking about.

Then after that creative and sensory experience, it is a pleasure to escape to the sanctuary that is the café and enjoy a cool drink or a coffee brewed with local beans and cakes sourced locally (top points!) or freshly made light lunches.

This is a boon for our local area and will attract tourists and art enthusiasts alike. It was a tragedy to lose our favourite local artist but what a legacy she has left behind for our little community.

'Impressive and courageous work of Brodie Quade!' Greta shouted. She'd heard all of the complimentary words but those stuck. The group of their most loyal and staunch supporters burst into applause and sang and shouted their congratulations. Everyone hugged and kissed, celebrating the achievement.

Greta only had eyes for Brodie. His gaze found hers and the cacophony of noise was lost. This was their world and they had created it. Overcome their demons together.

They had created their own good life.

EPILOGUE

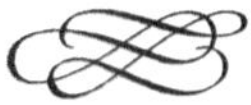

MAY 1970

Dearest Reggie,

I've kept a secret and I apologise profusely for not letting you know sooner. For escaping like a child and running away. I had good reason, or so I thought, but now I realise I was ever so wrong. How could I have been so blind?

I fled, left you because I discovered I was pregnant. I knew you would be overjoyed. You would have automatically thought that our life together would be cemented and we could be a family.

But Reggie, I was terrified. My life didn't involve a baby, domesticity or anything that could be described as an ordinary life. You know, I told you, repeatedly, I was only ever committed to my art. It is my life. I know you understand, but you think there's room for other things. Like love. I didn't believe you. But now I do.

Our daughter, Eleanor was born today. She is the most divine little creature and I have immediately fallen in love with her and realise that yes, I can have more. Art is not everything. Right up until the moment she was placed into my arms, my intention was to adopt her out to a family that wanted a baby, that would love her like I couldn't. Then I could continue on with my life and my art and you would be a deliciously lovely memory.

But in the instant I held her and she made a strange gurgle noise, I knew I could never let her go. And now I realise I should not have let you go either. You can love her too, be her father, be with me and we can raise her together. Can you come? And then we can work out the future.....

THE END

ACKNOWLEDGMENTS

I remember so clearly when inspiration struck for this story. I was at an art exhibit at GOMA admiring beautiful still-life paintings and interiors of timeless Queenslander homes. The older artist featured had befriended a younger artist and formed a true, long-term relationship.

Images immediately formed in my head of an older experienced female artist mentoring a younger emerging painter who had his own demons. Of course, enter a gorgeous young woman with her own difficulties and the three were thrown together in an amazing ramshackle cottage in the country. The images formed fast and so vividly and the main characters became real people in my head before we'd even left the gallery. It is such a wonderful feeling when this occurs and I cherish those moments. It made writing this book such a joy. However, I won't say it was easy, my main character, Greta caused me much angst until she formed into the character as she appears in the book. I hope, in the end, you love her as much as I do.

Thank you to the many people who helped me make this story the best it can be. To my home cheer squad who give me the space and time to write. To early reader, Sue Goldstiver, for her endless patience on suggestions for early versions and picking up plot holes I'd completely missed. For Annie Seaton for her editing skills and ongoing support. You remain an inspiration to me. To my neighbour, Liana for her helpful insight and proof-reading skills on later versions. To Susan Mackie of Small Town Publishing for her fabulous cover design and formatting skills. And to all of my writing friends who continue to encourage and inspire me, thank you. To all those writers who keep writing fabulous books, I love reading them! And most of all, to you, the reader, thank you for choosing this book out of the many thousands of wonderful books to read. I appreciate your faith and support in me. And if you've written a review, further massive thanks.

ABOUT THE AUTHOR

Leanne is a lawyer, wife and mother and a lover of romance and reading. Her law career created an addiction to coffee but provides countless story ideas. The author of three romance novels and two novellas, she likes writing sweeping love stories with happily-ever-afters featuring strong female heroines and set in the beautiful landscape of Australia.

You can find out more about Leanne and her books here:
Author page:
https://www.leannelovegroveauthor.com
Instagram:
https://www.instagram.com/leannelovegroveauthor/
FaceBook:
https://www.facebook.com/leannelovegroveauthor
Bookbub:
https://www.bookbub.com/profile/leanne-lovegrove